P9-DIB-399

SOAP FLAKES

★

"A night watchman at Shadowtown Productions was killed a few hours ago," Manders said.

Oxman searched his mental file, came up blank. "What the hell is Shadowtown Productions?"

"You never heard of 'Shadowtown'?"

"No. Is it near Buffalo?"

"It's a soap opera, Ox. One of the most popular on afternoon television. My wife watches it, her sister watches it, everybody female and most males watch it."

"I don't watch it," Oxman said. "Never heard of it till just now."

"They shoot the show over in an old converted warehouse off Riverside Drive. The inside is lined with plush offices, dressing rooms, and all the clap-trap that goes with shooting a major-league TV production. Boom mikes, lights, cameras, cardboard walls."

Lights, camera, and action, Oxman thought. "Is the corpse real?"

★

SHADOW-TOWN

Also By John Lutz

Time Exposure
Kiss
Better Mousetraps (Short stories)
Dancer's Debt
Scorcher
Ride the Lightning
Tropical Heat
The Right to Sing the Blues
Nightlines
The Eye (With Bill Pronzini)*
Exiled
The Shadow Man
Jericho Man
Lazarus Man
Bonegrinder
Buyer Beware
The Truth of the Matter

*Published by
THE MYSTERIOUS PRESS

ATTENTION: SCHOOLS AND CORPORATIONS

MYSTERIOUS PRESS books, distributed by Warner Books, are available at quantity discounts with bulk purchase for educational, business, or sales promotional use. For information, please write to: SPECIAL SALES DEPARTMENT, MYSTERIOUS PRESS, 666 FIFTH AVENUE, NEW YORK, N.Y. 10103.

ARE THERE MYSTERIOUS PRESS BOOKS
YOU WANT BUT CANNOT FIND IN YOUR LOCAL STORES?

You can get any MYSTERIOUS PRESS title in print. Simply send title and retail price, plus $3.00 for the first book on any order and 50¢ for each additional book on that order, to cover mailing and handling costs. New York State and California residents add applicable sales tax. Enclose check or money order to: MYSTERIOUS PRESS, 129 WEST 56th St., NEW YORK, N.Y. 10019.

SHADOW-TOWN

JOHN LUTZ

THE MYSTERIOUS PRESS

New York • London
Tokyo • Sweden • Milan

For Otto Penzler

MYSTERIOUS PRESS EDITION

Copyright © 1988 by John Lutz
All rights reserved.

Cover design by Barbara Buck
Cover illustration by David McKelvey

Mysterious Press books are published in association with
Warner Books, Inc.
666 Fifth Avenue
New York, N.Y. 10103

A Warner Communications Company

Printed in the United States of America

Originally published in hardcover by The Mysterious Press.
First Mysterious Press Paperback Printing: October, 1989

10 9 8 7 6 5 4 3 2 1

THE CAST

E. L. Oxman
Jennifer Crane
Art Tobin
Smiley Manders
Lana Spence .... Delia Lane
Zachary Denton
Arthur Sales .... Roger Maler
Linda Beller .... Midge Brown
Harry Overbeck
Sy Youngerman
Brian King .... Mayor Carl Smith
Jean Richards .... Mrs. Lois Smith
Shane Moreland
Manny Brokton
William Coats .... Louie Carter
Burt Lassiter
Lance Jardeen
Marv Egan
Calvin Oaks
Brad Gaines
Phil Malloy
Vince McGreery
Myra Deeber
Ernie Dickerson
Edgar Grume
Izzy Singer
Murray Felstein

Between the idea
And the reality
Between the motion
And the act
Falls the shadow.

T. S. Eliot

On the stage he was natural, simple, affecting,
'Twas only that when he was off, he was acting.

Oliver Goldsmith

Scene 1

Vincent McGreery—11:00 P.M.

He strolled halfway down the alley where little Ivy Ingrams had attempted abortion with a wire clothes hanger, only to lose her own life while her baby lived. Then he opened the door to Delia Lane's luxurious living room, where she'd seduced her best friend's teenage son, made phone calls revealing her sister's lesbian affair with the mayor's wife, and romped with the mayor himself in wild semi-nude ecstasy on her polar-bear rug while hidden cameras whirred. The mayor had hanged himself when Delia threatened to send the videotapes to the city council.

McGreery closed the door on the Lane residence, then stepped through a wall into Roger Maler's country cottage and swept the yellow beam of his flashlight around. Maler, the town's most eligible bachelor, had enjoyed some high times here.

Everything looked okay, as it had every night since retired New York cop Vince McGreery had been working as a watchman for Shadowtown Productions, Incorporated. The job paid nicely for this kind of work; McGreery knew several fellow retired policemen who wished they could do as well. The Shadowtown paychecks, plus his monthly pension checks, provided more than enough money for a sixty-eight-year-old former traffic patrolman and his wife, Annie. They still had their health, and their house out in Teaneck was paid for. Neither longed for travel or new sights. They often told each other there was plenty they hadn't seen in New York. But they never went to see any of it, choosing instead to spend evenings—days, since McGreery had landed the Shadowtown job—with only each other in their modest brick house with the daffodil-strewn backyard. They hadn't been out to

3

dinner in months, or to the theater in years. The quiet life; that was for McGreery and his Annie. McGreery had seen more than enough mayhem during his days on the force.

All McGreery had to do now was to look in on the Park Avenue apartment, and he could return to the well-lighted, cozy office and settle down with the mystery novel he was reading. Since retiring from the force, he'd become quite a fan of mystery fiction. He didn't like to read the occult stuff, though—all that supernatural malarkey. McGreery had had enough of nightmares when he was a kid and read too many scary stories and gone to ghoul and ghost movies. "It's tough enough living in the real world," his father had told him, "without borrowing trouble from your imagination and reading about things that don't exist." The old man was right, as usual. And McGreery had grown up to be a practical man who scoffed at, or observed with amused tolerance, the otherwise sensible people who fell victim to fortune tellers, phony mediums, and specialists in exorcising demons.

The Park Avenue apartment was a set that was no longer used. It had been the daytime home of Edgar Grume, a lothario who also happened to be a vampire, one with a power over women that enabled him to seduce a long string of willing and winsome young actresses who'd found brief fame on Shadowtown. And some of the victims had been established stars; falling victim to Edgar Grume had become a sort of running gag with show-business personalities. Rock stars and movie stars had exposed their lovely necks to Grume's fangs. Of course, McGreery had never witnessed any of this. It was Annie who was the soap-opera fan, and who daily filled in McGreery on what had happened in that insular little TV world while he'd been sleeping away the afternoon.

Edgar Grume had been lured to the dark bedroom of a sister of one of his victims and then destroyed by flashbulbs, intermittently decomposing before the audience's eyes with each brilliant eruption of light as the terrified but determined lass tripped her camera's shutter over and over. In the morning, they found her dead from shock, her hair as white as McGreery's. (So Annie said.) And on the floor by the window was only a small mound of dust that the maid wondered about briefly and then swept up and deposited with the trash. Ashes to ashes.

In the corpse's hand was a camera loaded with film that, when developed, turned out to be only snapshots of the empty bedroom. McGreery had laughed when Annie told him that; he could have predicted it. Everyone but Annie knew vampires didn't appear in mirrors or on film.

Thousands of letters had poured into Shadowtown Productions' mail room after Edgar Grume's death. There must have been something about the toothsome seducer that had touched women's hearts.

Everything was dusty and in order in Grume's swank apartment with its brass-embellished coffin resting on a table near the console TV. It was a real coffin, on loan from a mortuary in Queens. McGreery wondered when someone would come to pick it up. The Grume set would have been struck a long time ago if Shadowtown were pressed for space. But the huge warehouse the company had bought and then converted into a shooting stage enabled them to shuffle sets and props into dark corners and forget them. The show was high in the ratings, so the emphasis was on keeping up momentum rather than on squeezing pennies.

McGreery played his yellow flashlight beam over the modern furniture, the ceiling-to-floor red drapes, the bar in the corner where nighttime victims had gotten deliciously drunk on bourbon-colored tea before death by erotic transfusion. Some vampire, McGreery thought, his flesh-padded, seamed face widening in a smile. He ambled stiffly down the hall toward the prop room, which he'd glance into on his way to the office. His rheumatic knee was bothering him tonight. Bothering him more and more lately.

As he walked, he aimed the flashlight out in front of him at a downward angle. At his age a man had to be careful; one simple tumble he would have laughed at in his youth could now fracture a hip and lay him up for months. He would have turned on the lights to check the stage area, but there was some illumination here from outside streetlights, filtering in through the high slit windows. No point in walking around flipping switches on and off. And the main switch lighted the place up too bright for McGreery's aging eyes. Anyway, it would have been a waste of electricity for the ten minutes he spent on his initial round. At 3:00 A.M., in four hours, he'd make his detailed check of the place; that's when he always lit up the old warehouse like a partying cruise ship.

The prop department was a long, narrow room that had been created inside the warehouse with two-by-four framing and drywall. It had no ceiling of its own, and there was no lock on the hollow-core door.

McGreery opened the door, poked his head in, and swept the

flashlight beam around the racks of clothes, the makeup tables, and full-length mirrors. This was the costume department, too. The fitting-room door at the opposite end of the room was open. He aimed his light in there briefly, then closed the prop-room door and continued down the hall, pushing through the darkness.

His office was off the reception area of Shadowtown Productions' suite of offices in the north end of the building, close to the copy machines, desktop computers, and typewriters that would be a break-in artist's prime targets. On the sound stage itself, the studio, where the soap opera was "live-taped" every weekday, the company's main concern was the prevention of vandalism.

As he passed the row of dressing rooms along the hall, McGreery paused and cocked his head to the side.

A sound. He thought he'd heard something. There. Again. The faint scuff of a sole on cement. That was a sound any retired cop would recognize.

Except for the sets themselves, and the offices, most of the old building had concrete floors.

McGreery turned and started walking slowly back toward the sound stage. He wore soft-soled shoes and made very little noise.

He paused at the prop-room door, listening.

There was the sound again. Not from the prop room but ahead of him, where the set was arranged for tomorrow's indoor shooting after the picnic scene. In the park tomorrow, after packaged delicacies and iced champagne, Delia the ballbreaker was going to warn her lover, Roger Maler, to stay away from his college-age girlfriend.

It was probably something totally innocent that McGreery had heard. There was no reason yet for alarm, to suspect that someone had broken in. The sound might have been that of a precariously balanced object falling; a stack of papers slipping off the edge of a desk or table might make the same noise as they slid to the floor. Or it might have been McGreery's imagination. No sound. Nothing at all.

No, not nothing. McGreery stopped fooling himself. He knew he'd heard something. Probably somebody.

There was nothing in the alley other than some glued-down crumpled newspapers, and a row of metal trash cans that Special Effects had aged and battered.

Nothing in bitchy Delia Lane's plush living room.

Nothing in the resort cottage. Or in the Park Avenue apartment.

McGreery sighed long and loud and removed the heel of his right hand from where it had been resting on the butt of his holstered revolver. What the hell, maybe he hadn't heard anything after all. Old ears played tricks, sometimes heard sounds from memory as well as reality. The rhythm of his heart slowed, and he sidestepped a camera dolly, turned, and walked through the dimness back toward the offices.

That's when it opened the door and stepped out of Delia Lane's living room.

McGreery could only manage a startled "Wha—"

His mind whirled. This creature coming toward him must have been hiding in there. *But where?* McGreery thought he'd looked everywhere. Behind the drapes! That was the only possible place!

That information did McGreery no good now. His heart seemed to swell to ten times its size and battered at his chest like a wild thing desperately seeking escape. He fumbled with his holster, but a jolt of pain in his left armpit caused him to breathe in harshly and hunch over in terror. He forgot about the gun, and, for an instant, even about his fear of what he'd seen. The pain crept down his arm, so excruciating that it paralyzed the left side of his body. An iron grip closed on his chest and tightened. He realized what was happening. Everybody McGreery knew over sixty understood the symptoms.

Heart attack! *He was having a heart attack!*

The thing moved toward him, into slightly brighter light, and McGreery saw that what had appeared to be a huge dark bird with folded wings was actually a man wearing a long black cape. McGreery tried to take a step backward, managed only a clumsy lurch. The pain, the fear, rooted him where he stood.

The man in the cape made a deft circling motion with both hands. He was holding a piece of cord, McGreery saw, and stretching it taut to test its strength.

"*Please!*" McGreery hissed through grinding teeth.

His heart exploded over and over, driving him against the wall with pain. In a daze, he saw the man in the cape make a quick movement toward him with the cord, felt something brush the back of his neck.

And suddenly McGreery couldn't breathe. He tried again to fumble the revolver from its holster, but his limbs wouldn't function as he wished; they merely flapped around in stiff, awkward movements, his fingers spread wide and useless, as if they belonged already to death.

He could hear cartilage popping softly in his throat as the cord dug into his neck. *My God!* . . .

But it was the viselike pain in his chest that consumed McGreery, that drew him from life into darkness. In the dim, failing light he saw his assailant's lips curl away from white teeth in what might have been a smile or a sneer.

Fangs! Holy Jesus, the bastard had fangs! Fangs moving nearer, seeming to lengthen, as McGreery sank to the floor and the caped figure bent over him. Nearer.

That was Vincent McGreery's final vision, and almost his last wild fragment of thought.

Fangs!

He was swirling lightly into nothingness when he heard the voice: "Vincent? Are you there?" Annie's voice?

Annie? . . .

"Shadowtown" Episode No. 342 (In Reruns)

Edgar Grume glided nearer to the bed and smiled down at his victim-to-be. She was a buxom, dark-haired woman, lying rigid in alarm with her eyes wide, unable to believe Grume was there, in her own bedroom. Behind her the window was open, its filmy white curtains swaying gracefully in the night breeze.

Then a curious thing happened. As she met Grume's stare her fear seemed to disappear. His eyes were as gentle as they were hypnotic. Her sensuous mouth softened; the glistening pink tip of her tongue emerged and slid slowly across her upper lip.

"That's right, my darling," he told her in a soft voice. He didn't want to wake her husband, sleeping beside her. "There's nothing to fear. What's about to happen is a gift, from each of us to the other."

Still with her eyes locked to his steady gaze, she slowly ran her fingertips over her bare throat and down to where her half-exposed breasts swelled firmly above her thin nightgown. Her nails left scratches on her smooth flesh.

"I'll take from you what I must have," Grume told her. "And in return I offer you eternity, life for as long as time. Control of others. I'll give you another world. Another world, my darling, right here in this one."

He concentrated his gentle stare for the close-up, then moved toward the side of the bed. Gradually, so gradually.

The woman did that thing with her tongue and upper lip again, then returned his smile and raised pale arms to embrace him as he leaned over her.

Cut to the sleeping husband.

Fade to commercial.

9

Scene 2

"I thought I heard something," Zachary Denton said. "I called McGreery's name: 'Vincent.' I wanted to tell him I'd forgotten something and returned to the office to get it. Didn't want to surprise him. He didn't answer." Zachary hunched his bony but wide shoulders forward, as if to shelter his tall, lean body. "Guess somebody else surprised him."

NYPD Detective Sergeant E. L. Oxman listened quietly, his blue eyes patient in a face that gave away nothing. He was a fortyish, sandy-haired man, average size yet taller than he appeared, not fat, but with a thickset, deceptively powerful shambling quality about him. Because of his sometimes phlegmatic mannerisms, and his name, Oxman was often thought of as a plodder. But usually it was calmness and not slowness that was evident in Oxman. And he was plodding only in that he was painstakingly methodical; when he hung a collar on a suspect, it stayed.

He'd taken this squeal at home last night. His superior at the Twenty-fourth Precinct, Lieutenant Smiley Manders, had awakened him with the call.

Oxman was dragged from sleep by the jangling phone next to the bed. As he groped for the receiver with his right hand, he tried to glance at the luminous dial of his watch. But his left hand and wrist, and the watch, were pinned out of sight beneath Jennifer, who hadn't been awakened by the sound or his movement.

"We've got a homicide, Ox," Manders said in his sepulchral voice. The voice matched his basset-hound face. He was called Smiley precisely because his features seldom defied gravity and shaped a smile.

"I'm not on duty," Oxman said. "Didn't you notice the shift schedule?" But he knew Manders had noticed. The lieutenant's sad brown eyes noticed everything.

"This one's practically around the corner from you," Manders said, "so I'm giving it to you and Tobin."

"Damn near everything in the Two-Four is in my neighborhood," Oxman said. He was living now with Jennifer in her apartment on West Ninety-eighth, near the turgid Hudson and Riverside Park. Oxman had been instrumental in solving a mass-murder case in this neighborhood last year. That was how he'd met Jennifer, how he'd eventually gotten his divorce, how . . .

Manders interrupted his thoughts. "Sorry, Ox, but it's you and Tobin. Possible bad PR in this one; I need my best."

Departmental politics. Oxman hated them, and seldom played them or bent to them. That was why he was still a sergeant after two decades on the force. Manders could accommodate the politicos somehow without giving them an important part of himself. That was a talent not everyone had.

"A night watchman at Shadowtown Productions was killed a few hours ago," Manders said.

Oxman searched his mental file, came up blank. "What the hell is Shadowtown Productions?"

"You never heard of 'Shadowtown'?"

"No, is it near Buffalo?"

"It's a soap opera, Ox. One of the most popular on afternoon television. My wife watches it, her sister watches it, everybody female and most males watch it."

"I don't watch it," Oxman said. "Never heard of it till just now."

"They shoot the show over in an old converted warehouse off Riverside Drive; probably pumped a million dollars into the ramshackle joint, though you wouldn't know it from the outside. But the inside is lined with plush offices, dressing rooms, and all the claptrap that goes with shooting a major-league TV production. Boom mikes, lights, cameras, cardboard walls."

Lights, camera, and action, Oxman thought. "Is the corpse real?"

"It is," Manders said. "And still where it was found, waiting for you to drive over here and look things over. The ME's done with it, and the lab crew's finished, so it can be removed. But I thought the investigating officer should see the murder scene fresh. The ME says cause of death was possibly a heart attack, but more like asphyxiation. There's a cord—looks like venetian-blind cord—wrapped very tight around the dead man's neck."

Oxman worked his hand from beneath Jennifer's warm rib cage, swiveled on the mattress, and sat up on the edge of the bed. The bedsprings creaked, or was it his knees? He felt stiff, a little groggy. "Okay," he said. "I'll call Tobin and get over there."

"Fine," Manders said, as if Oxman were granting a favor rather than obeying an order. He told Oxman the address, said he'd stay on the scene with some blue uniforms until Oxman or Tobin arrived, then hung up. The broken connection sizzled in the receiver.

Oxman got the rest of the way out of bed and made his way into the bathroom. As he was removing his watch to step into the shower stall, he saw that it was 12:05. He cursed Manders, and people who murdered by moonlight, then he placed the watch on the toilet tank. Oxman always slept nude, so the watch was the only thing he had to take off. He adjusted the chrome faucet handles to a comfortable temperature, then stepped into the stinging cascade of water. It felt hotter than he'd imagined from testing it with his hand. In fact, it was too damned hot, almost scalding. He reached again for the faucet handles, twisted them, and was rewarded with a jet of ice-cold water.

Just dandy. Only a little past midnight, and the morning was starting off wrong.

Art Tobin was waiting for him when he reached the "Shadowtown" studio. He'd been Oxman's partner for the last four years. Tobin had been on the force about as long as Oxman, and he was black and let that bother him more than it should. His blackness, or his attitude toward his blackness, had held him back in the way that Oxman's stubbornness had been *his* stumbling block. And Tobin had something else in common with Oxman. He was a solid, conscientious cop.

Manders was right. The outside of the old building belied the money that had been spent on converting the inside. There was only a small, black-lettered sign mounted on the stained bricks near the front entrance: SHADOWTOWN PRODUCTIONS, INC. It was probable that even fans of the show wouldn't make the connection with this Shadowtown Productions and the "Shadowtown" that appeared weekdays on television. Oxman realized he'd have to watch at least a few episodes of the show. He didn't like that idea at all.

Inside, Art Tobin had been standing in a wide hall, along with two other men. Beyond them was sprawled the body of the murdered security guard. Two blue uniforms lounged nearby and chatted, casting occasional sideways glances at the corpse, as if they suspected someone might try to steal it.

Surprised by the size of the place, Oxman walked toward Tobin. Plasterboard walls fell far short of a ceiling from which were suspended steel catwalks and rows of heavy klieg lights. Oxman could see all of this only in dimness beyond the lighted area where the corpse lay, but he could sense the building's vastness around him.

Tobin introduced the two men with him as "Shadowtown's" co-producers, Sy Youngerman and Harry Overbeck. Youngerman was a sharp-faced, dark-haired man in his mid-thirties, wearing dress slacks and an expensive white sweater with dizzying diagonal blue stripes. He had on glasses that were tinted green at the tops of the lenses.

Overbeck was older, maybe in his fifties, with ruddy, even features beneath a military-short crewcut. The brush on his head was rusty brown, but his bushy mustache was almost black. He had on a rumpled brown suit with a red tie that was loosened and twisted at the neck. The top button of his shirt was unfastened. He'd missed another button just above his belt buckle. He appeared to have struggled out of bed and gotten dressed in a hurry in a windstorm. Youngerman looked as if he'd never gone to bed.

"Lieutenant Manders notified us of what happened," Overbeck said, "and we got right over here." He glanced back at his security guard's corpse as if he didn't want to look but must. "God, poor Vince. He'd just retired from the police department a few years ago; he told me he was enjoying life for the first time."

Oxman could believe that.

"I suppose this'll be all over the news," Sy Youngerman said. He couldn't help the note of calculation that crept into his voice. What made news made viewers made ratings made money.

A third man Oxman hadn't noticed approached from down the hall. He was tall, broad-shouldered, but extremely thin, wearing chinos and a cable-knit brown sweater and carrying a large leather portfolio. As he got near Oxman, he tried a smile beneath his unruly thatch of straight brown hair. He had bushy eyebrows, craggy features. Only in his thirties, when he got older he would be described as Lincolnesque. But there was none of the Lincolnesque somber dignity about him; there was more of a restless energy that made him seem vaguely discontent.

"This is Zach Denton," Sy Youngerman said. "He's our chief set designer."

"He discovered the body, Ox," Tobin added.

Denton rested the edge of his portfolio on the floor and described how he'd returned to the studio to get something he'd forgotten, some work he wanted to do at home, and as he was walking toward his office heard a soft scuffling sound. He'd gone down the hall, called the guard's name, and saw McGreery lying on the floor. He thought he was ill, maybe suffered a heart attack, so he ran to help him. In distorting shadows, he might have caught a glimpse of a fleeing figure, but thought little of that until he bent over McGreery and saw the thin cord wrapped around the guard's neck. He realized then what must have happened—McGreery had surprised an intruder, one who would kill and might still be in the building.

Denton had run back the way he'd come, then out into the street. He'd piled into his car, driven until he'd seen a phone booth, and called the police.

"What exactly was it you returned here to get?" Oxman asked.

"This." Denton nodded his long head toward his portfolio. "I wanted to make some detail changes on a scene we're going to shoot tomorrow. A picnic scene. We plan to do it in Riverside Park, and it has to be set up right so it appears the actors are in Central Park."

"Why don't you just go to Central Park?" Oxman asked.

"Well, grass is grass and trees are trees, and Riverside Park is closer." As he spoke, Denton shot a look at Youngerman that left little doubt he would have preferred Central Park. But a soap opera, like any other business, operated under constraints of budget and time.

"It's a brief scene," Youngerman said. "Delia warns Roger about seeing his younger-woman lover, then tries to seduce him and is rejected."

"Delia?"

"She's a character in the soap opera," Tobin said. "Delia Lane."

Youngerman nodded. "That's right, she's 'Shadowtown's' temptress bitch, out to roll in the hay with Roger Maler, the town's eligible bachelor. She's trying to find out if he's the real father of Ivy's baby."

"Ivy's dead," Overbeck cut in.

None of this seemed important to Oxman.

"What about this figure you glimpsed?" he asked Denton.

Denton shifted his long body uncomfortably. "I might only have imagined I saw someone."

"Now imagine you can describe him," Tobin said. He'd already heard Zach Denton's story and was looking forward to Oxman hearing it. His ebony features were expressionless, but Oxman knew there was a kind of hard-edged mirth going on behind them. There must be something about Denton's story . . .

Denton shrugged. "He was dressed in black, and I think he was wearing a cape."

"Uh, hm," Oxman said noncommittally, not giving anyone the satisfaction of his dubiousness. But he was thinking, *Oh, boy!* "You sure he wasn't just wearing a long overcoat?"

"Kind of warm for an overcoat."

"Okay, a raincoat, then."

"It's possible," Denton said. He hadn't considered that. "Maybe it was a long black or dark-blue coat, unbuttoned." He frowned. "Or maybe I was imagining things, in the dark, with a body. Hell, I was plenty shook up. Not every night you run into something like this."

"I thought you saw the running figure before you knew the watchman was dead."

"I, uh, did. But maybe a person somehow senses danger at a murder scene." He knew he was getting in deeper. "Yeah, I know that sounds crazy," he said apologetically. "It all sounds crazy, but there's Vince McGreery, dead." He began to sway his long body from side to side and shuffle his Nike-clad feet, as if he'd like to break into a sprint and purge himself of pent-up energy.

"No, it doesn't sound crazy," Oxman said. "I've experienced that same kind of premonition myself a few times."

Denton seemed relieved; he smiled.

"May I?" Oxman asked, nodding toward the portfolio.

Denton hadn't been expecting the request. He stammered, then said, "Oh, sure," and unzipped the portfolio for Oxman.

Oxman carried it to where the light was better and examined the contents. There were several large sheets of thick paper on which were sketches labeled "picnic basket," "blanket," "cooler." This was an overhead view, with dotted lines indicating camera angles. There was some black felt-tip scribbling Oxman didn't understand. The next sketch showed where the actors were to be in relation to the scheme of the outdoor set, along with some notes on lighting. Also in the portfolio were sketches of various other sets, lists of materials, a two-month-old *Newsweek*, and a magazine titled *Babes Fit to Be Tied*. This was a bondage magazine, with illustrations showing several models who looked suspiciously underage bound by thick rope in various uncomfortable poses.

Denton didn't appear at all embarrassed while Oxman was examining the magazine. "I bought that at a shop near Times Square," he said. "I'm interested in pornography."

"Just the sadistic stuff?" Tobin, who was standing nearby, asked. He was glaring at the magazine with interest.

"All kinds of erotica," Denton said.

"Erotica, shit," Tobin said.

Oxman shot him a look that Tobin ignored. Tobin was a straitlaced cop, almost a prude despite the things he'd seen on his job. Or maybe because of them. Oxman didn't mind what Denton read; it was only the kiddie porn that boiled his blood and made him consider transfer back to the vice squad. Consenting adults and all that.

He replaced everything in the portfolio and returned it to Denton. "We'll need you in the morning at the Twenty-fourth Precinct to give a statement," he said.

Denton nodded. "Sure. Whatever I can do to help. Hey, I liked Vince. I really did."

"That's it, then," Oxman said, when he saw that Denton didn't know whether he could leave. Denton nodded again, grinned his lean, handsome smile, and walked away toward the front exit. His pace was fast and his long arms were swinging in wide arcs. He was obviously relieved to get out of there.

"Whaddya think, Ox?" Tobin asked.

Oxman watched the ambulance attendants, who'd just arrived from more pressing duties involving live victims, zipping the watchman into a black plastic body bag. Like so much garbage, Oxman thought. The ripping sound the zippers on those things made always cut through Oxman like something cold and jagged. This time was no exception. *Riiiip!*

"Don't have enough facts to think anything yet," Oxman said. The attendants placed the watchman on a wheeled cart and headed for the door. "Maybe this McGreery surprised a prowler and got surprised himself. It figures that all kinds of nuts might break into the set of a soap opera. Maybe to act out their fantasies. A lot of kinks probably watch these things."

Tobin shook his head. "Ordinary people watch soap operas, Ox. I used to follow this one myself."

Oxman looked at Tobin, astounded. But he said nothing.

"Don't lay that look on me, Elliot Leroy," Tobin said. He always called Oxman by his given name when he was mad at him. He knew how much Oxman disliked that. "Anyway, it's a good thing I used to watch this show, or we wouldn't know about Edgar Grume."

Oxman sighed. He was getting tired of this. "Who the hell is Edgar Grume?"

"Was," Tobin corrected. "He was killed—I mean, on the show. He was a vampire, but the kind all the ladies went for. He lived by day in a dark luxury apartment on Park Avenue; at night he went looking for action in Shadowtown wearing the traditional vampire get-up. Including a black cape."

Oxman thought about that. "All right," he said. "That's something to remember."

He and Tobin walked back to where Youngerman and Overbeck were still standing. Seeing the watchman's body removed seemed to have upset Overbeck. He was pale. He ran a hand over his brush haircut and said, "If you're done with us, Lieutenant . . ."

"Sergeant," Oxman corrected. "Just one more thing. You still have the Edgar Grume vampire costume around?"

Youngerman raised his dark eyebrows above the frames of his tinted glasses. "Yeah . . . a guy with a cape. Zach said he saw a guy with a black cape."

"There were several outfits," Overbeck said. "You'll have to check with Wardrobe in the morning, but we can go into the prop and costume room and look around."

Oxman and Tobin followed the co-producers into a long room that became brilliantly lighted when Overbeck threw a switch. There were various chairs, tables, household items, and smaller painted backdrops lying about. There were also long racks of clothes and several fitting rooms. The place was packed with what looked to Oxman like miscellaneous junk.

"Everything we need for the show is contained in this one building," Youngerman said proudly, as if he were a tour guide. "We live-tape each episode and get it to the networks shortly thereafter. There's only a two-day lag time."

"How do you know what's going to happen?" Oxman asked. A naive question. He didn't mind playing stupid; it encouraged candidness.

"Oh, the show's written way ahead," Overbeck explained. "There's a book, a master plot, so we know where we're going with it over a period of months, and the writers use that as a guide and keep us several episodes ahead. One reason we do it that way is so we can adjust to viewer response. For instance, our polls told us our ingénue, Ivy Ingrams, was falling off in popularity after she was raped, so we had her bleed to death when she attempted to abort her illegitimate child." There was a hint of something in Overbeck's voice that suggested he enjoyed pulling the strings in his little made-up world.

"The viewers liked that," Youngerman said.

Oxman glanced over at Tobin, whose face was black stone.

"Ah, here they are," Overbeck said.

Near the end of the rack were two identical vampire costumes on hangers, covered with thin, clear plastic. Oxman examined each of them; there was nothing to indicate that they'd been worn lately, but then maybe there wouldn't be.

"There're only two of these?" he asked.

"I think so," Youngerman said. "But you'll have to talk to Velma in Wardrobe to be sure."

Oxman nodded and replaced the costumes on the rack. Velma.

"Another thing," he said. "Did the night watchman have a family?"

Overbeck swallowed and nodded. "A wife."

"Manders took care of that," Tobin said quietly.

Oxman appreciated the gesture; it was hell breaking the news to relatives of murder victims. This was apparently Manders's way of balancing the scales after rousting Oxman and Tobin from bed and assigning them to this case, which after all might turn out to be a routine murder-during-break-in.

Oxman told Youngerman and Overbeck he'd talk to them tomorrow, that he needed their statements. They said they were eager to cooperate and get this thing cleared up. Avenge poor old Vince McGreery. They had an immeasurably high opinion of him now that he was dead. Then Oxman and Tobin got out of there.

"Smells wrong," Tobin said, when they were standing out on the dark sidewalk. The night had cooled; from the west the scent of the nearby river wafted over to them. "That vampire bullshit."

"It really is possible some freako was playing vampire on stage, got surprised, and did in the watchman."

"I dunno," Tobin said. "Grume, the vampire, hasn't been on the show for about six months."

"Stake through the heart?" Oxman asked, playing along.

"Murder by flashbulb," Tobin said. "He was tricked into the wrong bedroom, reduced to dust by bursts of light from a flashbulb. You know how vampires can't stand daylight, or having their picture taken."

Oxman had heard rumors to that effect; didn't think it was information that might come in handy.

"And the dude is dead," Tobin added.

"I know. But why?"

Tobin arched a dark eyebrow. "Why?"

"Yeah, if he was so popular, a thirsty sex symbol, why'd the writers kill him off?"

"I mean the actor who played Grume is dead," Tobin said. "Killed in an accident. So the writers didn't have any choice but to do in Grume the vampire."

"I see."

Oxman began walking toward where he'd parked his car behind Tobin's. Riverside was fairly busy even at this early morning hour. Cabs whizzing by every ten seconds or so, carrying passengers bound for who knew where. The city sometimes reminded Oxman of a festering yeast-pile: virulent, frantic activity leading to decay. He had to catch himself at times or he'd slip into the old cynicism that had helped to destroy his marriage.

"Some wild place, that 'Shadowtown,'" he said to Tobin, when they'd reached the cars.

"So's the real world, Ox," Tobin said, getting in behind the steering wheel and slamming his car door. He started the engine, nodded to Oxman from behind the rolled-up window, and pulled away from the curb.

Oxman had to agree. Still, there was a difference. An important difference.

But as he lowered himself into his car to return to Jennifer, he wondered how many soap-opera fans couldn't make the distinction.

Ernie Dickerson—12:15 A.M.

Ernie's back hurt. The hard concrete of the alley where he lay didn't make much of a bed for a man pushing fifty. He rolled onto his side. He remembered how comfortable he'd been when he'd first staggered into the alley, full of cheap red and looking for a pad, and let himself sink against the brick wall of one of the buildings. But now he was awake.

He realized he was still more than a little drunk, and he thanked God for that. Cold sober, he would have been in even more misery.

For the last half-dozen years, after the youngest boy had died, and the wife had left him, Ernie had lived from bottle to bottle. He'd been a boxer in his youth, and the repeated left jabs to the head he'd suffered had caught up with him along with the alcohol. He knew he didn't sound sensible at times, but he *thought* sensibly, when he was sober. It was frustrating to hear his own thickened voice and rambling logic; he sometimes wanted to reach out physically and snatch the words back and reformulate them. Lots of times people assumed Ernie was drunk when he hadn't even begun his day's drinking.

In the corner of his vision he noticed a tall, dark form striding down the alley toward him. Ernie absently wondered what it was; vaguely, he suspected he should be alarmed but didn't know why.

The thing was a man, wearing a long black cape that swirled gracefully around his legs as he walked. He had wild white hair. Halloween, Ernie thought. Friggin' Halloweeen. No, it was too warm for that; Halloween was later in the year.

The dark form stopped and stood over him. Ernie clutched the hem of the cape and stared up with bleary eyes.

The black shape—he couldn't see the man's face—said nothing.

24

"Lishen," Ernie said. "If you could spare some change, I'd be 'ternally grateful."

"What would you know about eternity?" the dark figure asked. There was an edge of contempt and rueful humor in the question.

"Level with you," Ernie slurred. Then he tried to control his enunciation and spoke slowly and with deliberation. That only made things worse. "Bein' an honesht man. I need to buy whishky, and that ish what I will do with the money. On my honor."

"Pathetic scum, who are you even to touch my garment?" The caped form's voice was soft yet majestic, controlled yet vicious. Angry, yet having fun. That made the thrill of horror all the wilder as it raced up Ernie's spine. "Honor! It has nothing to do with you! If your blood weren't thin as cheap wine I'd rip you from asshole to Adam's apple and romp through your insides while they steamed cooling on the ground."

Ernie gathered some part of his senses then and pulled himself almost to a sitting position, focusing his eyes with effort to stare up into the face looming above him, into the lewdly grinning mouth, the white thrust of fangs distorting the lower lip. Not Halloween . . . Then what the hell? *Was this real?*

"Oh, Jesus!" he moaned. He began to tremble and sank back onto the concrete, hugging it as if he wished he could burrow into it. "Oh, sweet Christ!"

"Hardly," the dark figure above him remarked sardonically.

A long leg swung back, arced like a scythe, and a foot caught Ernie square in the throat. Pain cut through his alcoholic haze, grew heavy and searing in his neck. He rolled into a ball, gagging, his eyes wide and gleaming with fright, unable to unlock their gaze from that of the tall thing above him. He tried to say something but he merely retched. The warmth and stench of the vomit, spreading around his cheek that was pressed to the ground, rose from the pavement.

The figure bent over him, leaning close. "Damn you that I might end up like you!" it said. "Nothing. A wisp of nothing!"

Faint light caught the curved fangs, and the thing stood up. It seemed so tall!

Ernie, desperately sucking in air now, winced when the cape lightly brushed his face as the creature whirled and strode from the alley. Or maybe not *from* the alley. It seemed to get near the mouth of the alley and then suddenly become absorbed in the shadows, as if it had become a shadow itself. Something blacker than the night that moved through the night.

Ten minutes after the thing had left, Ernie, stone sober, staggered into The Bus Stop, a decrepit bar on Broadway, not far from the alley. The place was stifling and smelled of perspiration and stale beer. A dusty plastic fern that for some reason always reminded Ernie of a gigantic spider blocked any view out the front window. There was no music in here; it wasn't the sort of place where people drank to have a good time.

The half-dozen men at the bar, dressed shabbily themselves, paid no attention to Ernie. The bartender, a huge, paunchy man named Ben, only glanced at him.

"Didn't expect to see you till tomorrow sometime, Ernie," Ben said.

"Listen, Ben! Christ, you gotta believe what I just seen! A fuckin' werewolf! Big thing with fangs, wearing a black cloak, all dressed in black. It kicked me, cussed me out. It, it . . ." Ernie began stuttering and clamped his jaws to stop.

"Vampire," said a flat voice from down the bar.

"Huh?"

"Vampires is what dresses in black and wears a cloak. 'Course, werewolfs has got them long teeth too."

"Vampire, werewolf, whatever," Ben said. "Guys that drink like you have seen worse, Ernie. Hell, half my customers have seen vampires and werewolves—sometimes in the same night." He laughed at his own wisecrack, and most of the men at the bar managed a grin as they bent over their drinks. It didn't do to have Ben pissed at you.

"What you need, Ernie," one of the men said, "is a drink."

"Got the money for a drink?" Ben asked him.

"No," Ernie admitted. "I was putting the touch on this . . . thing, before I realized what it was."

"What it was," Ben said, "was the d.t.'s, Ernie boy. You wanna occupy a stool for a while, okay, but no booze."

"Jesus, on the tab, eh, Ben? Please!"

"Aw, you got no tab and you know it. Last time you paid a tab was when Kennedy was president."

Ernie slipped up onto a stool and sat trembling violently. He felt as if he might actually shake himself onto the floor.

"You're a fuckin' mess," Ben said. "Upchucked all over yourself." He laughed again. He had a wide mouth but it was very thin, and he didn't open it much beyond a slit even when he threw back his head to laugh heartily. When he stopped laughing, he screwed up his eyes and looked closely at the quaking figure on the other side of the scarred and glass-ring-marked bar.

"Please, Ben! . . ."

Ben drew a beer and placed it in front of Ernie. "Not on the tab," he said, "on the house. Truth is, you look like you need it more'n anybody I ever seen in here."

Ernie tried to say thanks, but the glass was already at his eager lips, the foam airy and cold in his nostrils. Ben was right, he needed this bad. He thought again of the black-cloaked thing towering over him in the alley. It hadn't been his imagination, hadn't been the d.t.'s; he was sure of that. He was sure! Everyone down the bar was watching him somberly and a little enviously now, guy with the free beer.

He drank.

Somebody said, "Maybe you oughta call the cops, Ernie."

Ernie decided maybe he should.

Tomorrow.

Jennifer Crane—7:00 A.M.

Music was sifting up through the building, a rhythmic throbbing conveyed by brick, concrete, and steel. One of the tenants had his stereo on too loud, even though it was early morning. It wasn't the first time; tenants in most New York apartment buildings couldn't choose their neighbors and usually had to put up with at least one decibel-numbed maniac. Part of the modern urban scene.

But this morning Jennifer found the music relaxing. She could barely make out the tune: Talking Heads singing "We're on the Road to Nowhere." Where she'd been before she'd met Oxman. The music wasn't loud in the apartment; the thoughtless stereo jockey was probably on the floor below, and across the hall.

"Want me to phone down to the super and have that noise turned off?" Ox asked behind her.

"No, I kind of like it," she said, not looking back as she removed two slices of whole-grain toast from the pop-up toaster.

"You didn't have to get out of bed just because I did," Ox said. She heard his weight settle on one of the creaking wicker stools at the breakfast bar.

"Had to get up anyway. I'm working against a deadline on those ad-agency sketches." The apartment doubled as a studio; Jennifer worked at home as a free-lance artist. Most of her work—at least the work that paid well—was for advertising agencies. She was telling the truth about the deadline; the macho diet-beer layout ("It don't take calories to be a man") had to be in by tomorrow afternoon. "You went out last night," she added.

"Didn't think you heard me leave."

"I heard you go out and come in," Jennifer said. She spread strawberry preserves on the two pieces of toast, then poured two cups of coffee. "Work?"

"Work," Ox said.

Jennifer wouldn't push for information, wouldn't complain about his unexpected absence. His former wife, Beth, had never been able to get used to Oxman spending so much time away from home. Absence hadn't made *her* heart grow fonder. Or Ox's.

Jennifer carried the toast and coffee to the breakfast bar, pulled up a stool, and sat down next to Oxman. Neither of them were much for a large breakfast; toast and coffee was all they usually had in the morning. She washed down a multiple-vitamin pill with a sip of hot coffee, grimacing.

"Think you really need those pills?" Ox asked.

"They can't hurt me," she said, thinking of all the Quaaludes she'd taken until she managed to get off the dark carnival ride, "and maybe they're keeping me from catching cold." *Or maybe I need the security of swallowing some kind—any kind—of pill in the morning.*

Oxman grunted and swirled his coffee in his cup. She knew he didn't believe in taking any sort of medicine unless there was no other way, but also that he'd never try to force that point of view on her. His wife had been some kind of hypochondriac, Jennifer knew, though she and Ox never talked much about it.

She liked sitting close to Ox, catching the subtle scent of his shaving lotion, sensing the reassuring, protective bulk of the man. Jennifer remembered her own marriage, the pain, both emotional and from her frequent battering at the hands of her husband. She remembered the years here in Manhattan after the divorce, the singles bars, the desperation, the sex with virtual strangers. The road to nowhere. E. L. Oxman had been her lifesaving detour. At the time, even her work had lost its importance to her. He was the one thing substantial in her life. That was the word for Ox: substantial. What Jennifer needed.

She said, "I love you, E. L. Oxman," for no reason other than that she felt like saying it. And she did love him.

He was preoccupied. "Ever watch soap operas?" he asked.

She grinned, a beautiful girl with green eyes and auburn hair that fell with light grace to beneath her shoulders. "That wasn't the response I was fishing for."

Ox smiled. "Sorry. I was thinking about the call I went out on last night."

She was glad he wanted to talk about the case. She knew that his wife had wanted to know nothing about his work, and that she'd resented his being unexpectedly called to duty at odd hours.

"I've watched the soaps from time to time. Not very often, though. I rarely turn on the TV during the afternoons."

"Ever watched 'Shadowtown'?"

Jennifer added cream to her coffee, stirred. "A few times. It's pretty much like all the rest of them. Sex, intrigue, sex, tragedy, sex."

"This case involves 'Shadowtown,'" Oxman said.

Jennifer listened as he told her about the McGreery murder.

"You actually met Lana Spence?" Jennifer asked. He'd talked about murders before; she'd picked up some of his professional detachment and kept sympathy for the dead watchman at a distance. There was so much murder in this city. It was like a backdrop to life.

Ox shook his head no and shrugged. "I don't even know who she is."

"She's Delia Lane, the program's bitch."

"Haven't met her, but I heard about her," Ox said. "That's the second time I've heard her referred to as a bitch. Delia Lane, that is, not Lana Spence."

"It's not necessarily derogatory in this context," Jennifer told him. "Every soap opera has its stock characters: the ingénue, the eligible bachelor, the matriarch, the patriarch, the middle-aged lech, the good girl, the bitch, and so on. It's the bitch who makes the whole thing go."

"What do you know about the show?" Ox asked.

Jennifer thought back to the time she'd had the flu and hadn't picked up pens and air brushes for several weeks. She'd gone almost crazy with boredom and cabin fever and had turned to the soaps to take her outside her world of prescription pills and Kleenex. "Let's see, that's the show that had the vampire. He was the ultimate dangerous seducer. The sort of bloodsucker women found irresistible. A good-looking guy, my kind of vampire, portrayed him."

"The vampire's no longer on the show," Ox said. "They had to write him out when the actor who played him was killed in an accident."

For a moment Jennifer thought inanely, you can't kill a vampire.

Then she said, "I didn't know about that. I thought he was still breaking hearts and blood banks."

"You know anybody who follows the soaps religiously?" He took a bite of toast and chewed while Jennifer thought.

She had several acquaintances who watched the soaps, though not religiously. At least, they claimed moderation.

Then she remembered Myra Deeber. She'd met Myra at a singles bar over on Forty-ninth about three years ago. The place hadn't been exactly crawling with men; or rather, it was full of the sort that slithered. So Myra and Jennifer had struck up a conversation and found that they liked each other's company. Myra was about ten years older than Jennifer, in her early forties, and had been single in the New York scene for years. She told Jennifer about that life, what to expect in the long run. She'd been candid, had used herself as an example of where the wrong moves could lead.

They'd visited each other's apartments several times, browsed through baroque antique shops on Second Avenue, gossiped on the phone; now, though, Jennifer hadn't seen or talked to Myra in at least six months.

Myra was always ensconced in front of the TV during the afternoons Jennifer had been there, always watching the soaps. She'd admitted her addiction to them once, calling them her complicated world that she could turn off with the press of a button. She said she wished she could switch off her own world like that sometimes, at least temporarily. It was oddly comforting, she'd said, to look in on people with more problems than she had. Wasn't that why people watched the news?

"Well?" Ox had finished his toast and was brushing crumbs from his fingertips, watching her.

"Myra Deeber," Jennifer said. She told Ox about Myra, then gave him her address in the Seventies, and her phone number.

"She home during the day?" Ox asked.

"Sure. She has to be to watch the soaps. She works evenings at the Hunan Experience over on East Fifty-seventh."

"I'm assuming the Hunan Experience is a restaurant and not a massage parlor," Ox said with a grin.

Jennifer sipped her coffee and gave him a level look. "Myra's a waitress," she said. She still felt a twinge of anger at anything that might pass as a judgmental remark about how she'd lived before she'd met Oxman. She knew now what had been happening to her, what she'd been becoming. She hadn't gone all the way down that Road to Nowhere, but far enough to have known its pitfalls and loneliness.

She was being oversensitive, she knew. Ox was a man who seldom passed judgment, a man with a passion for undeniable fact. And for simple justice.

"You mind phoning her later this morning and setting up an interview for me?" he asked. "I think that'd be better than the official approach. You know, me looming outside the door."

"I'll call her," Jennifer said.

Ox took a final sip of coffee, slid off his stool, and kissed her cheek. "I love you back," he said.

She watched him strap on his shoulder holster, then shrug into his brown sport jacket. He was developing a slight stomach paunch. For an instant she felt him getting older, and experienced the chill of the future. She was getting older, too.

When he'd gone out of the apartment, she waited a minute for him to descend in the elevator, then she walked to the window overlooking West Ninety-eighth Street.

She could see the building's super, Richard Corales, hosing down the sidewalk in front. The trash had been picked up last night, and someone's plastic bag had broken and there was the usual mess. She watched as Ox emerged from the building three stories below, saw him nod and exchange a few words with Corales, then saw Corales point to the wet sidewalk and wave his arms, complaining as he often did about cheap plastic trash bags. Ox listened patiently, then said something to Corales, patted his shoulder, and walked around to where he'd parked the car.

When he'd passed from sight, Jennifer continued staring out the window for a while. Then she let the curtain fall and carried her coffee into the large bedroom that was set up as her studio. She looked at the framed samples of her work hanging on the walls. She was good; she knew it and the people she worked for knew it. And she was doing okay at last, making a decent enough wage to survive comfortably in Manhattan, even alone if necessary.

But she knew that alone she might not want to survive.

She sat down at her drafting board, took a sip of coffee, and set the cup on its cork coaster. She had an uneasy feeling about this murder Oxman was investigating. She didn't know why. At least the poor old watchman hadn't had fang marks on his neck. Anyway, Jennifer didn't believe in vampires, or werewolves, or the Yellow Brick Road.

Well, maybe the Yellow Brick Road. Sometimes. She smiled, thinking of Oxman last night in bed, before they'd slept. She and Ox were, in the vernacular of soaps and singles bars, good together.

Before starting to work, she looked at her wristwatch, then set its alarm.

At ten o'clock, she'd call Myra Deeber.

E. L. Oxman—7:40 A.M.

Tobin was at his desk in the squad room when Oxman arrived at the Twenty-fourth. He was engrossed in paperwork and had his white shirt-sleeves rolled up, his tie loosened. Muscle and tendon played along his dark forearms as he shuffled the report he'd just finished typing from his almost illegible longhand. Tobin, usually neatly if conservatively dressed, looked unkempt for this time of the morning. Even his tie was wrinkled.

"Sleep at all last night?" Oxman asked, sitting on the edge of Tobin's gray metal desk.

Tobin glowered up at him, his intense brown eyes puffy and pink-rimmed. "I stayed up a while after I got home, E. L. Went over my notes from that 'Shadowtown' thing, thought about it."

A Narcotics officer names Jameson walked past and waved to Oxman. Oxman waved back. "And?"

"I figure a loony broke in there to act out his fantasy, got surprised and panicked, then killed the watchman."

"Why?"

Tobin looked irritated. "Hell, I don't know. Embarrassment, maybe. How would you feel if somebody walked in on you while you were dancing around a dark studio playing vampire?"

"Okay," Oxman said, "this should be easy. We question everyone till we get a suspect who blushes easily, and we know we got our perp."

"You be pokin' fun, Elliot Leroy."

Oxman stood up from the desk edge and sighed. He knew it was time to back off when Tobin lapsed into his self-deprecating parody of

34

street-black dialect. "Yeah, I guess I am. I just can't buy embarrassment as a motive for murder. A guy who lives in enough of a dream
world to put on his own private show, it seems to me he'd run if he
were surprised."

"People panic," Tobin said, "and act unreasonably."

"I think if he panicked he'd bolt, even if the watchman had his gun
out of its holster, which he hadn't." Oxman shifted the bulk of his own
holstered .38 Police Special. "You had coffee, Art?"

Tobin nodded. "But I'll have another cup if you're buying."

Oxman went into the precinct lounge, a tiny green room near the
booking area, and coaxed two cups of coffee from the balky vending
machine, black for him, cream and sugar for Tobin. Jameson the narc
was in the lounge, seated at the Formica table and sipping what looked
like hot chocolate but might have been anything.

"Heard you were up late last night, Ox."

Oxman nodded. "Or early. Depending on how you look at it."

"Need any advice in dealing with these show-biz types, just let me
know."

"You've dealt with TV celebrities?"

"Sure, Ox. I'm in Narcotics. There's enough snow drifting around
in show business in this town to start a ski resort. Part of that kind of
life. I never had anything to do with soap-opera stars, though. But their
kind are all the same; things won't be easy for you."

Oxman shrugged. "I think we'll wrap up this one soon. It's not all
that complicated."

"They can put on a show," Jameson warned, as Oxman was
walking out balancing the steaming coffee cups. "Remember, Ox,
they're all actors."

Oxman wasn't impressed. Some of the best actors he'd seen had
never been onstage or before a camera.

"Manders wants you," Tobin said, when Oxman had returned to the
desk.

Oxman nodded, but instead of leaving for Manders's office, he
picked up Tobin's typed report and read it. Oxman knew most of it, but
he hadn't been on the scene when Tobin had questioned the co-
producers and set designer.

There was nothing startling in the report. Zachary Denton was on
the scene when Tobin had arrived, had in fact interrupted the murderer.
Sy Youngerman and Harry Overbeck had been phoned at home and

had rushed right to the studio. It hadn't taken them long. Overbeck lived on Central Park South, Youngerman on West End Avenue. However, reading further, Oxman saw that both men had been at a cocktail party at Youngerman's place. Great. They could alibi each other, along with any of Youngerman's other guests.

Oxman scratched his chin. On the other hand, West End was near enough so anyone could have slipped away unnoticed from the party for a while, then returned after killing McGreery. Not much time for a costume change in that scenario, but there was no guarantee the killer had been dressed like a vampire, or had even worn a black cape. Denton might very well have been mistaken about that. An eyewitness account in a dim warehouse didn't count for much.

A button on Tobin's phone went into a riot of blinking. He lifted the receiver. "Yes, sir," he said, "he's right here now." He hung up and said, "Manders again, Ox."

Oxman laid the McGreery homicide report on a clear corner of Tobin's cluttered desk, then crossed the squad room and walked down the short hall to Smiley Manders's office.

Manders was seated at his desk, his hands laced behind his head, his eyes lightly closed. For a moment Oxman thought he might be practicing yoga, then he realized that wasn't likely in a harried police lieutenant who existed on a pizza-and-cigarette diet. More likely he was enduring pain while waiting for his antacid to work.

When Oxman shut the door behind him, Manders's eyes sprang open. He seemed startled; he might actually have been dozing.

"Didn't hear you come in, Ox." His hands came out from behind his head and he leaned forward and rested his elbows on the desk. He'd been up late last night, too, and he looked tired, but Oxman knew Manders often looked weary when he wasn't. "The McGreery murder," Manders said in his rusty-nail voice. "How do you read it?"

"Kind of early to get any kind of reading," Oxman said. "We need some facts."

Manders lit a cigarette, coughed violently, then balanced it on the lip of a glass ashtray. He delicately picked some tobacco crumbs off the tip of his tongue and rolled them between his thumb and forefinger. "Tobin thinks it was just some nut-case the watchman disturbed play-acting."

"It's possible," Oxman said. "You know how it is; most anything's possible in Manhattan."

"Yeah. Was anything missing from the studio?"

Oxman shook his head. "Nothing appears to be so far. The show's producers looked around last night and said everything seemed to be in place. They're gonna check more carefully this morning."

"The lab isn't finished with comparisons," Manders said, "but it appears there aren't any fingerprints we wouldn't expect to find at the scene. Of course, it'll take a while to identify some prints. Lots of people come and go in a place like that."

"Was the killer wearing gloves?" Oxman asked. The lab must have gotten that far.

Manders drew on his cigarette, then looked down at it as if dismayed that he was trapped by the filthy habit. He exhaled lustily and squinted through the smoke. "We can't even be sure of that, Ox, but it would seem so. Do vampires wear gloves?"

"I don't know," Oxman said. "Guess I'll take to watch some late movies to find out."

"Or some 'Shadowtown' tapes."

Oxman cringed.

"Actually," Manders said, "it looks like a simple B and E where the perp got interrupted before he had a chance to steal anything. Then he lost his head and killed the watchman."

"That's the way I see it," Oxman said, not sure if he did see it that way. Not sure if Manders did. This one wasn't quite right for a breaking-and-entry murder. Or maybe that was just the show-biz flavor making it seem as if there should be some sort of complicated plot.

"Get statements from the rest of the cast and crew and whoever else over there you need to talk with," Manders said. "We'll have to treat this one with a little care. You can understand why."

"Our friends the media?"

Manders nodded and drew again on the hated cigarette. "A contact at the *Post* tells me this afternoon's edition is gonna have a spread on the McGreery killing, playing up the soap-opera bit, the guy in the cape who was supposed to have been seen. But if we do our work quickly and neatly, the whole matter'll blow over in a few days."

"You think we'll find out who killed the watchman in a few days?" Oxman asked, astounded.

"I think that in a few days we'll get as far as the facts lead us and we'll realize the killer will probably never be caught. This is just another one of those panicky, spur-of-the-moment homicides that won't be cleared up until we happen to arrest somebody on an unrelated charge and he gives information in order to buy less prison time. That might be years from now, if at all.''

"You really believe that?" Oxman asked. He knew it was probably true, but he'd never heard Manders take a defeatist line. Or maybe Manders was simply being a realist.

"The captain believes it," Manders said. "Probably as firmly as I do.''

And Oxman understood. Politics again. A bad mix with police work, but one that persisted. Probably this really *was* a simple matter of a burglar surprised before he could do his work, then panicking and taking out the watchman. That was what the people from the top on down were telling themselves as they pulled strings to get this case as wrapped up as possible as soon as possible. A murder that would probably go unsolved like a lot of others carried open on the books. Probably.

That wasn't good enough for Oxman. Or Manders. Which was why Manders had assigned Oxman and Tobin to the case. He could give them all the innuendo that was passed down to him, play the game like a good soldier, and Oxman and Tobin would still go out and try to solve the crime no matter where it led them. Manders could maintain his political capital this way, and even increase it if Oxman and Tobin got lucky and solved the watchman's murder. McGreery had been a cop until recently; the department owed him more than a politically expedient rollover.

"Keep me informed on this one, Ox," Manders said. *But not too informed.*

Oxman nodded and left the office, hearing Manders choking on smoke again behind him.

Oxman filled in Tobin on what Manders had said. He knew Tobin wouldn't like it. Tobin figured it was politics that had kept him down in rank, a black man who'd joined the department too early to be regarded as one of the new minority hotshots. Tobin was one of those few who'd paid their dues long before the expression became popular, and now he had to stand back and watch younger, less capable men receive the benefit of his endurance. Some of the younger blacks assumed Tobin must have been an Uncle Tom to have survived on the force all those years, never guessing that Tobin had gone a longer, tougher route than they could imagine and had kept himself his own man in the bargain. Now here he was, in a department that had finally opened real opportunities for blacks, and he was enough of a fixture to be ignored. He was typecast and forgotten, a nonperson again. Tobin was bitter about that and figured he had a right to be. Oxman had never told Tobin he might have a point.

"Politics is shit, Ox!"

"We agree. Let's ignore politics. You go to the 'Shadowtown' studios and talk to the rest of the people over there, and I'll meet you soon as I can."

"Where you headed?"

"I'm going to read your report, carefully. Then I'm going to see a woman who knows and loves soap operas."

"Shouldn't be hard to find one," Tobin said. He got up to let Oxman take his seat behind the desk. They used each other's desks indiscriminately; no professional secrets among partners.

As Tobin was walking away, Oxman heard him mutter, "Fuckin' politics!"

Myra Deeber lived in the west Seventies, in a large brownstone that had been converted into small apartments. Oxman buzzed her on the intercom and identified himself, and she told him to take the elevator up; her place was at the end of the third-floor hall.

The old building hadn't been kept up well, or modernized. The tiny elevator squealed and rocked its way to the third floor. It stopped and its dented steel doors hissed open, leaving a step up of almost a foot. Oxman made a mental note to take the stairs on his way out.

At Deeber's apartment door he knocked, flashed his smile and his shield at the peephole, then stood listening while locks clicked, chains rattled, and bolts slid free. If a fire ever broke out in the Deeber apartment, Myra might burn to death at the door trying to work the locks in time to get out.

She opened the door and stared out at him for a moment, a tall woman in her late forties, lean from the waist up, but with a wide and fleshy lower body. As if somehow there'd been a mix-up and the physiques of two different people had been fitted together. There was a concave tightness about her jaw that suggested she wore badly fitted dentures. She was one of those women who, when dressed up, would be reasonably attractive, but who took on age and harshness without makeup and in ordinary clothes and natural light. Her face was lined as if she'd known pain, but her violet eyes were hopeful.

"A solid, kind cop with sex appeal," she said, smiling at him.

"That's how you were described. Jennifer's doing okay. She deserves it."

"I agree," Oxman said. Then he grinned, momentarily ill at ease. "I mean, she deserves to be doing okay."

Myra Deeber laughed and stepped back to let him enter the apartment. The place was a mess. Magazines were spread around the sofa, chairs and floor. Through a doorway Oxman could see unwashed dishes stacked precariously on the sink counter, next to a glass of milk and a plate containing a huge, half-eaten wedge of pie. Apparently Myra liked to eat. A gray cat lounged on the windowsill near a dead flower in a red plastic pot. The air was motionless and stale. The cat didn't seem to give a damn.

"Sit down, please," Myra said, sweeping a magazine off the sofa and onto the floor.

Oxman noticed it was a magazine devoted entirely to soap operas. Most of the magazines here were soap-opera oriented, some of them the chronicles of particular shows. "Will Lance Love Rhea Her Way?" was the caption on the nearest glossy cover. "Shana Chooses Gang Rape over Loneliness" was the lead for another story. The women on the covers all looked as if they'd just been done over at the makeup counter at Bloomingdale's; the males all looked as if they'd just stepped from the menswear section of a J. C. Penney catalog.

Myra sat down in a well-worn recliner and said, "Sorry, I didn't have time to tidy up. Jennifer just called a little while ago and said you were coming. She said you needed to know about soap operas. That right?"

"One soap opera, actually," Oxman said. He noticed that Myra's recliner faced a huge RCA console TV whose cabinet appeared to have been designed by Frank Lloyd Wright. The set had to have been expensive, a stretch for her budget.

"One soap's pretty much like any other," Myra said. "Television's a flat world without much innovation."

"Then why do you watch it?"

Myra shrugged her bony shoulders. "The soaps are a world I can turn off. And it's nice to be part of the everyday existence of people with more problems even than old Myra."

"Not so old," Oxman said.

"Nice of you to say, Sergeant Oxman, but I'm past it. At least I feel I've turned a corner and can't go back. Hell, I'm not so sure I even want to go back. Men. All that pain. It's better maybe to tune in on it every afternoon, and then tune out." She traced a fingertip over one of her meaty thighs.

" 'Shadowtown' is the soap I need to know about," Oxman said. He didn't want to listen to any more of Myra's self-pity and rationalization. But he wondered how many other people watched soap operas for the vicarious emotional wrenches that were disturbingly real, then reassuringly synthetic. For too many people life was a bad dream without escape; but life on the TV screen could offer that escape, in both directions. From this world, then from that one. Turn a knob, punch a button. Like travel through space and time, in and out of minds.

" 'Shadowtown' is a juicy show," Myra said. "Right now, Delia's making it with Roger Maler."

"Delia the bitch?"

"Check," Myra said, nodding. "Roger's every middle-aged woman's dream, the town's handsome bachelor without any kinks. What Delia's trying to do, secretly, is get him to admit he fathered young Ivy Ingrams's baby. Ivy was the sweet ingénue. She's dead."

"I heard," Oxman said, resisting the urge to add, "Sad . . ."

"The thing is, Roger *is* the father, and he's arranged for this young couple to adopt the child from the foster home. What Delia wants is to find out for sure that he's the legal father, then she can force him to take the child himself and later turn it over to her."

"How can she force him?"

"She knows about Roger and the mayor's wife."

"I thought the mayor's wife was dead," Oxman said. "Along with the mayor."

"This is the new mayor," Myra said. "His wife and Roger go way back, and took up where they left off a year ago. She and Roger were involved in a holdup in Miami and owe some drug dealers a lot of money." She waved a hand aimlessly. "But all that's really irrelevant. The question is, will Delia get the baby so she can give it to a man who wants to sell the child to a couple in Connecticut who're willing to pay fifty thousand dollars. The fifty thousand Delia owes this man from the time she was a high-priced call girl in Miami."

"Let me guess," Oxman said.

Myra's gaunt face lit up; she was into it, all right. "Exactly," she said, "the same man Roger owes money to, but neither Roger nor

Delia know they've got this creep in common. He figures this is the only way he'll get any money out of Roger, and when he's through using Roger and Delia for that, then he'll get even with Delia. Or thinks he will. Delia always comes out on top."

"What about the vampire?" Oxman asked.

"Edgar Grume? He's not in the show anymore. He was a dream, loved the girls and let them die. Half the housewives in America would have bared their jugs for Edgar—jugulars, that is. Then poor Allan Ames got himself killed in a subway accident. Fell under a train."

"Allan Ames?"

"The actor who played Grume. So they had to write the vampire out of the script. He didn't live in Shadowtown, which is a little place not far from New York; he lived on Park Avenue and sort of flew there from time to time." She sighed, heaving her bony chest. "He gave that show some real class."

"You mean the vampire character lived on Park Avenue, not the real Ames?"

"Sure. I don't have any idea where Allan Ames lived. Probably he was a jet-setter."

Oxman was somewhat confused. Well, more than somewhat. "This is all ridiculous," he said.

"Sure," Myra said. "Forget about all that blackmail and money-owed stuff; that's just background motivation. What 'Shadowtown' is really about right now is Delia trying to get the goods on Roger so she can get her bitchy hands on that baby. There's other stuff going on in the show, like Roger's sweet young thing, but for now the Delia and Roger affair is why everyone's watching it. The sweet young thing's gonna get her ass kicked out of Roger's life by Delia. And soon. You can count on it."

Oxman shifted in his chair. He looked at the blank TV screen. It seemed to look back at him.

"Get you some coffee?" Myra asked.

He said no thanks, he'd had enough coffee. Then he said, "Myra, how involved do the fans get with the soaps' stars?"

She grinned. "To a lot of fans, 'Shadowtown' is a real place, and the people are real. At least as real as the polticians and other public figures we see on television. How many viewers have seen the real Tip O'Neill or even the real David Letterman. Not much of a line between real and unreal on that TV screen. And sometimes real people even play themselves on soap operas, cross over that line. Is 'Shadowtown' real? Are all those starving kids in Africa real? What about all those strutting Arabs in the Middle East, and the terrorists in ski masks? They all share the same tube, Sergeant Oxman, sandwiched between commercials for beer and cars and laxative and aspirin. I'd say that, to some people, Delia Lane is as real as the Ayatollah Khomeini."

"Real enough for them to cross over that line you talked about? To think they can become a part of what they see on 'Shadowtown' between those commercials?"

Myra thought for a moment, then said, "Why not? There's all kinds of people in this world."

Oxman knew she was right about that. His years as a cop had convinced him there was no end to human variation. Just when you thought you'd seen it all, somebody would show you that you hadn't.

He stood up, careful not to step on a magazine from whose cover a smiling man with incredibly fluffed white hair stared up at him. "Thanks for your help, Myra." He glanced around at the array of magazines and a thought struck him. "Would you have a copy of anything featuring 'Shadowtown'?" he asked.

"Oh, sure." She rooted around for a few minutes in a stack of magazines beneath the coffee table, tossing them aside one by one and adding to the mess on the floor. "Ah, ha!" she said finally, and handed him a tattered copy of *"Shadowtown": Sins, Shame and Ecstasy*. On the cover was a color photograph of a man and woman kissing with such openmouthed enthusiasm that their features were barely distinguishable.

"Delia and Roger?" he asked Myra.

She studied the cover. "No, that's Clint and Carlotta. They're off the show now. Drowned when a cruise ship went down in the Bahamas. She's doing shaving-cream commercials now and he's on Broadway."

Oxman saw that the magazine was six months old. "May I keep this?" he asked.

"Sure. I don't collect them; they just pile up."

He assured Myra he'd tell Jennifer to call her again sometime soon, then headed for the door and thanked her once more for her help. The gray cat glanced over at him as if he could go straight to hell.

"Hey, that's okay," Myra said. "I didn't have anything to do anyway. 'Ryan's Hope' doesn't come on until noon. There's nothing on now but stupid game shows."

Art Tobin—10:15 A.M.

They were shooting at Shadowtown Productions when Tobin got there. Youngerman was nowhere in sight, but Overbeck, who was wearing the rumpled brown suit he'd had on last night, spotted Tobin through a wide window and waved him into the control room.

The place was bustling, but in an orderly fashion, and there was plenty of terse conversation at low volume, people coordinating activities, nodding and giving hand signals. There were fancy electronic gadgets all over the place, banks of dials and switches. And there were half-a-dozen TV monitors so the people in the control room could see on the screens what was happening on the other side of the glass wall that faced the sound stage.

Out there, beneath bright lights, a stunning brunette about forty was rolling on the floor of what looked like somebody's living room. She wasn't alone. A handsome young guy with his shirt off to reveal muscles and a flawless tan was trying to get on top of her and kiss her. Who could blame him? They were both laughing. Somehow the young guy's elaborate hairdo stayed in place. The woman's long hair was tousled, but on her it looked great. She had too much makeup on, Tobin thought. Then he noticed that the young guy with the engineered hair had makeup on, too. It was for the cameras, Tobin told himself; they didn't walk around like that in real life. Or maybe the guy did.

He wound up on top of the woman, grinned down at her. She brushed the gold chain dangling from his neck away from her face and they clinched and kissed. The shot on the monitors zoomed in tight.

A big, bald man in the control room raised a hand, lowered it slowly, and said, "Okay, fade." The images of the man and woman on the

44

monitors became faint and then disappeared. Everyone in the control room seemed to relax, though not completely. There was an almost palpable residue of tension in the air.

"Anybody got a cigarette?" a slim woman in skintight jeans asked.

"Smoke those goddamned things outside the booth," the bald man said.

"I was going to," the woman said. "Hold on to your balls and be patient. If you can. Be patient, that is." She accepted a cigarette from a grinning kid who looked about sixteen, then sashayed out of the booth.

On the sound stage, the brunette and her wrestling mate were standing. The woman was smoothing out her clothes while the man put on a silky blue shirt. He seemed preoccupied.

"We're into a commercial time-out," Overbeck said. "We leave spaces in the tape so there doesn't have to be any editing. Our show's live-tape; that means there's no editing at all unless something really bizarre happens."

"Such as?" Tobin asked.

"Such as when Delia's tit fell out of her dress," the young guy with the cigarettes said. Nobody laughed, or even smiled. Tobin saw that he wasn't nearly as young as he appeared at first glance. He just had one of those boyish faces that would stay that way until he hit senility. In fact, he might be well into his thirties. He looked unconcerned that his attempt at humor had fallen flat. Like he was used to it happening.

"Matt, get everybody coffee or whatever they want," the bald man snapped, and the youngish guy hopped to obey. He was taking drink orders and was out of the booth in no time.

The company gofer, Tobin thought. Damned white nigger. Tobin thought of any ass-kissing subordinate, whatever the color, as a nigger. He'd had to survive in a police department that had treated him as an inferior from the time of his academy days. Only in the years after the turmoil of the civil-rights movement had things gotten easier for blacks in law enforcement, but by then Tobin had developed his calluses. He'd gotten used to being a better cop than many of those around him, earning survival but not recognition. And the higher-ups had gotten used to seeing Tobin that way, too, as a survivor and not much else; it was assumed that he'd sought, and found, his level.

But they'd never had the opportunity to think of him as an ass-kisser. He'd never given them that. Never would.

"Alley scene," the bald man said. He gave a countdown as if the space shuttle were about to be launched. The booth quieted, he flashed some more of the fancy hand signals, and the brunette and a sleazy underworld type in a black turtleneck sweater appeared on the screen. She called him Louie. They made arch remarks to each other then began an inane conversation about somebody's infant girl.

Overbeck whispered to Tobin, "How's it feel to see the real Lana Spence in action?"

"Like when I used to watch the soaps," Tobin said.

Overbeck looked surprised and pleased. Fans were where you found them. Tobin stood with him silently and watched the scene develop.

The dialogue was predictable, and the acting ranged from simpering and mugging to wooden readings of lines. Yet it was all slick even if it was shallow. The actors were doing something close to live theater and were thinking on their feet, using quick wit and minor improvisation, maintaining a kind of balance that didn't appear as precarious as it was. Tobin felt a twinge of admiration for them; he knew he was watching a rare combination of nerve and professionalism.

"I need to talk to some of these people," he said.

"Certainly." Overbeck was all cooperation.

Sy Youngerman came into the booth, saw Tobin, and smiled and nodded. He was in a three-piece blue pinstripe suit today; he looked like a banker on his way to a foreclosure. An important lunch downtown, Tobin figured. Youngerman probably had a lot of those.

"How's it going?" he asked Overbeck.

"Okay." Overbeck glanced over at Tobin. "This is Friday's show we're taping."

"You into the cottage scene yet, Shane?" Youngerman asked the bald man in a soft voice.

"No, it's after the alley scene." Shane sounded annoyed.

Youngerman turned to Overbeck with an agonized expression. "Jesus, Harry, we got a schedule."

Overbeck nodded toward Shane the bald. "Talk to the director. I already have."

"This'll be wrapped up today," Shane assured them over his shoulder, then he turned back to study what was happening on the sound stage. For him, just then, nothing else existed.

Youngerman looked again at Overbeck, shook his head, and said again, "Jesus, Harry."

Overbeck shrugged helplessly, as if to say, "Who are we? Only the producers." But he gave the impression he felt secure enough in his authority to allow a little slack.

Another actress, a tiny blonde, was now talking to Lana Spence and the gray-haired man. The dialogue didn't improve.

"This is where it happened," the blonde said, holding back tears. "This is where my sister ran to so she could escape what was going on in that clinic, where she tried to abort her pregnancy herself. Where she bled to death because she was too drugged up to think straight. Oh, God, I wish it had been me!"

"Jesus, Harry," Tobin said.

Overbeck looked over at Tobin; he seemed angry for an instant, then he grinned and ran his hand over his stub haircut. "Come on outside and we'll talk," he said. He patted Shane on the back and led the way to the door. Shane didn't seem to notice. His heart and his head were in his job.

"Looks like hard work, putting out a daily soap opera," Tobin said. *But not as hard as pounding the sidewalk and asking questions and usually getting nowhere.*

Overbeck nodded. "Hard but lucrative. And nerve-racking. We watch the ratings like a nervous old maid watches her birthdays. Everybody in this business knows eventually the wrong number will turn up, the one that confirms you're without hope or a future."

"Speaking of people without," Tobin said, "did anything turn up missing when you checked for theft?"

"No. Except for a length of venetian-blind cord from the cottage set, the set you just saw. Zach Denton remembered it had been left over when the prop men hung the blinds; it had been lying on the windowsill, out of range of the cameras, for weeks."

"The murder weapon," Tobin said. The killer must have been hiding on the dark set, maybe behind the drapes, realized he might need to kill the watchman at some point in order to work his way out of the building, and armed himself with the cord. "Nothing else missing?" he asked.

"No. And we went over the place pretty damned thoroughly. Far as we can tell, nothing's been stolen. Maybe Vince got to the burglar before he or any of his confederates had a chance to steal anything."

"Confederates?"

Overbeck spread his hands. "There could have been more than one and poor McGreery scared them away."

That was something Tobin hadn't thought of, but there was no sense in making things more complicated than they were already.

"I'd like to talk to whoever's in charge of costumes," Tobin said.

"Certainly." Overbeck led the way down the hall. "So how about it?" he asked. "Do you have any clues?"

Tobin tried not to smile. "I guess I'm here looking for clues, Mr. Overbeck."

"Harry." Overbeck turned his head and smiled. "Call me Harry." Tobin couldn't help it; he liked the rumpled little easy-street jackoff.

A tall, sour-looking girl named Velma, in charge of Wardrobe, explained that there were five Edgar Grume vampire outfits. The hot lights caused the players to perspire heavily, she said; five were necessary. Tobin told her he'd seen some people perspire under hot lights, too. She didn't think he was joking and she got quiet and tense as she took him to a small, windowless room full of stacked cardboard boxes.

Velma seemed to know where to look. She read the black felt-tip printing on the boxes, then wrestled one out of the middle of a stack of three. She opened the box, then ripped tape loose from some plastic and peeled it aside. It took her only a few seconds to straighten up and say, "That's odd, there are only two costumes here. Want to see for yourself?"

Tobin said that he did, stooped low, and counted two vampire costumes. These two, plus the two on the hangers in the costume room, made the proverbial four. Not five. Tobin smiled slightly. He and E. L. were actually involved in a case where two and two made four, the kind of case that was supposed to be easy to solve.

"There's an Edgar Grume costume missing," Velma said, mildly bewildered. She was standing with her forefinger pressed to the point of her long chin, as if she were trying to use pressure to create a dimple. Someone had invaded her domain and she didn't like it. She might simmer over it for days.

Tobin thanked her for her cooperation and left her wondering.

He felt better about the case now. It was beginning to shape up as he'd supposed: some screwball broke in here to take an ego trip on the stage of his favorite soap, got surprised, and carried the role too far. Manders would be pleased. They wouldn't be able to catch the guy, but he'd turn up. His kind always did. Weeks or months would pass and he'd be arrested in Times Square for lascivious conduct wearing his vampire get-up, or he'd actually think he was a bat and try to fly and be no more problem to anyone. As far as the media were concerned, no one important on the "Shadowtown" set had been killed, not one of the actors. Just an old watchman, with an old wife who was now an old widow. A nobody was dead. So what?

Tobin had a sour taste in his mouth. He saw a drinking fountain in the hall, went to it, and tried to wash the taste away.

McGreery had been a cop. Tobin was a cop. Tobin wished one of those plastic assholes on stage or one of the backbiters in the control room had surprised the caped flake. The wrong people always died, the gentle people, the old and the very young and the unsuspecting and naive. Natural victims in a jungle that some of them weren't even aware existed.

He stood up from the drinking fountain and ran his tongue over the inside of his cheeks. The sour taste was persistent. So was his sense of rage and futility. He understood how the villagers in Transylvania felt when they took out after Dracula in that old movie.

Find the bastard and drive a stake through his heart.

E. L. Oxman—11:00 A.M.

Oxman showed his ID to the day security guard at the "Shadow-town" production facilities and entered the converted warehouse. He tried to imagine the place as it had been last night, when the murder had occurred, and he wondered how the killer had gotten in. So far no sign of forced entry had been found, though there was an unsecured window in the rear of the building that might have afforded easy access.

"Hope you catch the bastard," the day guard said, as Oxman stepped around him. "I liked Vince, what I seen of him, but it's more than that. He was a cop, like I was and you are, and cop-killers are the worst of all the human garbage we deal with."

Oxman turned and looked closely at the man. He was in his early sixties, with a weathered, veiny face that suggested long mornings directing traffic on cold corners. The plastic name tag with his dour snapshot pinned to his tan uniform shirt proclaimed him to be one Thomas Merritt.

"On the job here?" Oxman asked.

Merritt shook his head. A lock of his gray hair flopped down above his left eye. "I served in a little town upstate, but a cop's a cop wherever he did his job, and a cop-killer's a cop-killer."

Oxman wasn't surprised by Merritt's emotional reaction to his fellow guard's death. All cops held a particular hatred for someone who had murdered one of their number. It was a profound fraternal concern; it was the knowledge that a killer had struck at the very heart of what they represented. McGreery had no longer been on the force, but that didn't matter. His days on the beat, in the patrol cars, swallowing fear but seldom pride—that was what mattered forever in a cop's mind. Oxman felt the same emotion himself, the vague knowledge that with an old man he'd never met, some small part of himself had died. "Every man's death diminishes me," the poet said, and that was especially true about cops when other cops died violent deaths.

"Anything I can do to help . . ." Merritt was saying.

Oxman nodded. "Thanks. Maybe before this is over we'll take you up on that." He moved on down the long hall toward the offices and sound stage.

Beyond the white-paneled drop ceiling, the sounds of his footsteps changed somewhat and he could sense, as he had last night, the dim vastness of the building around him. Like the feel of an echoing cavern. Then he rounded a partition and saw Tobin standing with Harry Overbeck. He watched as Tobin looked up, saw him approaching, then said something to Overbeck and moved away so he and Oxman could talk privately. Overbeck stood at a forward angle for a moment, as if he wanted to follow Tobin, then moved toward a door to what looked like a control booth. Beyond the booth several of the cast were standing around a set made up to look like the rough-hewn and functional but trendy interior of a beach cottage.

"How you been spending your time here, Art?" Oxman asked.

Tobin shrugged. "Following the line of questioning, meeting all the charming people."

"What did you pick up?"

"If they're anything like their soap identities," Tobin said, "I suppose I might have picked up anything from herpes to the flu just standing around them. The truth is, though, they seem like normal, whacky show-business types who are too wrapped up in their careers to take time out to commit murder. Though they might consider killing one of their own number."

"Why do you say that?" Oxman asked.

"Professional jealousy, Ox. The air vibrates with it in front and in back of the cameras."

"Wouldn't you say that's more or less standard?"

"Never been on a soap set before," Tobin said. "Wouldn't know. I do know I've got no idea who's good for this murder. I did find out one thing. The woman in charge of Wardrobe told me an Edgar Grume outfit is missing."

"A vampire costume, huh?"

Tobin nodded. "More and more, Ox, it looks like some loony broke in here and killed McGreery. Kinda thing that happens all the time and doesn't even make the papers, only this time it happened where a soap is taped, so it's juicy news."

Oxman jammed his hands into his pockets and gnawed on his lower lip. He had to admit that what Tobin said made sense. It didn't figure that one of the cast or production crew would have any reason to murder a watchman, because it didn't figure they'd have a reason to be roaming around here after hours. And if one of them *had* wanted to kill anyone here at Shadowtown, why would he or she have gone to the trouble of stealing and wearing a vampire costume? That was apropos to murder, but a bit melodramatic even for a soap-opera star.

"Have you decided Edgar's come back again from the grave and is stalking the populace?" a woman's voice asked.

Oxman looked up from staring at a spot on the floor and saw a slender, fortyish woman of astounding beauty. She had a trim, almost waspish figure, penetrating blue eyes, and dark hair that cascaded with controlled wildness like a mantle of madness. She was wearing a low-cut blouse and tight slacks of some sort of silky material that showed off her legs. Legs worth showing off.

"You mean Edgar Grume the vampire?" Tobin asked.

"Only Edgar Grume I know," she said. "Knew, rather."

"Too bad for vampires," Tobin said in an admiring voice Oxman seldom heard.

But she wasn't looking at Tobin; she had her unwavering stare fixed on Oxman. This had to be Delia the bitch, he thought. Perfect casting.

"I should have said Allan," the woman said. "Allan Ames."

"The actor who played Grume," Oxman said.

"Ah, you're a fan."

"No."

"Which is why he probably doesn't know who you are," Tobin said, as if apologizing for Oxman's incredibly bad manners. "Ox, this is Lana Spence, who plays Delia on the show."

"Ox?" she said. "That's a curious name."

"My full name's Oxman. E. L. Oxman."

"What's the E. L. stand for?"

"Lana Spence your real name?"

"Of course not," she said, and smiled at his evasion. Oxman seemed actually to feel the impact of that smile. *Wham!*

Rumpled Harry Overbeck walked over, along with a hulking bald man wearing dark suit-pants and paisley suspenders.

"We're ready to shoot the argument scene," Overbeck said. He looked over at Oxman. "Any new developments in the case?" he asked, no doubt remembering the line from a thousand movies and TV cop shows. The bald man might have smiled, but Oxman couldn't be sure. He didn't look like a guy who smiled a lot.

"We're gradually putting the pieces together," Oxman said non-committally, giving him back some more movie dialogue. He noticed the bald man shift his weight from leg to leg, as if impatient.

"Come on, Shane," Overbeck said. "We better make a final check on the time sequence." Again he looked at Oxman. "Care to come into the control room and watch a scene being shot?" he asked. "Your partner seemed to enjoy the one he saw earlier."

Oxman nodded. "Thanks, I'd like that. My partner's more knowledgeable about the soaps than I am, but I'm learning."

Lana Spence seemed to glide in front of Oxman as he started to follow Overbeck and bald Shane. "I do need to talk to you alone after the scene," she said, loud enough for everyone to hear.

"About the McGreery murder?"

Lana laughed. "Not about some other murder. You didn't suppose I intended to seduce you, did you?" she asked. "That's Delia you're thinking of."

"Is it?" Shane asked no one in particular. Lana pretended not to have heard him as they walked toward the set and control room.

Five minutes later, from the regulated order behind thick glass, Oxman stared out at the scene unfolding before him in the cottage. Lana Spence—or Delia—was arguing violently with a man she referred to as Roger. Roger Maler, Oxman figured. The town's most sought-after bachelor, according to Myra Deeber. The argument seemed to be about whether Roger would go to a business meeting in New York over the next several days. Delia suggested that he was actually planning to meet another woman, his younger lover, and demanded that he spend the time with her. Roger was adamant about going until Delia mentioned something about a man from Miami who's been asking about him. He changed his mind about the New York trip in a hurry then. When Delia licked her lips and moved in on him and promised playfully to make their time spent together worth his while, Roger wound up clutching her to him and telling her how much he loved being with her. Oxman could see his point. As she ran her fingers over the back of Roger's handsome head and stared directly into the camera that was dollying in, she smiled wickedly.

"Great!" bald Shane said in the control booth. Then he threw a switch that carried the sound of his voice outside the glassed-in room and said "Great!" again with the same enthusiasm.

Roger and Delia started drifting off the set into the real world. Oxman glanced at the black-and-white monitor in the control room and saw that the cottage was empty.

"Restaurant scene in an hour!" Shane reminded them.

Neither of them seemed to have heard. Oxman wondered if Lana Spence *ever* heard Shane. Or anyone else she didn't want to hear.

"I'll meet you back at the Two-Four," Oxman said softly to Tobin. "After I see what Miss Spence has to say."

Tobin put on his wide and lascivious grin. "You devil, Roger—er, Elliot Leroy."

"Check with the earlier shift reports and see if there were any calls about vampires from anywhere else in the city."

Tobin nodded, somber again after Oxman's lack of response to his goading. "I doubt if that'll net us much, Ox. Whoever killed McGreery probably realized he might have been seen and would have ditched the costume as soon as possible. Still, I guess it's a base we oughta touch."

"If we want it to be legal when we score," Oxman said.

"Speaking of scoring . . ." Tobin worked his eyebrows Groucho Marx fashion.

"Can it, Artie," Oxman told him. What the hell was wrong with Tobin?

He waited until Tobin had left the control room before stepping out and looking around for Lana Spence. She wasn't in sight. Apparently she was waiting for him to come to her dressing room. A star was a star and was expected to act like one, he thought. But if she wasn't in her dressing room waiting for him, she'd find out a cop could act like a cop. Overbeck told him how to get there.

As he left the sound-stage area, he noticed Zachary Denton, the set designer who'd discovered McGreery's body, wandering around the cottage set carrying a clipboard and pencil. When Denton passed the sofa where Delia and Roger had clinched, he paused and ran his hand along where she'd been sitting, as if to find out if the leather was still warm.

Then he saw Oxman looking at him, grinned, and moved over to make a note about a quilt hung over the fireplace.

Oxman found himself wondering if Zachary Denton and Allan Ames wore about the same size clothes.

Zachary Denton—12:05 P.M.

Zach watched Oxman leave the sound-stage area and walk toward the dressing rooms. Oxman was going to talk with Lana Spence, Zach had heard a member of the sound crew say. And it was Lana who'd requested the conversation, which wasn't the way things usually occurred in a murder investigation. Lana should have hammed her way through enough low-grade thrillers to realize that much.

As Zach strolled around the cottage set, looking over the props, he was preoccupied, actually thinking about Oxman. He hadn't caught anything special in the way the homicide cop had stared at him; Oxman didn't know anything yet.

Or did he?

Zach again called up the vision of Oxman's features as they'd exchanged glances. That vision was reassuring: only the flat yet probing eyes of a cop, no spark of knowledge or emotion there along with the mild curiosity. It had been only a few hours since Zach had found out, so it wasn't likely that Oxman knew.

This morning, at breakfast in his apartment, Bonnie had been harping at Zach. They'd had an argument last night, over some spilled wine, and he'd lost his temper and struck her. Not hard, really, just a glancing blow off her upper arm. But it had left a large bruise that was turning an ugly purple, which Bonnie showed him indignantly as she poured his coffee.

Zach had prudently waited until she'd put down the potentially dangerous potful of scalding liquid before telling her that if she didn't like the way he treated her she could leave. Move out and find her own apartment. She'd gotten really mad then, and he thought for a moment

56

she might really walk out and not return, at least for several days, so he'd lightened up and laid on the sweet talk. Pressed the right buttons.

She was a pliable fool, like the rest of them, and after breakfast they were back in bed, making love. He was gentle with her this time, stroking her forehead as she bucked against his rhythmic thrusts into her. She kept moaning about how much she loved him. He listened to the music of the bedsprings and didn't answer.

What with Bonnie causing delay and confusion, he hadn't gotten a chance to read the morning paper until after he'd showered, and had only fifteen minutes before he had to leave for the morning's taping. He hadn't caught Oxman's name yesterday, and only when he read the news item about Vince McGreery did he realize who Oxman was. His, Zach's, name was in the paper, too, and he wondered if it had meant anything to Oxman. There was something unnerving about Oxman, about the methodical way the stolid, sandy-haired detective thought and moved. A kind of calm relentlessness. It was almost spooky.

"Honey," Bonnie said, close to Zach. She'd lowered herself onto the sofa and had sidled up to him while he'd been absorbed in the newspaper. She was a tiny, green-eyed girl with reddish hair and freckles across the top of her chest. She was still damp from her shower, wearing only her panties; Zach noticed the few freckles down on her breasts, above the pink nipples that were puckered and rigid from the coolness after the steamy bathroom.

When he didn't answer her, she coiled an arm around his neck and leaned close. He felt her tongue lick and then probe warmly at his ear.

"Jesus!" he said. "Didn't you get enough?"

She grinned. "Never enough of you, babe. I want you to be thinking about me all day long."

"I'll be busy," he said, "thinking about other things." He disengaged her arm from around his neck. "I'm thinking about other things right now."

"Such as?"

"Nothing that concerns you."

She moved away from him on the sofa. "You block me out, Zach. Unless you want sex, you treat me like some kind of pest."

Zach was still wondering about Oxman. "Sometimes you are a pest," he said.

"You don't mean that, baby."

"Sure I do."

"Damn you!" She rushed at him, feigning anger more than she was experiencing real insult. He'd called her worse. They'd fought. She'd forgiven him. Coming back for more was what she was all about.

Almost absently, Zach shoved her away, and she nearly lost her balance on the sofa, almost slid onto the floor. She stood up and kicked him in the leg with her bare foot. That hurt her more than it did him.

"You bastard!" she said, her anger stoked by the jolt of pain. She leaned forward and drew back her arm to slap him in the face. Too slow.

Zach caught her wrist, stood up, and cupped a hand beneath her chin. He pushed her and she struck the wall hard, causing his new Monet print to drop to the floor. The frame cracked and fell apart. First the wine, now the print. *Enough!*

"Wait!" Bonnie pleaded, but he was on her. He grabbed her by the arm, making sure his fingers dug hard into the purplish bruise, and slung her toward the sofa. She bounced off the cushions and sprawled backward onto the carpet.

Zach walked over to stand above her. He glared down at her and she raised her arms as if to ward him off and cowered back toward the corner. Her teeth were bared like those of a terrified animal whose only defense left was to bite. He saw, faintly, the familiar glint in her eyes.

"I don't want you here when I come home this evening." He spat the words at her. "Do you fuckin' understand?"

She nodded that she did.

Zach picked up the folded newspaper and flung it at her. It came half apart in midair and struck her in the legs, leaving her lower body covered with crimped pages. Then he whirled, snatched up his sport coat from where it was draped over a chair, and left the apartment, slamming the door hard behind him.

He knew Bonnie was watching him, so he didn't bother glancing back at her. The slut! The overbearing, interfering slut! She deserved far worse than he'd ever given her, and maybe she'd get it.

He knew she'd be there when he returned tonight.

They both knew.

E. L. Oxman—12:10 P.M.

Lana Spence waited, probably longer than was necessary, after Oxman's knock on her dressing-room door, then called for him to come in.

He'd found the right door only due to her name in small block letters, and was naively surprised to see that there was no star on the door's smooth surface. But he was equally surprised to see how plush the large dressing room was. He'd come to think of a place where actors and actresses changed as being small and functional, with exposed steam pipes and a large mirror surrounded by bare bulbs. Lana Spence's mirror was surrounded by concealed lighting, there were no exposed pipes, and the furniture in the spacious room was French provincial and obviously expensive. The carpeting was royal blue and deep. This room seemed not to be associated at all with the workplace outside where dreams were spun for Televisionland. Oxman, like most of the public, had a number of misconceptions about the show-business jungle and the animals therein.

"Sit down, please," Lana said. She was already seated before her mirror, removing makeup with some sort of strong-smelling solvent on a soft tissue. The acrid scent reminded Oxman of the airplane dope he used to apply to balsa-and-paper model aircraft he'd constructed as a kid.

He crossed the deep-pile carpet and sat in a rather uncomfortable wooden chair near her. He couldn't help feeling somewhat like a peasant in the presence of nobility. But then, that was the impression the room was meant to create.

As he studied Lana's reflection in the mirror, she seemed to get more beautiful as she removed makeup.

"Dorian Gray in reverse," he said.

She smiled at him in the mirror. "Why, Detective Oxman, what a nice thing to say. And from a policeman."

"We sometimes read more than crime statistics," Oxman said. Like the sports page. He'd read *Portrait of Dorian Gray* in high school and was surprised himself that it had just now bobbed to the surface of his memory.

"I didn't mean to imply I supposed you an illiterate," Lana said. She was smiling from behind the folds of the tissue.

"You wanted to talk, Miss Spence. Can we do that while you're removing makeup?"

She didn't answer, but instead spent the next minute and a half finishing wiping her features clean. Then she swiveled on her padded vanity stool to face Oxman. She waited, as if for another compliment. Oxman was getting fed up with this.

He said, "You had something to tell me about the McGreery murder."

"Did I?"

"So I was led to believe."

"I suppose it is about the poor watchman's murder—indirectly. At least, it could be."

"What is it, Miss Spence?"

"I've been threatened."

Oxman figured that probably wasn't so uncommon. "By who?"

"Well, that's just it, Detective Oxman, I'm not sure."

Oxman sighed. "But you're sure you were threatened?"

"Of course." She sounded barely tolerant of his mental sluggishness. She twisted her lean body, opened a drawer, and removed a plain white envelope. "I found this stuck under my dressing-room door yesterday." She reached into the drawer again. "And this and this the week before." She seemed to begin losing her composure, but Oxman had the feeling she was playing for effect, acting for him. Show biz in the blood. "I've been receiving these for the past two months."

Oxman took the stack of envelopes from her, opened them one by one, and read.

There was nothing particularly imaginative or interesting about the notes. They were all obscene, and whoever had written them threatened to do painful and humiliating things to the recipient and then kill her. The printing, in soft pencil, was simple and childish, the sort of thing that would be useless to a handwriting analyst, and the stationery was cheap stuff sold in drugstores all over the city. The notes were addressed not to Lana Spence, but to Delia Lane.

What *was* interesting was the signature at the bottom of each note, also done in the same crude scrawl: *Edgar Grume*.

"Grume's dead," Oxman said inanely. "I mean, even Allan Ames, the actor who played him, is dead."

"Being dead never stopped Grume before," Lana said archly.

"Maybe not, but he was sure as hell stopped when Ames died."

Lana stood up, walked to a closet with sliding doors, and took off her robe, as if Oxman weren't there. He swallowed hard. She was wearing a black slip and bra. Her breasts were larger than he'd imagined when seeing her fully dressed, and they seemed intent on escaping the bra's ample cups. She slipped a white sweater on over her head, bent immediately to check in the mirror and make sure her hair hadn't been too mussed, then said, "Someone in my position receives all sorts of strange mail, Detective Oxman, but the tone of those notes scares me. They're so straightforward and matter-of-fact about my—or Delia Lane's—dying. And they keep coming. They just keep coming." Again she pulled a distraught face, as she turned to the closet and began sorting through clothes. Hanger wire squealed across the metal rod; empty hangers pinged against each other.

"Any idea who might feel that strongly about you?" Oxman asked.

"I make enemies," she said. "It's part of my life, having enemies. Part of every actress's life. Especially if she's . . ."

"A star," Oxman finished for her. So modest she was.

"Exactly," she said, unsmiling.

Oxman knew there were certain beautiful women who, by virtue of their beauty, expected the world to tilt their way and all good things to come to them as if that were their due. Some of these women, along with their beauty, carried in their core an innate feeling of inferiority, and when they didn't receive what they expected, they needed to establish that the world and not they were at fault. When they weren't catered to, they got irritated. Sometimes very irritated. That was Lana Spence, Oxman figured: beautiful, talented up to a point, and insecure enough to be aggressive, even hostile. He could believe she had enemies. But a series of life-threatening notes, signed by a dead vampire (as if there were any other kind), was an extreme reaction, even toward a woman like this. Oxman wondered what Lana Spence had done, and to how many and what people.

"I'll take these with me, Miss Spence," he said, gesturing toward the stack of letters.

"Of course you may," Lana said, as if he'd asked permission. "I don't like having them around where I have to look at them. And since you're going to be investigating threats on my life, you might as well call me Lana."

"It'll be a privilege," Oxman said, only half seriously.

She hadn't picked up the note of sarcasm in his voice. "Don't force me to act like a star, Detective Oxman. Or may I call you Ox, as your partner does?"

"I'd answer to that," Oxman said.

"I just bet you would, Detective Oxman." She grinned wickedly, the same grin he'd seen earlier before the cameras; she thought she'd made an inroad.

"I need a starting point," Oxman said. "You must suspect someone, if even remotely, of writing these notes."

"No. I can't believe anyone would actually want to murder me. Or is he only trying to scare me? Should I take these death threats seriously, Ox?"

"You said 'he,'" Oxman pointed out. "Who'd be your leading candidate, or at least a possibility, to wish you any kind of harm? A rejected suitor, maybe? You must have an army of those."

She found a plaid skirt and stepped into it as she thought. She zipped it up the back and let the sweater hang out. With a shake of her head so her hair was slightly disarranged, she suddenly looked years younger. She got out a black pair and a red pair of high-heeled shoes. "These or these?" she asked, holding out both pairs for Oxman to see.

"Wear the black," Oxman told her. "Now, about these death threats . . ."

"All right, I'm sorry." She slid her stockinged feet into the black shoes, twirled before a full-length mirror, then nodded in satisfaction. "I'm not suggesting anyone I know wrote those notes, but there is what you call a rejected suitor; Christ!—that sounds like a term out of a Tennessee Williams play! Six months ago we had an argument on the set, and he struck me."

"With his fist?"

"Yes. I was surprised; no man had ever hit me until then. The night before, I'd told him we were finished. He didn't want to believe it. He walked up to me on the set between takes and wanted to talk it all out again. I strongly suggested he stop bothering me, and he got mad and all of a sudden I was curled up on the floor and couldn't breathe."

"This man was fired from the show, I presume."

"No, I wouldn't let Sy or Harry fire him."

"Why not?"

"He's one of the best at his job, and he apologized and promised never to harm me again. And he hasn't. He's been a gentleman since then."

"Okay. I suppose certain actors are indispensable to a soap opera."

"He isn't an actor," Lana said, "he's Zach Denton, our set designer."

Something, a vague stirring, rustled in the back of Oxman's mind. Something beyond the violent pornography Denton had carried in his portfolio. "Why did you break off the affair with him?"

"The earth had spun on its axis too many times," Lana said. "Time had passed, and I was bored with Zach. Simple as that. Sorry, but that's the way I am and I don't intend to change."

"You told him that?"

"Not quite so bluntly. But the message got across."

Someone knocked firmly three times on the door. "We're ready to leave, Lana."

"The cast is going to Riverside Park to shoot the picnic scene," Lana explained. "That's why I'm dressed like a cheerleader with the hots. Should bring back memories in the viewers. Everybody got fucked at some time or another on a picnic, don't you think?"

Oxman thought back to a day almost a quarter of a century ago. "Guess I'm no exception," he said. He stood up, stuffing the stack of notes into his sport coat pocket. "I'll talk to Zach Denton. Meanwhile, you take care, Lana."

"I feel better now that I've talked to you," she said, as he held the door open for her. The back of her hand brushed his thigh as she stepped past him. Not accidentally, Oxman knew. Her life was a reflection in the eyes of men, as was her sense of self-worth. It was the curse of many truly beautiful women.

Oxman watched her run down the hall to where a tall, distinguished-looking man with the bearing of a stage actor waited for her. They exited the place like royalty.

She might feel better now, but Oxman didn't. She had complicated the murder investigation. Death threats signed Edgar Grume, an Edgar Grume costume missing, and what appeared to be a man in a black cape seen fleeing from the scene of McGreery's murder. What had, an hour ago, seemed simple, had now become not only complicated but bizarre.

Oxman left the building, nodding a good-bye to Merritt the guard. This afternoon or tomorrow would be soon enough to talk to Denton, who was probably at Riverside Park anyway. Talking to him might lead somewhere, but the fact that he'd lost his temper and punched Lana Spence didn't necessarily make him a murder suspect or even a crank note writer. Denton was a big boy who'd probably been jilted before, and he'd had six long months to cool off since his run-in with Lana.

It was Lana Spence whom Oxman needed to find out about, and not from Lana Spence.

Arthur Sales—4:30 P.M.

Sales didn't feel like going home. Not to Wendy and her interminable bitching. Their marriage would never be the same, and that was fine with Sales. Maybe Lana had done him a favor, when she'd instigated, and then ended, their brief affair. Losing Lana had hurt at first, still hurt sometimes, but at least now he was sure he wanted to leave Wendy. Well, he thought he was sure. He'd always felt his heart tugged this way and that with Wendy.

Wendy Conroy, actress and sometime art dealer. Now full-time art dealer, really. But she'd done enough acting to notice genuine sparks between Sales and Lana Spence on "Shadowtown" and she knew Lana by reputation. A bitch. A classic bitch. Not at all unlike the character Lana played on "Shadowtown." Reality—or unreality—didn't end with the cutting of the scenes, Wendy suspected. Then she'd hired a scumbag private detective to get the proof she needed that Sales and Lana were having an affair. Sales still felt a rush of shame and anger when he thought about the photographs taken secretly at the motel in New Jersey. The things Lana had talked him into doing! Even soap-opera fans would have a hard time imagining.

Wendy had waved the photographs in front of Lana and threatened to give them to the *Enquirer* if Lana didn't stop seeing Sales. Lana laughed; she'd discarded Sales and moved on to other game the week before. And she knew Wendy was running a bluff and would never chance the consequences for herself of letting those photographs reach the press—the backlash of publicity, the potential slander suits. The hired thug who called himself a detective had broken the law to obtain the photos.

Then, apparently Lana had hired her own devious help; Sales couldn't imagine her sneaking into his apartment and stealing the photos and negatives herself. A few other items were taken, to make it appear to have been a common burglary. But Sales and Wendy both knew that somehow Lana had stolen the proof of the illicit affair between herself and Sales. She knew when to cover her ass as well as uncover it, Sales had to admit.

Sales parked his car and went into the Clover Lounge on West Forty-fourth Street. It was a dim place, with a long, curved mahogany bar, lots of wood paneling, and an Irish motif. It smelled, not unpleasantly, of cigarette smoke and spilled liquor.

The bartender, Jamie, seemed pleased to see him. He shot a deferential smile and waved a cheery hello as Sales hoisted himself up onto a bar stool and ordered a Scotch on the rocks. Above the bar, near the cash register, was a framed, signed eight-by-ten photograph of Sales with his arm around Jamie's shoulders. The Clover Lounge allowed Sales to carry a substantial tab here. Rather than face Wendy tonight, Sales had decided to add to that tab.

"Things going okay, Mr. Sales?" Jamie asked. He was a narrow, pimply young man with greasy black hair and the scraggly beginnings of a beard. He was always poised, always polite, an experienced bartender despite his youth.

"Going as usual."

"Could be worse, then," Jamie said optimistically.

"Guess you read about the 'Shadowtown' watchman's murder," Sales said.

Jamie placed the Scotch glass in front of Sales on a coaster and nodded. "A tough thing, all right. They gonna catch the guy that did it, you think?"

"They always do," Sales said, sipping his drink. "At least in every play or film I've ever been in."

He caught a glimpse of his still-lean handsome reflection in the back-bar mirror, like an image from one of his movies, lowering the glass from his lips. His flesh was still firm, but he was getting older and he could see it on close inspection. Anybody could see it on close inspection. He was forty-three. Soon he'd be out of young-stud parts and doing character roles, playing patriarchs and mature lovers without genitalia. Unless "Shadowtown" continued to run. Could the damn show run forever? Some soaps seemed to. Would Sales want to act in it forever? With Lana Spence? He shrugged and swallowed the rest of his Scotch. Why not? he told himself. He remembered how many cattle calls—auditions—he'd been to as a young actor. This wasn't an easy business and he figured he should be grateful for his part of eligible bachelor and consummate cocksman Roger Maler. Half the housewives in America were in love with him as Roger.

And here he was married to Wendy, who didn't love him. And recently spurned by Lana, who also didn't love him. Even Lana as Delia Lane didn't love him. Didn't love Roger. Sales started on his second drink. Sometimes even he momentarily confused the world of "Shadowtown" with his real world. What was it Poe wrote? Something about life being a dream within a dream? Close to that, anyway. Hell with Poe.

"I guess the police questioned you," Jamie was saying.

"What? Oh, sure, Jamie. In a preliminary way."

"No bright lights and rubber hoses, huh?" Jamie was smiling with his bad teeth.

"Not yet, anyway," Sales said. He tossed down the rest of his drink and motioned for another. He was knocking them down too fast this evening, he suddenly realized; better slow down. Damned bottle would get a hold on him again, if it didn't already have a hold. Booze, drugs . . . they were occupational hazards.

He wondered, what was that cop, Oxman, going to learn from Lana. It was Lana who'd asked to talk to him; what was the maneuvering bitch going to tell him? Maybe she was going to put some moves on him, get old John Law into the sack for reasons of her own. Turn him into a shell the way she had so many men. Sales wasn't sure if it was Wendy or Lana who'd been responsible for his falling off the wagon two months ago. God knew he still thought enough about both of them. Thought too much about too many things.

He and Wendy suffered through what might be described as a love–hate relationship, heavy on the hate. Still, you didn't live with a woman for five years without forming some sort of attachment and concern, at least on a subconscious level that affected your emotions. Hell, five years was a long, long marriage by show-business standards. He didn't want to see Wendy harmed by Lana, didn't want Lana to have that satisfaction, if that's what she had in mind. All Sales wanted to do, when he found the courage, was to leave Wendy and be left alone by her. And by Lana, the "black widow," as some of her former lovers referred to her.

"The black widow that feels compelled to destroy her lovers."

"Pardon, Mr. Sales?"

"Uh, nothing, Jamie. Line from a play. Can't get it out of my mind."

"We gonna hear it soon on 'Shadowtown'?"

"If they don't cut it."

Jamie freshened his Scotch.

Sales wondered what Lana could know about the murder of the watchman. And what was the deal with this vampire nonsense? What could she know about Edgar Grume—or Allan Ames. Had she ever made it with Ames?

No, not that Sales had heard. How had she missed him?

One thing Sales knew for sure: Lana was trying to use Oxman some way. He hoped Oxman was smart enough to see through it. Even a world-wise cop could fall victim to Lana's charms. Even a world-wise actor like Sales himself. He'd known what she was doing to him and he'd let her. That was part of the fascination. And now his marriage was beyond redemption, if it hadn't been already.

"The trouble with this world," Sales said to Jamie, "is that a man seldom can know anything for sure."

"That's for sure," Jamie said, and moved off to serve a couple who'd just come in and sat at the other end of the bar.

"Isn't that the guy on TV?" Sales heard the woman ask Jamie. "You know, on one of those soaps?"

Sales turned his head away slightly so they couldn't see his face. He knew he wouldn't look as good now as he did on screen. And of course he'd look closer to his actual age, not thirtyish like Roger. Jamie was whispering to them, explaining that Sales liked to stay anonymous in here; not that he wasn't a nice guy. Great guy! Hey, look at the photo behind the bar. Him and me . . . Jamie, protecting Sales's privacy.

Sales had to autograph a cocktail napkin brought down by Jamie, but he got by with a smile and a wave to the couple at the end of the bar and they didn't come over to join him, didn't force it. He was grateful for that. Good fans. Probably even watched the commercials.

Within two hours Sales was incapable of getting down off the bar stool by himself. The murder at the studio kept running through his thoughts. Jamie came to help him. "Vampire," Sales said to him, "fucking vampire."

"Sure, Mr. Sales, I already called you a cab."

Outside, on the sidewalk, Jamie stood supporting Sales, waiting for the taxi to show, trying to avoid the stares of passersby, trying to keep Sales conscious and under control. "How about them Mets?" he asked Sales. Sales knew what Jamie was doing; keep the man talking, thinking, upright.

Sales didn't care about the Mets right now. He wondered if Lana was going to tell Oxman that Wendy had threatened to kill her. Threatened her in front of witnesses. Would Oxman understand that Wendy hadn't really meant it?

The cab veered in tight on the puddled street, pulled close to the curb, and splashed water on Sales's cuffs.

"She wouldn't hurt anybody," Sales said earnestly to Jamie, aware that he was slurring his words. "Not really."

"No, sir. Specially not a lady-killer like you," Jamie said, helping him into the cab.

What the hell? Sales thought. My feet are wet!

Jennifer Crane—5:00 P.M.

"He doesn't keep me posted on his cases," Jennifer told Myra Deeber on the phone. "Not even juicy cases like this one."

Myra's voice flowed harsh and insinuating over the line. "I mean, Jennifer, you sleep with the man—he must tell you *something!*"

Jennifer laughed. She liked Myra and forgave her snoopiness and persistence. "Not about his work, Myra. Ox seldom talks about his job when he's home."

"Cops," Myra said wisely. "They're like that; keep everything bottled up. It's not good for them; not good for anybody."

"So I should get him to talk more about work," Jennifer said, "then repeat to you everything he tells me."

"Not *everything*, Jennifer dear. Some secrets are necessary between men and women. They help keep a relationship alive."

Jennifer knew better. Sometimes secrets could become dark and hideous monsters that devoured a relationship.

"Myra, listen, I've gotta go. I'm working on an ad layout." *And my ear might grow to the phone.*

"Artists!" Myra said with mock frustration. "Artists and policemen!"

"This is a magazine ad for Scrumpty-K dogfood, Myra. I don't know, you think that qualifies as art?"

"Yes, the way you do it, Jennifer. Your work's the best. Like that Smooth Shoulders Perfume ad that was in *Modern Woman*. Beautiful, with the mist, and the handsome hunk on the white stallion. I bet it sold perfume to millions of post–bra burners sitting at home regretting missing romance."

70

"Myra, I'm sorry, but I really—"

"Okay, dear, I'll call you tomorrow."

"Do that, Myra."

Jennifer made a mental note to screen her calls with her answering machine tomorrow, then said good-bye and hung up.

The "Shadowtown" case sure had Myra buzzing. Maybe it had been a mistake to send Ox to her. Myra tended to stick her nose, and then the rest of her, where she didn't belong.

But the phone conversation had made Jennifer curious about the case. It certainly seemed to have captured the public's interest, and she'd been so busy with the layout that she hadn't even read about it in the papers. Hadn't read about anything in the papers. Or caught the news on television, for that matter. Maybe Myra was right about artists being self-absorbed. An unhealthy habit to fall into.

Oxman was working tonight; he'd phoned and said he had an appointment to talk to one of the show's producers. Jennifer had done enough work, she decided. Her back was getting sore from bending forward, anyway. She'd build a dry martini, sit on the sofa with her feet up, and read the paper. Let herself relax.

She put the spare bedroom that was her studio in order, then went to the kitchen and found that they were out of gin. Out of everything but half an inch of bourbon, which Jennifer despised. She settled for a diet Coke and went into the living room. She'd read, catch up on the "Shadowtown" murder, then watch TV until Ox came home. Maybe she could convince him to go out for a late supper, try the new Pakistani restaurant over on Amsterdam.

She'd read only a few paragraphs on page two about the "Shadowtown" case when she sucked in her breath and spilled diet Coke down the front of her blouse. She looked again at the paper, ignoring the spreading cold stain, making sure she'd read correctly.

She had.

Zach was a set designer, among other things. But she'd never dreamed he worked on "Shadowtown." She hadn't been in touch with him in years. She'd heard some time ago that he'd gone to California. Los Angeles. For some reason, she'd always assumed he'd spend the rest of his life—or most of it—in California.

Jennifer concentrated. Tried to remember. She was reasonably sure she'd never mentioned Zach's last name to Ox. But would Ox find out anyway? Did he already know?

Should he know?

Jennifer mentally kicked herself for the shame she felt. She didn't like to think about Zach, much less talk about him with Oxman. And Ox had sensed the pain in her about Zach and didn't pry.

Zach. Lean and burning Zach. Who'd beaten her on a regular basis. Who'd caused her miscarriage and then left her. Who'd messed up her mind so badly that it had taken years, and then E. L. Oxman, to straighten out her life.

She put down the paper and hunched forward on the sofa as if suddenly cold. She didn't want to read any more about the "Shadowtown" case. Her stomach ached terribly, almost the way it had that day so long ago when she'd finally been rushed to the hospital. When she'd lost her baby. *Oh, God!*

Ox had to know about Zach, she decided. He'd find out anyway that Zach Denton was the same Zach they'd briefly and tentatively discussed. So Jennifer and nobody else should be the one to tell him.

Before it came to his attention some other way that Zachary Denton was her former husband, man of her dreams turned man of her nightmares.

Harry Overbeck—7:45 P.M.

Overbeck stepped out onto his narrow balcony twenty stories above Central Park South and squinted up at the sky. The shadowed clouds were traveling swiftly and it was beginning to rain; cool flecks of mist moistened his face gently, almost without seeming to have touched it. He glanced down at the miniaturized moving headlights and tiny foreshortened pedestrians, then beyond them at the view of a darkened Central Park with its winding trails of streetlights. Towering, mountainlike buildings blocked the sky on the west side of the park. He liked his expensive apartment with its expensive view.

And he liked not having to worry about paying the rent. He was living comfortably for the first time in his life. "Shadowtown" had been good to him and he wanted it to keep on being good.

Behind him the doorbell rang. He walked in through the open sliding door, brushing the mist from his damp, brown-tweed sport jacket. He used the intercom to confirm that the caller downstairs was Detective Oxman, as scheduled.

While Oxman was making his way past the doorman and up in the elevator, Overbeck wondered just what the persistent and insidious cop was going to ask him. He'd seen men like Oxman before, deceptive in their deliberation, easy to underestimate. From the moment he'd met Oxman he'd recognized an observant and calculating presence. He hoped Oxman could use those characteristics. On the other hand, there were certain facts Overbeck didn't want to be discovered.

But this was a murder investigation. And Oxman had talked to Lana Spence.

Damn Lana Spence!

Overbeck heard a firm rap on the door. The decisive command of The Law. He checked through the peephole and saw Oxman's sandy-haired, solid countenance, then opened the door to admit the detective.

Oxman smiled an uncoplike hello and stepped inside. He was wearing a light tan raincoat, which Overbeck took from him and draped over a hook on the hall tree by the door. Overbeck noticed that the coat seemed heavy, and he wondered idly if Oxman carried a gun in the pocket and maybe fired through the material if he got in a tight spot, just like on TV.

Without the coat to occupy his hands, Overbeck suddenly felt ill at ease. "Can I get you a drink?" he asked.

"Thanks, no. You just come up from outside?"

"Uh, no," Overbeck said, then remembered standing on the balcony. He realized Oxman had noticed the slight dampness on him. "Well, I was out on the balcony for just a minute. I like the view."

Oxman turned and gazed for a moment out the wide glass doors, at the mist-shrouded park and distant lights. "I don't blame you," he said. "Seems almost unreal."

Overbeck motioned toward the sofa, and Oxman unbuttoned his suit coat and sat down. Overbeck chose to remain standing, gaining the superior position.

But positions didn't seem to affect Oxman; apparently he hadn't read the how-to-get-ahead manuals. He leaned back at ease in the soft cushions and said, "Let's see, Mr. Overbeck, you were at Younger-man's party last night."

"That's right." Overbeck felt himself getting nervous; he didn't like being interrogated. Some cops could make *anyone* feel guilty.

"Where you there most of the evening?"

"From about seven until the police called, at about eleven."

"Who else connected with 'Shadowtown' was at the party?"

"Oh, let's see, there was Shane the director, and Linda Beller, who plays Midge Brown on the show. Quite a few of the production crew. And Arthur Sales was there early; I don't know how late he stayed. It was the sort of party where people came and went without a lot of notice."

"And only a short walk away from the 'Shadowtown' studio."

"Well, not exactly a short walk." Overbeck knew what Oxman was implying. "I suppose someone could have left the party, gone to the studio, then returned without anyone noticing," he said, before Oxman could ask. "But it would be taking a chance. I mean, someone *might* have noticed."

"Oh, sure," Oxman said amiably. "I'm not hypothesizing, Mr. Overbeck, just chewing on possibilities however remote. Would you do me a favor and write down the names of everyone you can remember from the party?" He held out a small, leather-covered notebook and a pen in one hand toward Overbeck.

Overbeck accepted them and began to write, pausing now and then to search his memory. The pen made a loud scratching noise on the paper each time a name was listed in his scrawled, slanted handwriting. The scratching seemed to get louder with every name.

Oxman was silent the five minutes or so until Overbeck had finished and returned the notebook. Then he studied what Overbeck had written. No reaction, though; his features remained immobile.

"Was Zachary Denton at Youngerman's party?" he asked.

"Zach?" Overbeck sorted through his recollection of all those faces, all those people drinking and milling about in Sy's small apartment. He'd drunk a few more martinis than he should have, and the scene was a kind of montage without detail or time sequence. Overbeck had listed everyone whose name he knew. "I don't recall seeing Zach," he said. "But that doesn't mean he wasn't there. You know how cocktail parties are sometimes; half the people aren't sure if they're even in the right apartment, and don't know the other half, but they sip drinks, get slightly loaded, and make small talk. And it isn't called small talk for nothing."

"Sounds as if you dislike cocktail parties."

"I do."

"Then why'd you go to Youngerman's?" Oxman asked.

Overbeck had no ready answer. "Guess I didn't want to hurt Sy's feelings," he said, knowing the inadequacy of that explanation. He cautioned himself to be more careful talking with Oxman. Still, he had to ask: "What, uh, did Lana Spence have to say to you?"

"Something that might not be pertinent," Oxman said. "What do you know about her?"

"Lana? She's the show's star. Her Delia Lane character is what everything else revolves around."

"What's she like off-camera, though?"

Overbeck ran his hand over his close-cropped hair. Why not level with Oxman about this? It was sure to come out anyway, float to the surface like something bloated and undeniable. "She's not all that different on- or off-camera, if you want to know the truth," he said. "A bitch. The black widow."

"Black widow? As in spider?"

"As in Lana. That's what some of her former lovers—and there are plenty—call her. Because of how she leaves men when she's done with them. When she's finished and there's only the husk. I know it sounds trite, but it's the truth."

Overbeck didn't like the way Oxman was staring at him. As if he could look past flesh and blood and bone and into the gears of the mind.

"So who are some of the spider's victims?" Oxman asked.

"There's Zach Denton. Then after him it was Arthur Sales, until Sales's wife Wendy wised up and got after them."

"What about before Denton?"

Overbeck felt a weight drop through him. He sighed. "All right, it's not that big a secret anyway. I was involved with Lana for a short while. Until she got tired of me. That's the way she is with men, she simply drains them, gets tired of them, then discards them. They stand in line for that, the ones who haven't been there before."

"She the one who broke off your affair?"

"Of course. She's always the one who ends affairs. Nobody walks away from Lana Spence." Overbeck was aware of the bitterness in his voice. "And she never ends affairs cleanly; she has to leave her lovers, even what little remains of them, crushed."

"How'd she crush you?" Oxman asked softly, almost as if he really wasn't interested. Overbeck knew better.

"The rumor began that she'd slept with me to get the part of Delia. That, anyway, wasn't true; Lana had the part before we became lovers. But she didn't like the rumors and how they might affect her career, so she stopped seeing me and spread her own rumor—that I was a homosexual and we'd merely been good friends."

"Nice lady," Oxman said. "You sure the rumor started with her?"

"Oh, I'm sure." Overbeck noticed his hands were trembling. He jammed them deep into his pockets. "I wouldn't be surprised if someday it might be Lana Spence getting murdered," he said.

Oxman looked up at him sharply, and Overbeck laughed to signal he'd been kidding about Lana getting killed.

"What kind of man was Allan Ames?" Oxman asked.

Surprised, Overbeck said, "Allan? He was a decent enough sort. He had dark and moody good looks, and his Edgar Grume role really took off with the viewers. It was a shame he had to die when he was at the top of his career. I mean, 'Shadowtown' isn't *King Lear*, but it sure pays a lot better."

"Was there anything between Ames and Lana?"

Overbeck shook his head. "I'm sure there wasn't. That was at about the time Lana and I were . . . close."

"But can you be absolutely sure?"

Smiling sadly, Overbeck said, "There are no absolutes, are there?"

"Yes," Oxman said. "In every homicide case, someone is absolutely guilty."

He stood up and thanked Overbeck for his time, then told him they'd probably be talking again.

"You're working late," Overbeck said, walking with him to the entrance hall and handing him his coat. "Guess it'll be good to get home to your family."

"I'm not married. Not quite, anyway."

Overbeck watched Oxman walk down the carpeted hall to wait for the elevator. Then he closed the door and drifted back out onto the balcony.

He didn't stay outside more than a few seconds. It was raining harder now, not just misting. And a chill wind was rushing along the high corridors formed by building walls.

Just as Overbeck was about to step inside, he noticed a dark figure crossing the street and entering the park. Whoever it was must be crazy; no one sane walked through Central Park at night. Especially on a night like this. A cold sensation moved along the back of Overbeck's neck; there was something familiar about the striding figure in the long dark coat.

Or was there?

Overbeck focused his gaze on the blackness where the man had disappeared, but he saw nothing. Maybe he'd only imagined someone was down there. It wouldn't be any wonder, the way his life had gone lately.

Back inside, Overbeck stared out through his own reflection on the glass and remembered the way Oxman had glanced up at him when he'd mentioned the possibility of Lana someday being murdered. And how he had tried to make a joke of it.

He knew Oxman hadn't been amused.

Art Tobin—7:15 P.M.

Tobin forged out into the rain and turned up the collar on his topcoat. He stuffed his note pad deeper into his left-hand coat pocket, lowered his head, and made for the car. The cool drizzle managed to find its way down the back of his neck. He shivered, dragged the polished toe of a shoe through a puddle, and cursed.

What in Christ's name was he doing wandering around interviewing soap-opera producers in the middle of the night—well, in the evening, anyway—when he could be home on the couch watching a Mets rain delay? Sometimes Tobin wished he were back on the burglary detail. Sometimes you could actually catch the bad guys in the act on that duty, if a burglary-in-progress squeal came in and you were close by the scene. But murderers, they were almost always long gone by the time the crime was discovered. And the victim wasn't around to cry foul and help the law.

He hadn't learned much from talking to Sy Youngerman. He wondered if Ox had had any luck with Youngerman's co-producer, Overbeck. This was all probably a waste of time, anyway. It seemed more and more likely that some loony-tune pretending to be a soap-opera star had been surprised in the act and took it all too seriously. The city was crawling with people who belonged in mental institutions.

Youngerman had simply stated that he'd been at his cocktail party in his apartment all evening, straight through the time of the murder, and he spit out a lot of names to substantiate his story. But Tobin knew how it was with cocktail parties in Manhattan; people entered and left, and if a host played it right, he or she was in the easiest position of all to come and go without attracting attention. People at cocktail parties were involved with each other, themselves, or with their sore feet, and didn't notice much else.

Still, here Tobin was with a story that was probably true, and a list of people who'd been at the party. A party that was within walking distance of the murder scene.

Tobin climbed into his Datsun, ignoring the parking ticket waving at him from beneath the windshield, and pulled away from the curb. Didn't the dumb blue uniforms ever think of running a check on his license plate? He was going to quit using his personal car for department business and sign out one of their unmarked clunkers that might as well have "Police" printed all over it, if he kept having to explain parking tickets. He was supposed to be a goddamned public servant, not a victim.

Halfway down the block he switched on the Datsun's wipers. He watched with satisfaction as the soaked traffic ticket worked its way out from beneath the flailing wiper blade and slid along the side of the windshield to disappear into the night.

Tobin figured he'd check in at the Two-Four with Manders, who was on late duty, then wait for Ox to phone in, as they'd agreed, with any useful information from Overbeck. They would compare notes. Then Tobin would organize the file on the McGreery case and head for home and bed.

He had to park almost a block away from the precinct house and was in an even gloomier mood as he walked into the squad room. He shook water off the undersized umbrella that hadn't done much to shield him from the rain. "What you get when you buy something from one of them outlaw street venders," he mumbled. "Unlicensed fuckin' crooks!"

Sergeant Felstein, who was working the desk, grinned and said with exaggerated concern, "I got a real umbrella I'll sell you if it's still raining when you want to leave."

Tobin didn't answer. Murray Felstein was the kind of guy who strove to be personally responsible for anti-Semitism.

"Galoshes, too, if your feet are wet," Felstein said. He didn't like being ignored. "But for you, they won't be cheap."

"How come you're such a fuckin' stereotype?" Tobin asked, peeling off his coat and tossing it onto a brass hook.

"How come *you* are, Uncle?"

Tobin stopped short and glared at Felstein. Felstein was smiling. Good thing.

"Too bad you couldn't have been a doctor like all your brothers," Tobin said. He moved down the row of green steel desks toward his own.

"I coulda been a doctor," Felstein said, "like you coulda been a real basketball player instead of just dribbling when you piss or drink coffee."

Tobin was getting tired of this bullshit, even from Felstein, with whom denigrating banter had become a subtly supportive routine. "Listen, Murray—"

"You listen, Art. There's somebody here to see you."

Tobin stopped near his desk, surprised. "See me?"

"He was referred to you. You *are* an officer in this precinct, aren't you? You *are* on the 'Shadowtown' case, as I recall."

Tobin looked around and for the first time noticed the man slumped on the bench beneath the wall clock. He had on a threadbare coat that looked as if the Salvation Army had given it away at least twice. His hair was long and ragged, his eyes were bloodshot, and he was a week past needing a shave.

"This is Mr. Ernest Dickerson," Felstein said. "Mr. Dickerson, meet Detective Art Tobin. He's the fella I suggested you should talk to."

Dickerson nodded and tried a grin that shorted out.

"Come on over to my desk, Mr. Dickerson," Tobin said. This guy looked so deep down and so far out that Tobin couldn't help feeling sorry for him.

While Tobin sat down and rearranged some papers, pencils, and file folders, as if refamiliarizing himself with his work space after a long absence, Dickerson shuffled across the cork floor and lowered himself into the chair a few feet from the desk. Tobin noticed the man smelled unwashed, but there was no scent of alcohol about him. And he seemed sober enough, which was a condition that probably wouldn't last long. This wasn't the sort of guy that usually walked into a police station voluntarily.

"How can I help you, Mr. Dickerson?"

Dickerson blinked, as if the light hurt his eyes, and didn't answer. Tobin was patient. He knew talking to the police was difficult for a man like this.

"Do you have information pertaining to the McGreery murder?" Tobin asked nonchalantly, as if he lived in the precinct house and had plenty of time.

"I don't know," Dickerson said in his low, hoarse voice. "The sergeant there, he seems to think so." He glanced toward Felstein, then back. "But that's not why I'm here."

Tobin was puzzled. "Well, did you come here to report a crime?"

"Uh, yeah. I guess you could say that."

Tobin glanced over and caught Felstein grinning at him. Oh-oh. "Say what?" Tobin asked Dickerson. "What kind of crime did you want to report?"

"What kind of crimes are there?" Dickerson asked, as if inquiring about ice-cream flavors.

Christ! Tobin thought. "Well, let's start with murder. Then there's robbery, rape, assault, embezzlement—" *Want that in a cone or a cup?*

"Wait a minute," Dickerson stammered, interrupting Tobin. "That'd be it, I guess. Assault. Assault by a vampire."

Tobin saw that Felstein was whistling tonelessly now, pretending to read a report like the one Tobin would have to spend the next half hour typing up.

Tobin was in the mood for a little assault himself.

Jennifer Crane—8:40 P.M.

She heard Oxman fumbling with his key in the door. Not like him; from only that sound Jennifer could tell he was tired.

He took the burdens of his work too seriously sometimes, she knew, and this was one of those times. An ex-cop, a member of the fraternity, had been murdered. Ox hadn't said much about it, but she knew how it bothered him that a cop-killer he was supposed to catch was still free, how it burned in him.

She drew in her breath as the door opened.

Ox saw her, nodded, then closed the door and locked it. He didn't look weary, but then his exterior seldom revealed how he felt.

"You act as if you were expecting me," he said. He walked over to her, leaned down, and kissed her forehead.

She wanted to clutch him, cling to him, and tell him everything in a rushing relief of words. She'd felt that way as a little girl, with her father. Too long ago.

Ox had crossed to the phone on the table near the door when he stood still and looked curiously at her. "Something wrong, Jennifer?"

"I need to talk to you." She felt her breath catch in her throat, making her voice strained. "It'll keep till after you make your phone call."

He came back to stand near her. "The call can wait." She touched the back of his hand, and he sat down next to her on the sofa.

She sensed, and heard, his arm move around behind her, but he didn't encircle her shoulders, didn't press her to talk. Instead he rested his arm on the back of the sofa, letting her know he was ready to comfort her if she needed it. Jennifer suddenly loved him almost overwhelmingly. She had to take a few seconds to compose herself. Her throat was tightening.

"I hadn't read any of the details about the 'Shadowtown' murder until this afternoon," she said.

"Quite an assortment of elements, isn't it? Vampires and soap-opera stars and a dead watchman. But we can talk about all that later, if you want to." He must have thought she was changing the subject.

"What I want to say has to do with 'Shadowtown.'" She felt the cushions shift as his body got rigid. His forearm was now lightly touching her shoulder. "When I was reading about the murder a name caught my attention," she said. "Zachary Denton, the set designer who found the body."

Ox sighed and leaned back, causing the sofa to groan. She knew he'd made the connection. Just like that. He hadn't been aware of it, she was sure, but it must have been on the edge of his consciousness. The air in the room got heavier and harder to breathe.

"Zach Denton's my ex-husband," she said.

Ox's arm did go around her now, but almost absently. She could tell he didn't know quite how to react, how to feel about this. She wasn't sure herself how she *wanted* him to react.

"Should you take yourself off the case?" she asked.

He thought about it for a moment. "No, I think I can be objective." He didn't sound sure.

"Is Zach a . . ."

"A suspect? No more than anyone else is, at this point." He shifted on the sofa so he was facing her. "Lana Spence told me she'd had an affair with him," he said. "When she broke it off, he didn't like it. They argued and he punched her, in front of most of the production crew."

Jennifer felt an old anger well up in her and tried to force it back into the past where it belonged. "I'm not surprised; same old Zach. He doesn't mind at all beating up on women." She was aware of the subdued rage in her tone.

Ox stood up, obviously feeling his own anger. "The bastard!" he said.

"I knew he was a set designer," Jennifer told him, "but I'd heard he'd gone to California. I assumed he was still there, working in Hollywood."

"He still *would* probably be there if he hadn't gone to work for a soap opera," Oxman said. "Soaps are about the only major regular series that originate from New York."

Jennifer stood up and he moved to her and held her. The past had come after her and she needed him, needed him badly. And he was there, obviously yearning to help.

She pressed her head gently against his chest, then began to sob, worming closer and digging the point of her chin into him. He held her tight and made soothing sounds in her ear, not really saying anything intelligible, but stroking her where she was injured nonetheless.

Finally she stopped crying. She tried to swallow the lump in her throat as she leaned back away from him. He kissed her on the mouth, then he rested his hands on her shoulders and looked down at her. Down *into* her.

"It doesn't matter, Jennifer. The past is dead and over; it no longer exists in any way that can hurt us unless we let it."

She smiled somberly. "Very philosophical. Very true. Also very true that I love you."

The telephone rang shrilly, startling her and causing her body to jerk.

Ox grinned and exerted a brief, reassuring squeeze with both hands. "Want me to answer it?" he asked.

"Unless you want to let it ring," she told him. "I don't feel like talking to anyone."

"Me, either." He took her hand and led her into the dark bedroom. Before they were undressed and in bed, whoever was on the line had given up and the phone was silent.

He made love to her gently but insistently, sensing the urgency of her need and entering her almost immediately. He caressed her face lovingly as he lunged in and out of her. Jennifer heard herself sigh, heard Ox's deeper breathing and felt his heightening tension. There was reassurance in their lovemaking.

Then something found its way free in her. She began thrusting her hips up at him in violent rhythm. The rush of her desire was new but familiar and overwhelming. "Grind it!" she moaned. "Grind me into the goddamn mattress!"

He increased the pressure of each downward thrust. Again and again. The headboard slammed into the wall; who cared if the neighbors heard? She was aware that she'd screamed, and her orgasm carried her far out into an endless warm sea. A roar of receding tide. A low groaning in her ear.

Ox had gripped her hair and had her head pulled back at an unnatural angle. He seemed to realize it at the same time she did and released her.

He pulled out of her, rolled to the side, and gasped for breath. After a while, he looked over at her, a little puzzled by her ferocity and desperation. By his own, perhaps.

"You okay?" he asked.

She nodded and reached for the box of tissues by the bed.

He stroked her cheek, her breasts, then kissed her stomach, flicking lightly with his tongue, and climbed out of bed. As he padded barefoot into the bathroom she saw for a moment, in the wash of light when he clicked the wall switch and closed the door behind him, deep scratches on his back. The shower began to run.

Jennifer didn't have to worry about pregnancy; Zach had taken care of that. She lay alone with a wad of Kleenex pressed between her thighs and stared terrified into the darkness, as if something might be hiding there, staring back.

Ox switched on the lamp and got dressed, but Jennifer elected to wear only her robe and slippers. He touched her hair gently, smiled his slow smile. "Sure you're okay?"

"Sure."

They'd returned to the living room when the phone interrupted them again; the outside world refusing to be ignored.

She watched Ox reluctantly leave her, walk to the phone, and lift the receiver.

She could tell by the expression on his face that it was his partner Tobin on the phone. She'd been able to do that within a few months after Ox had moved in with her, able to read the all-business, intense expression on his features, the paleness at the corners of his mouth, the fine parallel vertical lines above the bridge of his nose. He could never be sure what Tobin was going to tell him, and always there was that first second or two of tension when he answered the phone and learned who was on the other end of the line. And when the call was routine, as it usually was, Jennifer would watch Ox relax.

But the tension didn't go away this time as Ox listened to what Tobin had to say, and Jennifer knew the call was serious, that it was about "Shadowtown."

E. L. Oxman—9:30 P.M.

Oxman stood holding the phone to his ear and listening. Though he was still a bit thrown by what Jennifer had told him about Zach Denton, he'd sensed immediately that Tobin's call meant trouble.

"I was about to phone you, Art," he said, glancing over at Jennifer, "tell you I'd meet you tomorrow morning instead of tonight."

Tobin said, "Thought I'd better get in touch with you as soon as possible. Got a Mr. Ernest Dickerson here with me at the Two-Four. He's a man you're gonna want to talk to tonight, Ox."

"Why tonight?"

"Because he's here now. And he's the type who, uh, might not be available tomorrow."

Oxman got the impression Ernest Dickerson, whoever he was, must be sitting next to Tobin listening to the conversation. "So what's this about, Art?"

"Seems Mr. Dickerson saw a vampire."

Oxman felt suddenly very, very tired. "He the sort who might see one?"

"He is," Tobin said.

"Did you check his neck for puncture marks, Artie? To make sure he's not one of the walking dead?"

"That's the first thing I did, Elliot Leroy."

"I'll just bet. Where'd he see this vampire?"

"In an alley around Third and Broadway."

"I know the area. Was he sober?"

"Nope. Seldom is, I suspect."

That was what Oxman figured. "How come you're bothering telling me about this, Art?"

"Because he saw the vampire last night."

Oxman had to admit that could be more than coincidence, even in Manhattan.

"And the description, such as it is, fits in with the missing Edgar Grume costume. White wig and all."

Oxman looked again at Jennifer, who was sitting limply on the sofa watching him. She seemed okay now, but the knowledge that it was her former husband who'd discovered the "Shadowtown" victim's body, and the strain she'd felt telling Oxman about it, had worked its effects. Her desperation a while ago in the bedroom gave evidence to that. She hadn't gotten used to the notion that Zachary Denton was again, through Oxman, a part of her life.

Oxman placed his left palm over the phone's mouthpiece. "Will you be all right if I leave?" he asked softly.

Jennifer nodded.

He removed his cupped hand and told Tobin he'd be down as soon as possible, and to hold on to Ernest Dickerson.

As soon as Oxman walked into the squad room and saw Dickerson sitting near the desk, he had his doubts. The guy sure looked like the most wasted kind of alky. Looked as if he might see a vampire per night.

"Maybe a pink vampire," Sergeant Felstein said from behind the booking desk, where he'd been reading Oxman's thoughts. Irritating bastard.

Oxman nodded to him and walked toward where Dickerson sat near Tobin.

Tobin saw him, said something to Dickerson, then got up to meet Oxman halfway to where Dickerson waited in his chair.

"Jesus, Art," Oxman said, "the guy looks like he was born a wino."

"Does at that. But I don't think you'll wanna brush off what he has to say." Tobin was so tired he appeared to have been on a drunk himself. His face was drawn and his dark-brown eyes peered out blearily like half-moons from beneath fatigue-hooded lids.

"Third and Broadway's a long way from where McGreery was killed," Oxman said.

"But the times work out about right. And even though Ernie's a hard drinker, I get the impression he's telling the truth. I don't think he could have made himself walk into a police station otherwise."

" 'Ernie,' huh?"

Tobin seemed slightly embarrassed. "You gotta feel sorry for the poor dumb bastard. And if you listen to him a while, you gotta believe him."

Oxman trusted Tobin's instincts about people. And Tobin had a point about a beaten-down alky like Dickerson having to screw up considerable courage just to walk into a police station.

Tobin led the way to where Dickerson sat. As they got near, Oxman picked up the faint, rancid odor of the wino, but he didn't smell alcohol. Oxman took the desk chair, letting Tobin stand alongside Dickerson. Tobin made the introductions.

"Okay, Ernie," Oxman said, "tell me what you told Detective Tobin."

Dickerson ran the back of his hand across his grizzled chin. He seemed sorry he'd come here and started things rolling, but he began his story. His voice was thick, halting, but sober.

"Wait a minute," Oxman said, when Dickerson had gotten to the part about trying to beg some change from the vampire. "You mean he spoke to you?"

Dickerson nodded and eagerly repeated, word for word, what the vampire had told him before kicking him in the throat.

"Our vampire isn't very charitable," Tobin said. "And he has an odd way with words. 'Garment,' no less. Talks like somebody outta the nineteenth century."

"Or like a would-be actor hamming it up." Oxman stared at Dickerson, wondering if the man actually had such good recall, or if what he was relating was an alcohol-wrought delusion that had taken on the weight of reality. It wasn't easy to know about these men and women who lived on the streets, who moved in a world that was only on the edges of society's consciousness. They were, to most people, invisible. But they saw things. Felt things. They were real, all right.

After Dickerson had given a statement, and an address Oxman knew was a roach-ridden flophouse off Broadway, they watched the occult-touched wino make his way out of the precinct house. Oxman figured Ernie Dickerson would head straight for a bout with a bottle, if he could afford one.

Before Oxman and Tobin had a chance to go in to see Manders, prior to hanging it up for the night, Manders wandered out into the squad room and over toward them. The lieutenant looked weary, too. But he always did, with his basset-hound, downturned features and his sad, sad eyes.

He sat on the edge of the desk. "Ox. Tobin. Any movement on the 'Shadowtown' thing?"

Oxman handed him a copy of Dickerson's statement.

Manders's features seemed to sag to even longer, more formless proportions as he read, as if the bone structure beneath his flesh were dissolving. The incredible melting lieutenant.

"I don't like this," he said, giving the statement back to Oxman. "Damned news media will get hold of it and pound the public over the head with it for weeks. Vampires! Whole case sucks!"

Oxman wondered if Smiley Manders knew he'd cracked a joke. He doubted it. The lieutenant wasn't known for his sense of humor.

Manders abruptly stood up from the desk, as if he'd just remembered he shouldn't be sitting on furniture other than chairs. Oxman knew he wasn't doing it from good manners; Manders had been bothered by piles lately and feared seeing a doctor and having that operation where he'd have to sit on a miniature inner tube for weeks and dread having a bowel movement. "So what do you make of this?" he asked.

"Could be something," Oxman said. "We have to check on it, send some troops down around Broadway and Third and see if anybody else had a run-in with a vampire lately. It's possible whoever killed McGreery was wearing the missing Edgar Grume costume, and left it on while he traveled to lower Manhattan after leaving the crime scene."

"So maybe we have a description of the killer," Manders said, cheering up a little. "I can stall the media with that, keep the bastards at bay for a while."

"Not much of a description," Oxman said. "Tall—only the guy who saw him was lying on the pavement. Lean—only Dickerson was so shook up he can't really recall his face, and the so-called vampire was wearing black clothing, including a cape. Oh, and white hair, of course."

"Don't forget," Manders said in a flat voice, "fella had fangs."

"Vampires don't always have fangs," Tobin said. "Sometimes only when they're riled up or about to suck blood from a victim."

Manders looked at him as if he were crazy. "I seriously doubt if Vince McGreery was killed by a genuine vampire." He felt in his pocket for change for the coffee machine, found some, and jingled it in his tobacco-yellowed right hand. Manders was smoking heavily again, trying to end up in the cancer ward. Couldn't stop. "The media and commissioner will suck all the blood outta *me* if we don't wrap this up in some way or other so it at least drops outta the news. Does anybody look like the collar might fit?"

Oxman was tempted to name Zach Denton as the most likely suspect. Only it simply wasn't true. "Nobody special yet, Lieutenant; we're still working on the crew and cast of the show. Everyone seems to have had an opportunity to kill McGreery, but no one seems to have had a motive. Could be some whacko broke into the place, got surprised by McGreery, then killed him."

"But you don't believe it," Manders said.

"No. And there are the threatening notes to Lana Spence. Something's going on at 'Shadowtown,' Lieutenant, and it isn't over yet."

Manders glared at Tobin. "You share that view?"

"I lean toward the surprised whacko theory," Tobin said. "The letters to Lana Spence might not have any connection with the murder."

Manders ran his hand down the loose flesh of his face. "*Might* is the word that's giving me ulcers over this," he said. "And *celebrity*. Too many damned celebrities involved in the case. That's what keeps the press and politicians on my ass."

Oxman knew Manders hadn't seen anything compared to what would happen if whoever wrote the Lana Spence letters made good on his or her word.

"One thing that *has* been made clear," Oxman said, "is that almost everyone has plenty of motive to murder Lana Spence. The 'black widow,' as some of her former lovers call her. She's apparently one of those women who has to leave a man in ruins after an affair, so there isn't much left for whoever gets him next. It goes against her grain to leave behind a usable discard."

"That's the word I get on her, too," Tobin said. "A genuine ballbreaker."

Manders sneered. "'Black widow,' 'ballbreaker.' Sounds like something out of the *National Enquirer*."

"It might be," Tobin said.

"I think we better assign someone to watch her," Oxman said. "Whoever wrote those threatening notes is serious."

"You sound sure of that," Manders said.

Oxman nodded. "I feel sure." He looked over at Tobin.

"I agree," Tobin said.

Manders tugged at a long-lobed ear, then said, "I'll put Austerman on her for a while. Think we oughta tell her she's being watched over?"

"Not yet," Oxman said. "She'd probably alter her behavior pattern so drastically that whoever threatened her would simply lie back and wait."

"Not tell her, huh? . . ." Manders said. "We're talking about using her for bait."

"Only if we're fishermen. I'm a cop, talking about the most logical way to catch a killer—and to prevent Lana Spence's murder either now or later."

Manders raised a long-fingered, yellow hand. "Don't get your nose outta joint, Ox. I agree with your suggestion. Austerman will latch on to her tomorrow and stay out of sight."

Oxman was satisfied. Austerman was young, but he was a good cop who had the patience to conduct a solid stakeout. Lana Spence would be as safe as she could be, under the circumstances.

Some circumstances! A killer, maybe one who fancied himself a vampire, determined to spill her blood. And a world full of people who wouldn't care. Who would, in fact, be glad to hear of her death.

"Keep me informed," Manders said, and walked away toward the lounge and its coffee machine.

"It should be easy to keep him informed," Oxman said, "considering how much we don't know."

"I know this," Tobin said, shoving a desk drawer all the way closed with his knee. "I'm going home and get some sleep, before Smiley comes walking outta that lounge bitching about the coffee and in an ugly mood generally."

Oxman was two minutes behind him. He knew when to lead and when to follow.

Jennifer Crane—11:00 P.M.

Jennifer felt the mattress shift and heard the groan of the springs as Oxman slid into bed beside her. She moved over close to him, feeling the subtle draw of his body heat. He was lying on his side, facing away from her. She scooted over until her breasts were pressed against his back, and rested an arm around him. He patted her hand.

"You all right?" he asked.

"I think so. You?"

"Tired."

She snuggled nearer and closed her eyes, listening to his deep, even breathing and trying to go to sleep. She thought Oxman might be asleep already; he could do that, sleep almost on command. He began to snore lightly. She envied him the control he had over his life.

Half an hour passed, and Jennifer still couldn't sleep. She climbed out of bed, padded into the kitchen, and heated some water in the kettle for a cup of caffeine-free tea. The tiled floor was cool on her bare feet. After adding plenty of cream and sugar, she carried the cup into the carpeted bedroom and walked to the window.

The city was always awake. She could see lights across the Hudson in New Jersey, and a boat of some kind was making slow progress upriver. Faint, restful sounds of traffic filtered in from the street below. She wondered how many people like her were out there, unable to sleep, standing at darkened windows, staring blankly out at the night. Thousands of them, perhaps, with thousands of reasons not to sleep.

Jennifer knew what was keeping her awake. Zach. Zach Denton back in her life. She'd thought he was relegated to a deep corner of her mind where he wouldn't bother her. Thought she'd come to terms with that part of her past.

But she realized this wasn't true. Since Oxman had entered her life, Jennifer had faced up to everything. She knew this couldn't be an exception. Ox had taught her to stand firm and rely on her sense of worth and her honesty with herself.

It had worked. It had changed her life.

She'd made up her mind never to run again, from anything. It was a commitment she'd been sure she could keep.

But now, tonight, sipping tea at a dark window and listening to Ox breathe, she felt the old puzzlement and hatred and self-incrimination when she thought about Zach. She didn't want to face up to his re-emergence in her existence. She felt—God help her—guilty, and with no logical reason!

And for the first time since falling in love with E. L. Oxman, she felt like running.

Scene 3

Sy Youngerman—8:35 A.M.

Youngerman waited at his desk in his office at Shadowtown Productions, wondering just what sort of questions E. L. Oxman would ask him. He'd handled the black guy, Tobin, okay. Talking with the police made Youngerman uneasy; had since those drug busts in his early days. Cops were a source of trouble for everyone, the guilty and innocent alike.

Of course, they weren't the only source of trouble for the innocent. Anybody, by virtue of his or her job, could wind up in the wrong place at the wrong time. Could wind up dead, like Vince McGreery.

The intercom buzzed and Youngerman's secretary told him Oxman was in the anteroom.

Youngerman stood up, put on a relaxed kind of smile, and went to the door and opened it.

Oxman nodded a good morning to him. The detective had on dark brown slacks, a tan sport coat that was a bit wrinkled around the elbows, serviceable brown dress shoes. Serviceable—that was Oxman. Maybe the job had done it to him.

"Come on in, Lieutenant," Youngerman said, injecting some morning cheer into his voice. The important executive, eager to begin a new day and meet fresh challenges. He remembered last night, when he'd orchestrated the consumption of alcohol and cocaine with a precision that had opened new interior worlds.

"Sergeant," Oxman corrected.

Youngerman walked back behind his desk, waited until Oxman was seated in the nearby leather-upholstered chair, then sat down in his Danish desk chair with the built-up lumbar support. He swallowed; he was tremendously thirsty, though he didn't feel at all hung over. Still, maybe he'd been tripping and boozing it up too often lately; maybe that explained what he'd seen, or thought he'd seen, this morning. There must be *some* explanation.

"What can I do for you, Sergeant Oxman?" he asked casually.

"I have some questions."

"Of course." *What else?*

Youngerman put everything out of his mind except the task of fielding Oxman's questions.

They were the same questions Detective Tobin had asked him yesterday. Sometimes they were even worded the same. Oxman was insistent. Youngerman was running low on patience.

"Seems I've already answered all these questions," he said, finally. "Your partner Tobin asked them. Is it standard police procedure to ask the same questions of the same . . ." Youngerman almost said "suspect."

"Yes, we do that. Then we compare notes."

"Ah, to see if anyone's lying." *Like in a low-budget thriller.*

"It works out that way sometimes, but other times whoever's answering the questions phrases something differently, in such a way that it will shed some light. And you'd be surprised how much more people remember when asked the same questions twenty-four hours apart. Memory's an unpredictable thing."

"I'm afraid I don't remember anything more."

That didn't deter Oxman. He continued in his calm way to fire the same questions at Youngerman. Where was Youngerman when this happened? When that happened? Who was with him? Who'd remember him? How well did he know McGreery? What time was this? What time was that? Youngerman felt like calling Security and having Oxman tossed out of the office.

Then, suddenly, a new tack:

"What do you know about Lana Spence?" Oxman asked.

Youngerman was a little confused. Was Lana a suspect? "I know she's a good actress," he said. "Not great, but good. She knows her lines and picks up on her cues. And she's the backbone of the show as Delia Lane."

"Is Lana the kind of bitch she plays as Delia?"

Youngerman hesitated, then figured he might as well be candid.

Oxman must have questioned other people about Lana. "She can make Delia look like Mother Teresa," he said.

"You sound as if you know her well. Lana, not Mother Teresa. Were you ever . . . involved with her?"

Youngerman smiled. "I assume you mean Lana. Involved romantically?"

Oxman nodded.

"For God's sake no, not after what I've seen her do to other men. I've known Lana for years, Sergeant Oxman, watched her operate on her victims."

"People often use the word *victim* in describing the men in her life," Oxman said.

"She likes to make sexual conquests," Youngerman said, "and that's all. I doubt if she's capable of what you or I might think of as love."

"But your partner Overbeck got involved."

Youngerman realized that Oxman knew a great deal about Lana already. The detective would be comparing answers. "Harry was dumb enough to fall for her," he said. "She used him and then threw him on the scrap heap. I don't think he lasted six months. When he didn't want to let her go, and the fact that their relationship might have proved harmful to her career, she pretended they'd only been friends. To back up that fabrication, she spread the rumor that Harry was a homosexual. Which, incidentally, is only a rumor."

"You and Overbeck are the producers. Didn't you consider firing her after she did this to Overbeck?"

"Not for a second," Youngerman said. He knew it was probably hopeless to explain the nature of show business to a cop like Oxman, a plodder. "Harry never considered firing her, either. Lana means that much to 'Shadowtown.' Our ratings would plunge without her. And in this game, ratings are everything."

"So you keep personal relationships separate from business."

"We try. Though it isn't easy at times. Let's face it, many people in our business are . . . temperamental. They have big egos."

"And Lana Spence, being somewhat temperamental and egotistical, is likely to get involved with that same sort of actor."

"Sometimes, anyway, Lieutenant."

"Sergeant. What about Sales?"

"Arthur? Oh, he had his turn with Lana. But he's used to callow show-business affairs. He escaped with some dignity, though his marriage might still be suffering. His wife, Wendy Conroy—Conroy's her maiden and stage name—used to be an actress, and she knew how to deal with Lana Spence. I don't know exactly what she did, but the Sales and Lana affair ended abruptly after she found out about it." Youngerman sat and watched Oxman jot some kind of shorthand in his note pad. "What's with all the questions about Lana Spence?" he finally asked.

Oxman glanced up from his notes. "She might make the world behind the camera go round," he said, "just as she does the world in front of the camera."

"How cryptic. Are you implying that she's somehow central to the murder of poor Vince McGreery?"

"It wouldn't be cryptic anymore if I answered that," Oxman said, smiling.

Oxman was holding something back. Something big. Youngerman could sense it, and not just on the basis of what Oxman had said about Lana Spence. For a moment Youngerman thought he might hold something back from Oxman, then he decided he'd tell him. *Here goes . . .*

"As I was getting out of my car in the parking lot this morning," Youngerman said, "I, uh . . . Well, you're going to laugh at this, but I thought I caught a glimpse of a tall figure dressed in black, with a long cape and flowing white hair."

Oxman didn't laugh. In fact, while he didn't seem too surprised, he appeared to become rather serious.

"It was just for a second," Youngerman said. "I can't be sure."

"What time was this?" Oxman asked.

"About seven-thirty. I often come in very early to work."

"Broad daylight, huh?"

"Not exactly. Because of the fog this morning, it was gloomy. And the area where I saw the figure was pretty much deserted. I doubt if anyone else saw it."

"Can you remember any details?" Oxman asked. "How tall was the figure?"

"Seemed tall, but it was impossible to tell for sure."

"Did you see any of the features?"

"Oh, no. It was too far away, and this all happened too fast. It was something I saw, yet didn't see because my mind wouldn't accept it right away. It just wouldn't register as real. Do you know what I mean?"

"Yes," Oxman said. He seemed pensive, even somewhat worried.

"Anything else, Sergeant?" Youngerman asked. "I need to get busy for today's shooting. Delia's going to bribe Midge Brown to stay away from Roger Maler."

"Will Midge do that?" Oxman asked. Youngerman could tell he was only half serious.

Youngerman smiled. "She will when Delia threatens to reveal Midge's secret passion for the bottle."

"Sometimes," Oxman said, "I feel as if I'm walking a dotted line and now and then I wander out of the real world and into 'Shadowtown.'"

"You and forty million viewers," Youngerman said. "That's the idea."

"Guess it is," Oxman said. He stood up.

Youngerman felt relief that the interview was over. He held out his right hand to Oxman and they shook. The cop's firm grip was warm but dry.

"Thanks for your cooperation," Oxman said.

"Anything to help find whoever killed Vince McGreery," Youngerman told him. "I guess, him being an ex-cop, you guys are especially anxious to get his killer."

"Especially," Oxman confirmed, with a quiet relentlessness that scared Youngerman.

"Just like in the movies."

"Or in a soap opera," Oxman said.

After Oxman had left, Youngerman sat down again in his desk chair and leaned back, closing his eyes. He didn't like what was playing in the theater of his mind. He could see again the dark figure near the building corner, but he refused to admit to himself the resemblance it had struck in his startled mind.

He shivered. Maybe he was going crazy. Maybe, like Oxman, he wandered now and then into another world.

Delia—uh, Lana Spence—had driven plenty of directors and producers crazy.

Youngerman felt sorry for Overbeck and Sales and all the others. And he was glad he hadn't allowed himself to be lured into Lana

Spence's web. He'd had his chance, and probably would have fit in somewhere between Overbeck and Sales. Like brunch.

He wondered again why Oxman was asking questions about Lana. What did Oxman know?

E. L. Oxman—9:15 A.M.

Oxman was told by "Shadowtown's" bald director, Shane Moreland, that Lana Spence wouldn't be in until noon, to tape the scene where she threatened Midge. So Youngerman may have been faking in his conversation with Oxman, telling him time was short because of the imminent taping. That could mean nothing, Oxman knew. Only a busy executive who didn't want his time wasted by a persistent cop. *Tough shit.*

He hung around for a while, chatting with various crew and cast members, trying to pick up some morsel of information that might help. But everyone seemed guarded, and no one rose to any bait Oxman put out suggesting they might know about the threatening Edgar Grume letters to Lana. Oxman learned nothing other than that Tobin was right: there was no shortage of egos in conflict, or of professional jealousy on the "Shadowtown" set.

Oxman used the phone to check in at the squad room with Tobin, and learned there was nothing new on that front, either. He called Jennifer then, and she seemed to be in a normal frame of mind. Almost. There was a shade of something in her voice that made Oxman uneasy.

Around eleven o'clock, he decided to go out for a short lunch before returning to talk to Lana Spence. After leaving Shadowtown Productions, he walked away from Riverside Drive. The day had warmed into the sixties, and a rare blue sky was swept clear of clouds by a southeast breeze.

Oxman found a bar that featured a short-order grill and went inside and ordered a hamburger, French fries, and a Heineken.

The barmaid brought the beer first, and as Oxman settled into his booth he noticed that the TV mounted behind the bar was tuned to "Shadowtown." Lana Spence—rather, Delia Lane—was reclining in a lounge chair, wearing a scanty bikini. Dappled light playing over her lush body was supposed to represent reflection off water in a swimming pool. A handsome blond boy carrying a towel walked up and stood next to her. They began to talk; the volume was too low for Oxman to hear what they were saying, but Delia was obviously flirting with the boy and he was gradually picking up on the fact. Fast as the script allowed, anyway.

Just as the boy was beginning to rub suntan lotion on Delia's shoulders, the barmaid arrived with the hamburger and fries.

"I thought that program was on later in the afternoon," Oxman said, motioning toward the TV.

"It is, on network," the barmaid said, setting down the plates on Oxman's table. "Those are reruns. On a local station. I heard that's where the money really is in television programs, in the reruns. Specially cable."

Oxman studied the barmaid. She was a pretty, dark-haired girl with friendly brown eyes and a round, amiable face. "You a 'Shadowtown' fan?" he asked.

"You betcha."

"So am I."

She perked up. "So what do you think of the murder, and that creepy business about Edgar Grume?"

"You mean the vampire? I thought he was dead."

She smiled. "All vampires are dead. Question is, why's Edgar Grume back to haunt 'Shadowtown'?"

"Publicity stunt, maybe," Oxman offered.

The barmaid looked skeptical. "Featuring a real murder?"

"Guess not," Oxman said. "So what do you think?"

"I think it's possible to make something seem so real it becomes real."

Oxman stared at this apparently normal young woman. "I don't follow."

"I mean, maybe if enough people pretend hard enough, long enough, that something is real, it can take on a kind of reality of its own. Now, 'maybe,' I said."

"Kinda bizarre," Oxman told her.

She smiled and turned to walk back behind the bar. "That's why I said 'maybe,'" she lobbed over her shoulder.

Oxman glanced back up at the TV. A commercial was on. A woman was comparing nasal sprays and seemed enchanted by the one that had instantly cleared her sinuses. Nasal sprays were, at that moment, the most important thing in the world to her, pivotal to her existence.

He looked away and took a large bite of his hamburger.

Where was this case going? he wondered as he chewed, trying not to think about the nasal-spray commercial. If the idea of Edgar Grume walking around outside "Shadowtown" had gotten something of a grip on soap fans now, wait until they learned that Grume—or at least someone resembling a vampire—had been sighted since the murder. Publicity about the murder and about Grume would explode, and Smiley Manders would be unbearably depressed, and the pressure to solve the case would increase so much you'd need a computer to figure it. And even a computer might not be able to figure how hot the case would get when the media learned that Grume had been sending imaginatively threatening letters to Lana Spence.

Oxman sipped his beer. He was uncomfortable about the way the line between "Shadowtown" and reality seemed to be getting vague.

After lunch he returned to "Shadowtown" and was told Lana Spence was in her dressing room, preparing for the Midge Brown scene.

"Ah, my friend and protector, Ox," she said, after he'd knocked on the door and been royally summoned with a "Come!"

She was seated at her dressing table, where a makeup artist in a red T-shirt was applying coloring to her features with a soft brush and then skillfully blending the edges of the smears into flesh tones. Oxman watched as the man brushed dark makeup beneath her cheekbones, then softened it with deft twirls of the bristles so that her strong bone structure was emphasized. Oxman sat down and observed silently as Lana the bitch was transformed into Delia the bitch. The difference was, he decided, only a matter of degree.

Finally the makeup artist left, and Lana sat primping, licking a forefinger and making minor adjustment in whatever had been applied beneath her eyes. She caught Oxman looking at her in the mirror and said, "If they don't get this just right, the overhead lighting makes it appear that I have bags beneath my eyes." She made it seem as if bags beneath the eyes could be equated with cancer.

"Some very attractive women have bags beneath their eyes," he said.

She didn't answer. He'd given no solace.

"Received any more notes?" he asked.

She surprised him. "Yes. This morning I found this slipped under the door." She turned from the mirror, got a plain white envelope from the middle drawer of her dressing table, and handed it to Oxman.

He read the note. It graphically explained the things that were going to be done to Lana Spence with a straight razor. Not to Delia Lane this time, but to Lana Spence. That could mean that the genuine Lana and soap-opera character Delia had merged in the killer's deranged mind, making him all the more out of touch with reality and all the more dangerous.

"There's a reference there to a strawberry birthmark on my left breast," Lana said in a tight voice. "I do have such a birthmark, exactly where whoever wrote the note said it is."

Oxman thought about asking to see the birthmark. Line of duty. *Not a good idea; not professional*. "Have you ever done any film work nude?" he asked.

"No. Stage, either. But when I was very young I did some posing for a magazine layout. Nothing really undignified."

"But nude? So the birthmark showed?"

"Yes." She bit her lower lip, then said, "An acting company is close, Ox. Almost anyone here in the crew or cast might have seen that birthmark. During a costume change, for instance. We get busy sometimes and don't think much about modesty."

"Did you find this here or at your apartment?" Oxman asked, putting the note and envelope into his pocket.

"Here. Slipped beneath that door behind you. So far the monster has left me alone at home. Thank God." She turned back to the mirror and began nudging her long, wild hairdo into an even more flattering arrangement.

"Youngerman thought he saw someone in a long black cloak outside the building this morning," Oxman said.

He had to admit he found some satisfaction in the thrill of fear that momentarily brightened her eyes. At least he had her full attention now, even though it was via her mirror.

"What time this morning?" her reflection asked.

"Early. About seven-thirty."

"Do you think Edgar might have been in here, delivering the note?"

Oxman was getting confused again. "Who do you mean by 'Edgar'?"

"Edgar Grume. Or whoever's pretending to be him." She suddenly slammed a hairbrush down. "Shit! I don't know! That's the trouble, I don't goddamn know!"

Oxman went to her and rested a hand on her shoulder. He wasn't sure if she was acting, doing a bit from an old script. "Don't cry," he cautioned her, "you'll cause your makeup to smear."

But she was crying. Or at least she'd summoned tears. Not quite enough, though, to mess up her makeup. She stared up at him. "Oh, Ox, can you help me? Protect me?"

He knew he had to tell her about Austerman, now that she'd requested protection. "Someone *is* watching you," he said, "looking out for you. He's a good man, so you'll be safe as possible. I want you to pretend he isn't there; that's the way he can do his job best." But he knew Lana would need heavier protection now, publicity be damned, and would get it as soon as he had a chance to clear it with Manders.

"And I can do my job better knowing he's there," Lana said. She laid a hand on Oxman's and squeezed. "I realize it seems crazy, to get so upset about some crank notes . . ."

"I'd be upset if they were written to me," Oxman told her.

"I know what everyone's been telling you about me," she said. "About how cruel I can be in love."

"How do you know that?"

She seemed surprised. "What else would they tell you? It's all true. It's the way my affairs seem to go, I'm afraid. After a while, men—all men—seem to want more of me than I'm willing to give. I react, go on the offensive, sort of. It's a compulsive and protective thing in a woman such as myself. Can you understand that?"

Oxman felt as if he were talking with Blanche DuBois. "I understand what you're saying," he said.

"I don't want to hurt anyone at first," she said softly. "It isn't in my nature. And then, I *do* want to hurt—to hurt back!"

"Zach Denton injured you physically. You want to hurt him back?"

She laughed. "Physically! That's nothing. That was only Zach's childish reaction. I bear him no ill will at all, Ox. I swear it."

"You think he's capable of greater violence?"

Her eyes widened; they were beautiful. "You mean murder? Did he kill Vince McGreery, you're asking." She lowered her head for a moment, then raised it and focused her gaze to bore into Oxman. "I don't think he'd kill," she said. "Zach's violence is aimed at women, if you know what I mean. Sometimes it's erotic, sadistic, sometimes merely a temper tantrum. But I don't think he would or could kill anyone, male or female. Men like Zach, they're actually cowards trying to affirm their masculinity."

"Maybe," Oxman said. Not that it made a difference. Cowards could kill.

"Is Zach your main suspect?"

"No. As of now, there are no suspects." But Oxman wondered if Zach Denton was shaping up to be the prime suspect. And if so, was it the facts of the case pointing to him? Or was it Oxman's loathing for the man and what he'd done to Jennifer?

"What about other men in your life?" Oxman asked. "Before your 'Shadowtown' days."

"I was married once, a long time ago. The man's name is Calvin Oaks. After a few months I felt trapped, and I began to take it out on Cal. He initiated me in the use of drugs, and I resented that, too. After I left him, it took me two years to get free of them."

"Where's Oaks now?"

"Last I heard, he'd found God and was in some kind of religious cult in the Midwest. In the Ozarks, I think. I guess that's where you go to find God—among the acorns."

"Think he's capable of writing those notes?"

"I doubt it, but I don't know him anymore. And it's been almost ten years since we saw each other."

"What about other men in your past?"

She grinned with deliberate wickedness. "In alphabetical order?"

"I get the point," Oxman said. "Never mind. But is there any one of them specifically, other than Denton, who might threaten you?"

"I'm afraid they all have at least some smidgeon of motive."

Great! Oxman thought. Makes it easy. He was intrigued by Lana Spence, but he wasn't sure if he liked her. Or even if he felt sorry for her.

"I suppose you've heard those awful show-business stories about how leading ladies sleep with the leading men?" Lana said.

"Sure," Oxman said, "to make the love scenes more realistic."

"Usually those stories are false, but in some cases they're true."

"Are they true in your case?"

"More often than not." If she'd glanced up to see if he was shocked, she might have been disappointed. After deftly playing a mist of hair spray over her head, she said, "Why did you become a cop, Ox?"

"Why do you ask?"

"I'm interested in why people do things. That's one reason I'm an actress. One of many reasons."

"I like things to be the way they should be," Oxman said. She'd have to settle for that simple answer. It wasn't inaccurate. He'd become a cop because of his persistent feeling that the world was unfair to the wrong people and should be set right. As a policeman, he was one of the few who could help set it right—as right as possible, anyway. It ran deep in him, this passion for order and justice, like something stamped on his genetic code. Even before he'd put on the uniform, he'd been a cop. He didn't think Lana would understand that. He wasn't sure if he did. One thing he'd learned: People usually did things for reasons they didn't really understand.

There was a knock on the dressing-room door, and a male voice told Lana she was needed immediately on the set.

She gave Oxman's cheek a pat in parting, stood before the full-length mirror, and twirled artfully.

"Thank you, Ox," she said, then she flounced out the door. The room seemed excruciatingly devoid of her presence, emptier than empty.

Oxman was left standing and wondering if he'd been witness to reality, or if he'd been part of a well-played scene.

Jennifer Crane—3:15 P.M.

Jennifer knew what she had to do. She had to face the fear to make it stop gnawing at her insides, permeating everything she'd done since learning about Zach being at "Shadowtown." She checked her appearance in the mirror, as if it mattered how she looked for this. But her navy-blue dress fit her well, and with her dark-blue high heels and simple string of pearls, she was dressed up just enough to project the attractive but subdued image she thought appropriate.

She absently fluffed her long auburn hair, and, slightly irritated with herself that she'd been so particular about her appearance, snatched up her purse and left the apartment.

Though it was a nice enough day to walk, she took a cab to Shadowtown Productions.

When he came through the door and saw her seated in a chair in the reception area, his craggy features creased into the smile she remembered, and she raged inwardly at the old emotions that welled up in her. She knew again why she'd forgiven him for all the beatings, why she'd believed each time was the last.

"Jennifer!" he said, and extended both hands toward her. "I was shocked when I heard who wanted to see me."

She couldn't recall getting to her feet, but she was standing and her hands were in his. When he kissed her cheek she recoiled slightly, but he didn't seem to notice. She was of average height, yet she felt dwarfed by him; he was even taller than she'd remembered.

"I'm glad to see you!" he said.

It sounded so genuine. As if the past didn't matter. As if it had all

110

happened to two other people. She had to remind herself that it had been real, and very personal.

Now that Jennifer was here, with him, she didn't know quite what to say. "I saw your name in the paper," she told him. "That's how I knew you were back in New York."

Gripping her elbow, he guided her over near a small sofa and a potted rubber plant, where they could talk privately. "Yeah, that McGreery thing. A hell of a business."

And then, quickly, she told Zach about her relationship with Oxman.

Denton shrugged. He hadn't put on an ounce of weight; he looked as lean and youthfully loose-jointed as he had when Jennifer watched him walk out of her life. That made seeing him all the more unsettling.

"It won't matter," she assured him. "Ox is a professional."

Zach smiled warmly down at her from his lanky height. "I didn't suppose he'd try to frame me for McGreery's murder." But there was a trace of something in his voice that suggested to Jennifer he feared exactly that.

"I suppose that's why I wanted to see you," Jennifer lied. "To assure you that Ox wouldn't let our past relationship color his investigation."

"Is that the only reason, Jennifer?"

The bastard knew she was lying! He could always tell. "It wasn't because I miss you," she said, more sharply than she'd intended.

"Sure," he said.

What did that mean?

Zach leaned down toward her until she could feel the warmth of his breath. "Listen, Jennifer, how about having a cup of coffee with me in about an hour and putting the past to rest. I know I didn't behave well—"

"That's a hell of an understatement," Jennifer interrupted.

"Yeah, it is. I can understand why you wouldn't cherish any memories from those days. I was under a lot of pressure then, and I did some things I'm sorry for. Things I'm . . . well, things I'm ashamed of, Jennifer."

"That's how you used to talk each time after you beat me. And each time, I believed you." She shook her head. "Jesus!"

He spread his long arms in a pleading gesture. "I'm different now. Really. I'm not sure why. I suppose I've grown up. I'm not the same hostile young guy who acted and then was sorry."

"You hurt me, badly, Zach. And probably killed our unborn child. God, I can't forget that!"

He brushed a strand of straight, lank hair from his forehead, a boyish gesture that sent a thrust of memory through her. "I understand," he said. "But we oughta bury the past, since we can't change it. Now that the emotional tug-of-war's over, there's no reason we can't be friends."

"I don't think going out for coffee's a good idea, Zach."

He seemed surprised and hurt, as if she'd turned him down for a first date. "Okay," he mumbled, and briefly tried a smile that didn't quite manage to take form.

"When I heard you were in town," Jennifer said, "and involved in a case Ox was working on, I thought I ought to see you, talk to you."

He did grin at her now. "Well, you have," he said.

She couldn't help smiling. Looking at the gentleness in his eyes, it was impossible for her to fully comprehend what had happened. It seemed no more important or real to her just then than an unpleasant dream remembered in the light of day.

He held out his hand and she took it. For an instant he rested his other hand on top of hers, then he pulled both hands back.

"Guess it's good-bye again, then," he said.

"Good-bye, Zach," she told him, and turned quickly and walked toward the exit.

She knew he was watching her as she pushed open the glass door and walked down the short flight of steps to the sidewalk.

She was outside without immediately realizing it. The visit with Zach had disturbed her more than she anticipated.

When she reached the corner, she stood for a moment leaning against a traffic sign. The motion of the cars rushing past made her dizzy and slightly nauseated. Was she the only thing in the world not moving?

The light winked to red, and the traffic stopped. Jennifer straightened, breathed in deeply, and crossed the intersection. She decided she'd walk back to the apartment; she needed the physical exertion to clear her mind.

Coming here to talk to Zach hadn't been a good idea, she realized. She hadn't faced only her fear. She'd also faced the past and, unexpectedly, found not the Zach of her hate and imagination, but the kind Zach, the familiar Zach who seemed somehow disassociated from his occasional brutalities, who perversely inspired guilt and self-revulsion in *her* for the things *he'd* done. As if she'd caused them simply by being herself.

Jennifer realized she was walking very fast, slamming her heels down on the pavement with each long stride. She'd found a different fear, a greater fear at "Shadowtown" than the one she'd gone there to lose.

Because she'd found the old Zach Denton. The old familiar set of emotions, in perfect working order after all these years.

The old yearning.

Smiley Manders—3:30 P.M.

Manders sat behind his wide, cluttered desk, wondering if there was anybody in the world who wasn't on his ass. Only the people who didn't know about him, he figured.

The mayor and the police commissioner and the chief knew about him. Every newspaper reporter, talking-head TV anchorman, news-magazine journalist, gossip columnist, crime buff, crackpot, and people who could read or just see or hear in general seemed to know about him. They were all on his ass.

He sighed and decided it was time to quit feeling sorry for himself. God helped those who helped themselves—unless God felt like having a good joke.

Manders got up out of his chair, burped and tasted again the greasy pizza he'd had for lunch, then walked to the door and peered out into the squad room and booking area. Felstein was busy behind the desk, collecting and writing out receipts for the valuables of two suspects who looked like hookers who'd just been brought in by a rookie patrolman named Anderson. Hookers in the middle of the day, yet. If they were street workers it might be hard to make a soliciting charge stick. Somebody had better talk with Anderson.

After Felstein had placed the sullen women's valuables in large brown envelopes and sealed the flaps, Manders called to him: "Send me Ox and Tobin immediately when they check in, Murray!"

"They're coming in the door now, sir," Felstein called back.

Manders waved a hand languidly at Felstein, glanced again at the scantily dressed suspects, and turned to reenter his office. He burped again, sat back down, and waited.

Within a minute there was a knock on the door. Manders called to enter, and Oxman and Tobin stepped in. Tobin was gnawing on a toothpick and seemed preoccupied. Oxman appeared as stolid and quietly observant as ever, a tough man to read. Manders liked both men; they were his best, though he seldom let them in on that fact. Better to keep them striving.

He mentally crossed his fingers. "Tell me you've driven a stake through the heart of the 'Shadowtown' vampire," he said, "and now all the villagers can sleep securely."

Oxman smiled faintly and shook his head. "Sorry, Lieutenant, can't say that."

"Ernest Dickerson would sleep better," Tobin said.

Manders felt a vague resentment toward Dickerson for confusing the "Shadowtown" case and supplying the media with something juicy to write up and to yak about on TV. One of the New York papers had run an interview with Dickerson, before the publicity-shy wino had wisely disappeared into the wilds of the Bowery to find privacy.

"We're going to have to step up protection for Lana Spence," Oxman said.

Manders didn't want to do that. More and obvious protection meant the threats on her life would be made public, and the media would do cartwheels of delight.

Oxman must have interpreted the expression on Manders's face. "More publicity, Lieutenant," he said, "but I don't see how we can get around it. She received another threatening note, signed 'Edgar Grume' like the rest, only this time it was addressed to Lana Spence instead of Delia Lane, and it made mention of a strawberry birthmark on her breast. It had to have been written by somebody who knows her, and wants her to realize it. Not by some crank fan getting his kicks."

Manders cupped his long face in his hands, bowed his head for a moment, then looked up and nodded. The media would be even more ecstatic if some brain-fried fanatic murdered a celebrity like Lana Spence. "We'll keep Austerman on her for now. This evening some extra manpower will be assigned, and the uniforms in the area will be alerted."

"Speaking of Lana Spence," Tobin said, the toothpick bobbing in his mouth. "I spent the morning digging into her life, and it ain't pretty. Seems she hopped in the sack with every leading man she ever played opposite, then she managed to break off the affairs some way that left them pissed off for life. I mean, this beauty liked to maim. Her poor husband—"

"Husband?" Manders interrupted.

"Former husband," Tobin amended. "They been divorced over ten years."

"Calvin Oaks?" Oxman asked.

"Yeah." Tobin looked surprised.

"She told me about him this morning," Oxman said.

Tobin winked at Manders. "Ox is halfway in," he said.

Manders looked at Oxman, saw nothing in his eyes. It wouldn't do to have one of his detectives getting mixed up with the object of death threats in an active murder case. Manders decided not to ask Oxman about that possibility. Oxman was a pro and had learned the hard way not to free-lance or get personally involved.

"Anyway," Tobin was saying, "she drove this poor bastard Oaks into some kind of religious cult in Missouri."

Manders began tapping a pencil on the desk, holding it loosely between two fingers. He watched it bounce until the lead broke. A religious cult member with a motive. Had to be covered. "I'll have Missouri law question Mr. Oaks," he said. "Maybe they can give us some idea of his whereabouts when McGreery was killed."

"This Lana Spence really is some ballbuster," Tobin said. "That's what comes across stronger than anything when you question men she's worked her magic on. Not a one that I can remember said anything in her favor, and I talked to plenty of them. The producers sure as hell cast her right in that soap opera. I felt like I was hearing about Delia Lane most of the morning."

"Lieutenant!"

Felstein's voice. He was standing in the doorway, looking smug in the way of a kid with a big secret to tell. Felstein could do that better than anyone Manders knew.

"So what is it?" Manders finally asked, aggravated.

"Thought you oughta know, a call just came in. A landlord over on West Forty-fifth dicovered the body of one of his tenants, a guy named Burt Lassiter, in an apartment."

Manders waited, raised his eyes to gaze at the ceiling. "And? . . ." he said.

"There was a vampire costume hanging in the closet."

Manders was trying to figure out what that could mean, if anything, in this bizarre business, when he saw Tobin remove the toothpick from his mouth.

"Burt Lassiter's the name of one of Lana Spence's former lovers," he said. "He was on my list of people to talk with this afternoon."

"You got the address?" Manders asked Felstein.

Felstein handed him a folded sheet of memo paper. Manders glanced at the West Forty-fifth Street address and gave the paper to Tobin, who squinted at it.

"Same address, same guy," Tobin said. "I didn't figure there could be that many Burt Lassiters."

"Not with Lana Spence in their past," Oxman said.

"Lassiter is—was—an actor," Tobin said. "He was Lana Spence's leading man in some off-off-Broadway play about a guy who imagined he was a St. Bernard. She played a poodle."

Manders tried, but couldn't believe that one. He frowned at Tobin.

"Really," Tobin said, as if insulted by being doubted. "Dogs."

"I know what St. Bernards and poodles are."

Manders's phone rang. Somebody in the booking area was yelling for Felstein. A siren singsonged outside, not more than a few blocks away. The cadence of the dispatcher's voice on the police radio in the next room picked up. Manders reminded himself that the "Shadowtown" case wasn't the only crime in town.

"Ox. Tobin," he said, ignoring the jangling phone for the moment. He pointed toward the memo sheet with the address scrawled on it, still in Tobin's hand. "Go. Find out what the hell's the deal with this Lassiter guy, other than that he's dead."

He lifted the receiver and waited until Oxman and Tobin had left the office before saying hello.

Someone who identified himself as an aide from the mayor's office said hello back.

Manders tasted pizza again.

E. L. Oxman—4:15 P.M.

What was left of Burt Lassiter was dressed in yellowed jockey shorts and a T-shirt. It was lying on the bed in harsh light from a shadeless, drapeless window. The brilliance of the scene made it all too vivid. The dominant color was red; Lassiter's throat had been slashed.

Felstein's information was off the mark. The apartment turned out to be in a small residential hotel on West Forty-fifth, the Penmont, and the "landlord" who'd discovered the body actually had been a weasly little gray desk-clerk who'd sometimes played chess with Lassiter. When he'd come upstairs after getting off duty, to meet Lassiter for their weekly game, he'd gotten no answer to his knock, tested the door and found it unlocked, and then discovered that Lassiter had already been checkmated that afternoon.

The photographer, fingerprint crew, and lab men had come and gone. Two white-uniformed orderlies were gingerly fitting Lassiter into a black plastic body bag, trying to keep their rubber-gloved hands out of the mess. They weren't having much luck. Oxman looked away.

"Any idea about time of death?" he asked Wellman, the assistant Medical Examiner who'd made the prelim on Lassiter's body.

"Couple of hours is my guess," Wellman said. He was a short, wiry redheaded man whom Oxman disliked. There were times when Wellman seemed to enjoy his job too much.

"Ox," Tobin said, and stood aside from the open closet door.

Oxman saw hanging among a sparse and mostly threadbare wardrobe an impressive black outfit complete with red-lined cape. The lapels of the old-fashioned suit were of the same silky material as the long cape. There were even pointy-toed shiny black shoes to go with the outfit. Laceless dress shoes. Had Dracula worn slip-ons?

"Guy's throat was slashed with a knife, not fangs," Wellman said. "Big blade. Quite a grin; damn near ear to ear." He laughed softly, somewhere between a chuckle and a giggle.

"Not funny, though," Oxman said.

"Oh, I dunno. Lassiter'll smile forever."

Oxman ignored Wellman and looked around in vain for the murder weapon. He hadn't really expected to find it.

Wellman said, "Sorry to leave good company, but I was on my way to pick up some carry-out chow mein when I got this call. Hope it's still warm. Warmer'n Lassiter, anyway." He gave his soft, weird little chuckle, hoisted his black bag, and left.

A few seconds later, the morgue attendants got the body bag zipped with the usual grating, ripping sound, and wheeled out Lassiter's corpse.

Oxman walked over to the closet and brought down a square cardboard box from the top shelf. According to the illustration it had once held a Sony portable tape player, a medium-sized ghetto blaster. The box was light now, and felt almost empty. Oxman shook it back and forth gently, then he pried up the interlocking flaps. Inside was a luxurious white wig. He held the box out so Tobin could see its contents.

Tobin craned his neck to stare, then grunted.

"What do you know about this guy Lassiter?" Oxman asked.

Tobin glanced at the unmade and bloodstained bed, as if to make sure Lassiter was gone before they talked about him. "Like I said, he played opposite Lana Spence in this play. It ran about four weeks, which wasn't bad, considering where it opened. This was about nine years ago, probably right after she sent Calvin Oaks on his way. It's the first role her present agent, Manny Brokton, got her. Everybody I talked to says Brokton's a snake, incidentally, so it's no wonder he's represented Lana all these years. Changed her luck for her, too; moved her up from acting with guys like Lassiter into bigger parts. She ditched Lassiter, and the play, when Brokton got her a film role in Los Angeles. The play folded right after she left, and the way I hear it, Lassiter held her responsible and figures she ruined his career. He drank a lot, got into drugs, and used to talk all the time about how Lana ran out on him, and that the play was his turning point, where his life started to go sour."

Oxman remembered the bony, ravaged features of the dead man on the bed. "Lassiter looks pretty rough, and old, to have been one of Lana's leading men and lovers."

Tobin shrugged. "He was forty-five, Ox, even if he looked sixty-five. Drugs, remorse, and sudden loss of blood through a gap in the throat will do that to a man."

True enough, Oxman thought. Or maybe Lana did that to her men. Black Widow Lana. "Didn't Lassiter land any good roles after his affair with Lana?"

"I was told by other actors who knew him then that Lana cooked up a story to put what she did in a better light. She blamed Lassiter for ruining the play, and said that was why she left it without notice. She spread the word he was a temperamental no-talent and impossible to act with. It worked well enough to send him into a spin that hit ground in the crash we just saw here."

Something like the way she'd treated Overbeck, Oxman thought. And Arthur Sales. Draining them of their worth to her, then moving on and leaving them with blame and innuendo.

He walked to the dirty, drapeless window and looked out at an airshaft and the stark zigzag of wrought iron that served as a fire escape. He felt uneasy about what they'd found here. This wrapped it up too neatly.

Tobin must have known what he was thinking. "It's convenient, Ox. Lassiter stays full of hate and drugs and goes whacko. Envies Lana's success and pictures himself in 'Shadowtown,' in the part he might have had instead of Ames, if his life had gone differently. So he gets his jollies sneaking onto the set and dressing up like Edgar Grume. And leaving threatening notes for Lana Spence. It's our most likely solution to McGreery's murder; this Lassiter guy was twisted."

"So twisted he slit his own throat with a knife?" Oxman asked.

"Hell, Ox, anybody might have killed a dopehead like Lassiter. Maybe the desk clerk did it over cheating at chess. Maybe some fellow junkie did it for Lassiter's stash. People have been killed for less. You and I have both seen it. Maybe Lassiter was dealing and got the wrong people pissed off at him."

"It's all maybe," Oxman said.

Tobin snorted and crossed his arms. "Okay, let's change it to probably. We both know Smiley will."

Oxman had thought of that. Manders would have no choice but to hang everything on Lassiter; everybody in the chain of command above Manders, all the way to God, would be pressuring him to close the case. Manders was a good cop, but also one practical enough to have made lieutenant.

"Let's have the lab pick up the vampire costume," Oxman said. "See what they find when they go over it."

Tobin nodded and walked to the phone.

Maybe it really was this simple, Oxman thought, looking around the tiny, fleabag room. The way Lassiter had lived was pathetic. Peeling paint and wallpaper, sagging mattress. Dirty and depressing. It was easy to believe the man had been a candidate for the twitch bin. Easy to believe McGreery's murder and the threatening notes to Lana Spence had come about the way Tobin had theorized. Easy because it was so logical.

All that tightly constructed logic in such a random world scared the hell out of Oxman.

Jennifer Crane—9:00 P.M.

Wind-driven rain was beating against the living-room window of Jennifer's apartment. It made a sound like something with huge wings trying to get in. She walked to the window and looked outside. It was raining so hard the lights of the traffic below were barely visible— unreal, moving glimmers of yellow.

Behind her, Oxman said, "It was foolish of you to go see him."

Jennifer turned away from the night outside. "I can't explain it any better than to say it was something I felt I needed to do, even though I sure wasn't looking forward to it. I didn't like the idea of avoiding thinking about those years with Zach, rough as they were. And my mind was avoiding them the way the tongue avoids a sore inside the mouth: instinctively, but unable to keep from touching now and then. That's no way to live. I wanted to put Zach Denton to rest with the past."

Oxman settled deeper into the sofa and sipped his hot chocolate. "And did you?"

"I'm not sure," Jennifer lied. She was sure she *hadn't* buried the memory of Zach with the rest of the past. Ox was right; she'd been foolish to see Zach at Shadowtown Productions. Instead of making the past easier to live with, she'd stirred it up, along with emotions she hadn't suspected were still attached to Zach Denton. Her conversation with him had sent a subtle but profound shock wave through her.

But the "Shadowtown" case was over, and that was her salvation. She knew she could at least push Zach Denton back to that remote part of her mind where he'd resided all these years, and she could control him there, even if she couldn't exorcise him. It was his connection

122

with Ox that had sprung him loose, revived the frightening potency of his memory. It was as if he'd always be a part of her. But now Zach and Ox would probably never meet again, and somehow that made getting up each morning easier for Jennifer.

"You should have had the bastard thrown in jail after he beat you," Oxman said.

"I wasn't thinking clearly then," Jennifer said. "About anything." It was funny, she mused, how a person couldn't really remember pain. It was the psychological abuse that lingered. And it was the very truth about that abuse that Zach could twist and pull and shape to his selfish design. That was why women so often stayed with men like Zach, even as they were dragged through hell. Somehow the situation got shifted around so they saw themselves in some way to blame for their own victimization. And even though they could see that their perspective was being warped, they were powerless to stop it from happening.

That was the force Jennifer sensed Zach was exerting on her the day she'd seen him at "Shadowtown." And she'd recognized the familiar lure of it, the temptation to forgive and succumb and to drift beyond all decision-making in her life. Even if that drifting occasionally carried her onto the rocks. He'd long ago engendered in her, more deeply than she'd known, a capacity for punishment and self-deception.

She suddenly felt the need to feel Ox's arms around her, to press herself tight against the protective warmth of him. He was solid; he was sanity.

But as she moved toward the sofa, the phone rang.

She changed direction and answered it.

A woman's voice, asking for Ox. An oddly familiar voice.

Jennifer watched Ox's face as he talked on the phone. She knew that this was business. The fine, parallel lines appeared above the bridge of his nose; his eyes were alert. She'd gone back to stand near the window and couldn't quite hear what he was saying.

The conversation was a short one, in which the caller had done most of the talking. Ox got his bulky tan raincoat from the entrance-hall closet before returning to the living room.

Jennifer didn't want him to leave. "You don't have to go out in this rain, do you?"

"Afraid so," Ox said. "That was Lana Spence. She wants to see me."

"About what?"

"She wouldn't say." He smiled. "She likes to wring maximum suspense from commonplace situations. It probably isn't anything, Jennifer, and I'll be back in an hour. She's in her apartment over on Lexington."

"Why didn't she call the precinct, let them send somebody over?"

Ox came to her and kissed her forehead, holding the bunched material of the folded coat between them. "Because she's smart like you and wants only me." He stepped back and worked his arms into the coat, then straightened it and adjusted the collar. "Actually, she's got me cast as the detective in her personal real-life drama. Just the detective, nothing else."

Jennifer considered asking him if he was sure about that, then she decided she didn't need to. Ox would play whatever role he'd chosen.

He walked toward the door, buttoning his coat.

But there was something else Jennifer had to ask. "Ox, before Lassiter was found, did you suspect Zach?"

He turned and stuffed his hands into his coat pockets; she could tell by the material that he'd clenched them into fists. His shoulders were hunched, as if it were raining inside the apartment. "Logically, no more than some of the others." His steady eyes met hers. "Emotionally, I'm not sure. Maybe I wanted Denton to be guilty."

She watched him walk to the door and open it. His movements were studied, deliberate. The coat was stretched taut across his wide back.

Before he left, he paused and said, "I would have acted on the facts, Jennifer, on logic and not emotion."

"I know that," she told him, and watched him leave.

And she did know it.

She only wished she could be as sure about herself.

E. L. Oxman—10:15 P.M.

Oxman had to awaken the doorman at Lana Spence's apartment building on Lexington. He was a hatchet-faced old man who'd fallen asleep watching the television monitor mounted above his desk. The screen was glowing but blank. The set was probably closed circuit, trained alternately on strategic points of the building, but Oxman noticed that the elderly doorman had a video recorder hooked up to it; he might have been watching a tape of a show he'd missed earlier and had dozed off.

To shake up the old guy, Oxman identified himself as a detective and said Lana Spence was expecting him.

"You won't, uh, mention to Miss Spence I was resting my eyes, will you?" the doorman asked, standing up straight and using the backs of his frail knuckles to brush off his tan uniform.

"Don't worry about it," Oxman told him. "But try to stay awake, huh?"

"Yes, sir," the doorman said. He told Lana over the intercom that Oxman was on his way up and buzzed him through the door from the glitzy lobby.

Oxman took the elevator to the thirtieth floor, wondering why exactly Lana wanted to see him. He knew what Tobin would think, and he decided not to mention this visit, whatever it was all about. Was it possible that this big-time soap-opera star actually had the hots for a New York homicide detective? A middle-aged and not-all-that-handsome one at that?

Oxman dismissed the idea. The stuff of fantasies. A "Shadowtown" slant on life. Things didn't happen in the real world the way they did on television.

As the elevator slowed and stopped, and its doors glided open, he heard a woman scream.

He was startled, then he realized Lana wasn't above arranging theatrics for him. He stepped from the elevator and looked down the hall to his left, in the direction of the scream.

A tall figure in a black cape was rounding the corner toward the fire stairs. Moving fast—gone! Like a fleeting hallucination.

The door to Lana Spence's apartment was hanging open. As he rushed to it, Oxman was relieved to hear Lana scream again, even though the shrill sound made his scalp crawl. She was alive!

Not only was she alive, but she was standing just inside the door in a sheer pink nightgown and gripping a large ceramic vase with her arm drawn back to strike.

As Oxman swung his body in through the door, she hurled the vase at him.

He was barely able to duck out of the way as it exploded against the doorjamb.

"Jesus!" he said.

She held both hands to her gaping mouth when she saw the identity of the man she'd almost brained with the vase.

"I'm sorry . . . Oh, God! . . ."

"You all right?" Oxman asked.

She nodded frantically. Mindlessly. "Yes, I scared him. Held him off. Then he heard the elevator door open and he ran."

"Phone the doorman! Ask him to watch the fire stairs! Then call the police!"

"Won't you stay with me? . . ."

Oxman didn't bother answering. He was already sprinting down the hall toward the fire stairs. They were probably the type with one-way, locking doors, and could be opened only from inside the halls; the dark-caped figure might be trapped in the stairwell and forced to descend all thirty flights of stairs before he could leave the building.

Oxman hunched low as he ran and hit the horizontal brass bar on the fire door with his forearm. As he began taking the steps that angled down the narrow stairwell, the door's pneumatic closer hissed behind him.

He paused.

From far below might have come the faint clatter of hurried footfalls.

He drew a deep breath and flung his body forward, taking the stairs two, three at a time, maintaining his balance only by playing his grip along the handrail. His palm warmed and squeaked against the smooth steel.

At every landing, the floor numbers were marked in red on the cinder-block wall. By the twenty-fifth floor Oxman was gasping for air, almost stumbling as he hurled himself down the stairs. He heard his shrill, rasping intakes of breath echoing around him.

On twenty-two he glanced down the stairwell and thought he caught a glimpse of black movement, like the wild swirl of a cape, several floors below.

He cursed and pushed himself harder, feeling a deep ache in his thighs. Out of shape. He was too old and too damned out of shape for this kind of thing. There was a stitch in his right side, and his heart was bashing a mad rhythm against his ribs.

On sixteen Oxman had to stop and lean on the handrail. His chest was heaving and his legs trembled weakly.

Rough. God, this was rough!

After a few seconds, when he pushed away from the rail and tried to run again down the stairs, he found he could barely keep from falling. His legs were rubbery, sending him lurching in undesired directions. Someone else's legs.

On twelve he had to stop again, this time to sit down. His entire chest burned and his heart was hammering at such a rate it was almost like one sustained vibration. He was old enough to be in heart-attack country, he knew, but he tried not to think about that.

Forcing himself to his feet, he took a few awkward steps, stumbled, and fell to a sitting position on the small concrete landing.

He tried to stand, but his vision wavered and he became nauseated. Slumping against the hard wall, he tried to catch his breath and concentrated on not vomiting.

Then he told himself the man in the black cape would be hurting just as badly as he, Oxman, and he rose and lurched on down the stairs. Maybe he was closer to the bastard than he'd thought. He managed to draw his service revolver from its holster, but it dropped from his quaking hand and clattered down the steps ahead of him. He paused to stoop and pick it up, then he staggered on.

It took Oxman as much time to descend the next two floors as it had the previous eighteen.

On the landing at ten, his body finally rebelled. His legs buckled and he felt himself sagging. Closing his eyes to his swimming vision, he groped for the wall to lean against.

Then he doubled over and retched, trying to ride out the ache in his gut as he struggled for breath. The air around him was foul, like thick liquid he had to suck into his lungs. He smelled the vomit he'd dribbled onto his shirt.

Oxman couldn't remember hurting all over as badly as this, ever, and he welcomed the blackness that claimed him.

He wasn't sure how much time had passed when he sensed motion around him and opened his eyes.

Large dark shapes hovered over him. He gasped and tried to sit up, but he was so weak he merely fell back and banged his head against the cinder-block wall. The pain settled behind his eyes.

He calmed down when he realized the dark forms were New York City firemen in slickers.

"Take it easy, hoss," one of them said.

Something soft was fitted over Oxman's mouth and nose. He fought it at first, then he realized he was being given oxygen. He relaxed and tried to breathe deeply and evenly.

Eventually he felt revitalized enough to push away the oxygen mask and try to stand up.

He had to lean against the wall, but he made it.

"We get him?" he asked the fireman who'd administered the oxygen.

The firefighter was a stocky guy with blond hair and a friendly pug face. He looked puzzled. "All I know is we answered an alarm that was phoned in by the doorman. Old guy seemed confused when we got here."

"No, sir," a voice said to Oxman. A blue uniform appeared behind the fireman. "We didn't get him. There was a fire door on the twenty-ninth floor wedged open with a child's building block. It might have been set up that way on purpose."

Oxman bowed his head and leaned with both palms against the rough, cool wall. He cursed silently. The bastard had figured he might have to escape via the fire stairs and had taken precaution. The footfalls Oxman had thought he heard, the glimpse of shadowy movement far below—all that had been his imagination. None of it real.

From the twenty-ninth floor down, Oxman had been chasing a phantom.

Tobin was with Lana Spence in her apartment when Oxman took the elevator back up to the thirtieth floor.

Lana was sitting on the sofa with her knees primly pressed together. She'd put on a flowered silk robe over the see-through nightgown. Oxman suddenly realized she'd been expecting him when she opened the door in the nightgown and encountered the man in the black cape.

"You recovered yet, Ox?" Tobin asked. He was standing near Lana Spence; he'd been asking her questions.

Oxman nodded. "Got my breath back, anyway."

"Grume got clear," Tobin said. "Must have sneaked past the doorman to get up here. And the doorman was watching the fire-door exit after Lana called him. That gave Grume the opportunity to slip out another exit. That old doorman's about as alert as my twelve-year-old hound."

"And without the good nose." Oxman sat on the end cushion of the sofa, away from Lana Spence. His lungs still ached with each breath, as if they'd been seared. He looked up at Tobin. "You said 'Grume' got clear."

"That's what Miss Spence called him," Tobin said.

"See his face?" Oxman asked Lana.

"No, not exactly. He held his cloak up over it when I opened the door."

"The Bela Lugosi act, eh?"

She shook her head. "Nothing theatrical about it; more as if the light from the apartment startled him, scared him. I was going over some publicity photos at the table and had the chandelier on full wattage."

Oxman remembered how bright the apartment had been. He looked at the dimmer switch controlling the many-bulbed chandelier. Now it was turned down about halfway, casting a restful light over the apartment. There was a pile of bound scripts on the table beneath the chandelier, but no photographs. Lana probably read in the brilliant light rather than admit to herself that she'd reached the age where she needed glasses. Her vanity might have saved her life, allowing Oxman a few seconds' time to come along and frighten away her weird and dangerous caller.

"Did he say anything to you?" he asked.

"No," Lana said. "I was so scared—numb—and he just sort of backed up when all the light hit him, then he stopped and raised the knife."

"Knife?"

She shuddered and massaged her upper arms. "A long one with some kind of bone handle. Then he heard the elevator stop on this floor and he whirled and ran."

"You recognize him?"

"No. It all happened in such a hurry. I saw Edgar Grume when I looked at him, but maybe that was my nerves, and all the scenes I played opposite Grume—Allan Ames."

Oxman rubbed his forehead. The case was opening up again, becoming even more complex. For the first time, he found himself wondering if Allan Ames was really dead.

"Did you go to Ames's funeral?" he asked Lana.

"Of course. The entire cast and company did."

"Was there a service at a funeral home? With the coffin open?"

"No. Allan was mangled by the subway train. The family requested a closed-coffin ceremony."

Oxman looked at Tobin, who nodded. Something to be checked out. One of a thousand pieces the department would pick up, examine to see if it fit, and probably put back down. Police work was as painstaking as archeological exploration, only the human folly was more recent, and sometimes what you found when you dug or turned over a rock might kill you.

Oxman glanced out at the blue uniform in the hall. He recognized the cop, a heavyset guy named Colter; sharp and reliable.

"We're going to assign a detail to watch you," Oxman told Lana. "This building's actually pretty tight; no one should be able to get to you up here if the people downstairs are competent."

"Sammy the doorman—"

"Is okay for keeping out pesky insurance salesmen," Oxman interrupted. He stood up. "Try to get some sleep now," he advised. "We'll talk to you again in the morning."

"It won't be easy to sleep. I'll have to phone for some prescription pills."

"Make sure they're left downstairs, so they can be brought up by the man on duty."

"Don't worry, Ox, I'll be careful." For a moment she seemed about to cry, then she composed herself. "I thought this was all over. I mean, after Burt Lassiter was found . . ."

"We thought it was over, too," Tobin said.

Oxman stepped close to rest a hand on Lana's shoulder. She was trembling, or his hand was. "It'll be all right," he assured her, in a not very professional tone.

Tobin had moved to the door and was out of earshot. "Why did you want to see me tonight?" Oxman asked Lana.

"I wanted to thank you. I guess that turned out to be premature. But it was damned lucky."

Oxman remembered the vanilla lushness of her body beneath the sheer nightgown. How had she intended thanking him?

Tobin was waiting for him in the hall. Oxman nodded to Lana and backed out of the apartment. "Lock your door," he reminded her. He wondered if she'd intended locking it with him inside the apartment tonight. The black widow spinning her web for another blissful victim.

As he closed the door behind him, she was getting up from the sofa to obey his instructions, showing a lot of leg where the robe gapped.

"We better leave by a side door," Tobin said, as Oxman walked beside him toward the elevators. "The media's gotten wind of this and they've assembled downstairs with all their electronic shit."

Oxman grunted agreement. He didn't feel like facing a horde of persistent journalists pounding him with questions he couldn't or didn't want to answer.

"Back in the pressure cooker," Tobin remarked.

"And at a higher temperature."

They stood and waited for the elevator. Oxman's legs were throbbing and felt as if they weighed several hundred pounds each.

"Maybe this case is simpler than we think. E.L."

"How so?" Oxman asked.

"Maybe we're dealing with a genuine vampire."

Oxman looked at Tobin. Tobin wasn't smiling. Swell.

The elevator arrived, its doors growled open, and Oxman stepped inside. "Coming?" he asked Tobin. "Or are you going to fly?"

They managed to avoid the media, but they had to walk down a dim, littered alley and around the block to get to their cars.

On the sidewalk, Oxman and Tobin agreed to let the case sleep for the night. They'd meet at the Two-Four tomorrow morning to suffer through the wrath and agony of Smiley Manders, then they'd drag out the file on "Shadowtown." They'd start over.

The rain had stopped; no need for the wipers. As Oxman drove away from the apartment building and made a left to get to the transverse at Ninety-sixth Street, he saw a tall figure stride down the sidewalk and turn the corner.

Oxman hit the accelerator, swerved to avoid a delivery van, and then drove slowly down the dark street where he'd seen the man.

The street was empty except for a shabbily dressed bearded guy rooting through a wire trash container.

Oxman drove around the block and back to Ninety-sixth. The figure he'd glimpsed hadn't worn a cape. It had, in fact, been dressed in slacks and a light-colored Windbreaker. But Oxman was reasonably sure of the identity of the lanky, striding form:

Zachary Denton.

"Lana," Overbeck said into the phone, "I heard it on the news while I was waiting to watch Johnny Carson. Good Lord! Are you all right?"

"Of course I am," she said. "As if you cared."

Overbeck felt a rush of relief. He cared not about Lana Spence, but about her continued existence and ability to act. "Shadowtown" could ill afford to lose its resident vixen. The character the audience loved to hate and envy. And sometimes emulate. Delia Lane—Lana—had even inspired a line of designer fashions. The country was teeming with Delia Lanes.

"What did the newscast say, Harry? I haven't even seen a reporter. The police wouldn't let them upstairs."

Stupid cunt! "Haven't talked to the media? Listen, Lana—"

She laughed. "It's all right, Harry, sweet, I'll hold an 'impromptu' press conference tomorrow in the lobby. The show will reap the benefits of the publicity. Now, what did the newscast say?"

Overbeck smiled faintly. "Aging actress Lana Spence claims to have been threatened by a vampire at her apartment in Manhattan. Police Detective E. L. Oxman arrived on the scene and scared the supernatural creature away! Or something like that, Lana."

"You bastard, Harry."

Overbeck's grin widened. He did hate this bitch, he realized. When he let his emotions about her really run, he was surprised at their depth. She'd used him, dumped him, spread terrible rumors about him—and now he needed her. Only the spiraling numbers in his bank account and mutual-fund statements made the situation at all bearable.

133

"The news also mentioned that you'd identified the vampire as Edgar Grume," he said. "Did you say that?"

She didn't answer right away. "Not exactly." Her voice sounded strange. Scared, Overbeck suddenly realized. That wasn't like her. He'd never heard Lana sound frightened unless she was faking it.

"What did you say to the police, Lana?" he asked.

"I don't remember exactly. But, Harry, so help me it *did* look like Grume."

"Like Allan Ames, you mean."

"Of course like Allan! I'm not going crazy, Harry."

"You saw his face?"

"Not really. He held his cape over most of it."

"Christ!" Overbeck said.

"The light seemed to bother him."

"Of course." He wanted to sound skeptical, make her feel he wasn't taking her seriously. In the vampire, or whoever was pretending to be a vampire, Lana had finally encountered a man she couldn't bend to her will. That was something about all of this that Overbeck enjoyed immensely.

"He had a knife, Harry."

Overbeck sobered. That she'd seen a knife was serious; it posed a definite threat to the show. "The news didn't mention that," he said.

"Maybe the cops didn't tell the reporters about the knife."

"How'd Oxman scare the guy off?"

"Grume—I mean the vampire—heard the elevator arrive a moment after I opened my apartment door. Either that or the light made him run. Oxman saw him and chased him. Did everything but fly after him."

"Your hero, huh?"

"Yes, that's what he is." She sounded indignant, defensive. "There *are* real-life heroes, Harry."

"There's no such thing as real life," Overbeck said, wondering about Lana and Oxman. Did she have her hooks out for that poor cop? If so, he wouldn't have a chance. Big soap-opera star beds average working cop. Big soap-opera stars did that sometimes, Overbeck knew. For erotic sport. And Mr. Average, whoever he happened to be, almost always tumbled for the rich and famous. People like Lana knew how to use the magic that came with fame.

On the other hand, there was something different about Oxman. A steadiness. An equilibrium not easily upset. If he were an actor, Overbeck would have cast him precisely as what he was: a resolute police detective, the modern-day, big-city Mountie who always got his man. A sort of shorter, stockier Randolph Scott.

"What was Oxman doing at your apartment?" Overbeck asked.

"I was going to thank him for what he did for me. Be polite to him, shake his hand. Then we were going to sample some coke and fuck our brains out." She laughed, knowing she'd shocked Overbeck. Knowing, he suspected, that she could still evoke a pang of jealousy in him, a reminder that a piece of him was hers forever because he was foolish enough in the center of his being not to want it otherwise. She could have him again, she was letting him know. What was left of him now that he'd experienced and then lost her. If the black widow thought there was something more of him to nourish her or her career, she could have it. On a whim.

She was wrong about that, Overbeck told himself. Goddamn her, she was wrong! He was ashamed of his anger. He fought it down. "I assume the police protection is back on for you," he said in his normal voice.

"Is it ever," Lana said. "I'm guarded like little Miss Fort Knox."

Worth more gold to me than to yourself, Overbeck thought. He couldn't wait to see how high the show's ratings would soar after tonight's incident at her apartment. Lana was one of life's users, so Overbeck had no compunctions about using *her*. In fact, other than that he had to see her, talk to her, every day, he rather enjoyed using Lana Spence to further his *own* career. His turn now.

"I'm glad you're all right," he said, in an unctuous tone he didn't try to disguise. She knew what he really thought of her. Good. He wanted it that way.

"What're you going to do now, Harry?"

"Go to bed, I guess. I saw the news, Lana, and I was worried about you and just wanted to make sure you were okay and you'd be at the studio for tomorrow's taping. The scene with the Louis Carter character is tomorrow, when he arrives from Miami and puts pressure on Delia to work harder on Roger Maler. It's a pivotal scene, Lana."

"I'll be there, Harry. See you then. Good night."

"Night, Lana."

"And Harry?"

"Yeah?"

"Shove the phone up your fat ass."

Overbeck felt himself flush with surprise and rage. "What the hell was that for, Lana?"

"For that 'aging actress' remark." She slammed the receiver down hard enough to hurt his ear.

Overbeck hung up his phone slowly and then walked into the kitchen and poured himself a glass of milk. A pain in his jaw made him realize he was clenching his teeth.

He sat at the table and gulped down the milk without tasting it, too furious with Lana to know whether what he was drinking was hot or cold. She really was a despicable bitch. In what she called "real life," as well as in "Shadowtown."

It was too bad so many people needed her.

In so many ways.

Scene 4

E. L. Oxman—1:10 A.M.

Oxman saw the tall, lanky form of Zachary Denton cross the shadowed street and head toward the entrance to Denton's apartment building. Denton was wearing dark slacks and a light-gray Windbreaker, indicating that he was indeed the figure Oxman had seen earlier that night near Lana Spence's apartment.

Denton had been leaving the area only about an hour after Oxman had chased but lost the man in the vampire costume who'd brandished a knife when Lana had opened her door to him. It was possible that the man in the vampire getup had been Zach Denton, and that he'd taken refuge near the apartment building, hidden his costume somewhere, then tried to get home unnoticed.

Oxman sat in his car and watched Denton glance up and down the street, then push open the door and disappear into the foyer.

After a few minutes, during which Denton would have made his way upstairs to his apartment, Oxman got out of the car and walked to the building entrance. The air smelled fresh after the recent rain, but Oxman barely noticed. He was thinking only about Zachary Denton.

When he knocked on Denton's apartment door, he heard a woman's voice inside. But it was Denton who opened the door.

He was obviously surprised to see Oxman. His features lost all composure for an instant, then they set in lean, unreadable planes and sharp angles. Young Abe Lincoln about to put one over on Douglas.

"Hello. I, uh, was just about to go to bed," he said.

"You been home all evening?" Oxman asked.

Denton's eyes narrowed and grew cautious. "That sounds like a line from 'Shadowtown,' Sergeant."

"Maybe it is."

"Well, yeah, I've been home most of the evening. Bonnie will verify that." He moved back and motioned with a hand for Oxman to enter. A come-in-if-you-must gesture.

"Bonnie would be lying," Oxman said, stepping inside the apartment. He looked around. It was the kind of apartment he would have figured for Denton. The furniture was modern and color-coordinated in beiges. The walls were decorated with framed prints of what Oxman was sure were famous paintings. It all blended together smoothly, like the components of a stage set.

The girl named Bonnie went well with the rest of the room. She was small, with red hair and considerable breast development. In her late twenties, probably. She was wearing a short bathrobe, floppy green slippers, and a frightened expression. The robe's sleeves were short and loose, kimono-style; Oxman saw dark bruises on her arms, like acid stains just beneath the flesh.

"What would I be lying about?" she asked.

"About the whereabouts of your friend Denton here, for the past several hours," Oxman said.

"How would I know where Zach's been?"

"Go back into the bedroom," Denton told her. He was rattled. His protruding Adam's apple bobbed and he ran his hands nervously over his thin hips.

Bonnie smiled at Oxman and backpedaled on her green slippers into the bedroom and closed the door.

"Obedient," Oxman commented. "Train her yourself?"

"Have you been watching my apartment?" Denton asked. He seemed to have decided to put on the irate-citizen act.

"Only since I saw you near Lana Spence's apartment this evening."

Denton arranged his long, craggy features into an expression of innocence. "Something wrong with me being in the neighborhood?"

"Why did you tell me you were home most of the evening, when actually you walked through that door only minutes before I knocked on it?"

" 'Most of the evening' doesn't necessarily mean the last part of the evening, Sergeant."

"The part of the evening I'm interested in," Oxman said, "is around ten o'clock. You were at Lana Spence's place then."

"I thought you said you saw me *outside* her building."

"I might have seen you inside," Oxman said.

"You didn't." Denton began to pace, his long arms swinging loosely. As he took a few strides this way, then that, he kept his eyes fixed on Oxman. They were direct, appraising eyes; you had to look closely to see the cruelty in them, like a shifting dim light far back of the irises. Something intense lived there, watching like a carnivore for weakness. "I went to see Lana; that much is true. I got to her place, but I didn't go upstairs."

"Why not?"

"There were police cars parked out front. Then I heard more sirens, and fire engines arrived. They wouldn't have let anyone into the building then."

"You thought there was a fire?" Oxman asked.

"No," Denton said. "There were too many police there for the primary reason to be a fire. I figured Lana might be involved, but either way there was no sense in me sticking in my nose. So I turned and walked to a bar, had a few drinks, then came home."

"I believe the part about the bar," Oxman told him. "There'd be plenty of witnesses, I'm sure, who'd say you were drinking there tonight. Though they'd be confused about the time. But what did you do with the vampire costume before you went there?"

Denton didn't answer. He crossed his arms and smiled his handsome smile. "Look, Sergeant, let's drop the pretense and the bullshit. You know I'm Jennifer's former husband, and there was a time when I wasn't quite in control of myself. That cost me a lot. It cost me Jennifer. But it's all over and I'm trying to live it down. It's too late after the offense for you to be badgering me about it."

"Jennifer went to 'Shadowtown' to talk to you," Oxman said.

Denton shrugged. "That was her idea. And not a bad one. It's time for us to forgive each other."

Oxman felt a rage beginning to boil inside him. "What has *she* done that requires *your* forgiveness?"

"That's a private matter," Denton said.

"So's beating a woman until you cause her to have a miscarriage."

Denton appeared uncomfortable, as if his clothes had suddenly begun to make him itch. "I told you, that's all over."

"Maybe something like that is never over for some people. And maybe there are certain people it simply doesn't bother. It might have been over for you a day after it happened. But it wasn't you who suffered pain and lost a baby.''

"I get a definite impression, Sergeant, that because of who I am you've singled me out for persecution."

"I haven't singled you out," Oxman said. "And you haven't told me what you were doing outside Lana Spence's apartment, either."

"I said I was on my way to talk to her when I saw the commotion, the police and all."

"Talk to her about what?"

"Tomorrow's taping. There are a few special props she needs to know about."

"Why wouldn't you wait to tell her in the morning?"

"She arrives for a scheduled scene late sometimes. The truth is, the great Lana Spence comes and goes almost as she pleases, except for the time slots of the actual taping. I couldn't count on her showing up early enough to provide time for instruction."

"What kind of instruction?"

"There's a scene where a car's supposed to turn over. She has to know just how we're going to shoot it. We won't use a double, and she'll be in the mock-up car as we vibrate it and then tilt it on a hydraulic jack. We'll do the rest with camera work and stock footage, the car spinning and tumbling down a cliff. She has to learn how to make it appear as if she jumps free just before the car goes over."

Oxman watched Denton carefully. He seemed confident of his story, and if this was a lie, it was an elaborate one.

The trouble was, Denton was right about Oxman singling him out, and Oxman knew it. Not that Oxman had acted on that personal perspective. Not yet. He would have arranged a conversation as soon as possible with anyone from "Shadowtown" he'd seen in the vicinity of Lana Spence's apartment tonight. But he did want Denton to develop into the main suspect, and Denton was looking better all the time for that distinction.

Denton had access to the Edgar Grume costume. He was about the right height and weight, considering the sketchiness of the witnesses' stories. And he had motive. He hated Lana Spence for jilting him, and he might have been surprised by Vince McGreery while trying to plant one of the threatening letters in Lana's dressing room.

There was circumstantial evidence pointing to Denton, all right.

Plenty of it. Oxman had to keep reminding himself it was only circumstantial.

"I saw on TV in the bar what happened at Lana's," Denton said. "Really, I had nothing to do with that. I'm not in the habit of running around in a vampire outfit—or in any other kind of costume."

"You haven't asked me if Lana Spence is all right," Oxman said.

"That's because the news report stated she wasn't harmed." Denton had raised his voice. He realized it, and he shook his head and laughed. "This is fuckin' ridiculous. Am I your chief suspect, Sergeant?"

"You're climbing on the charts," Oxman said. "Good night, Mr. Denton." He turned and walked toward the door.

"Oxman," Denton said, stopping him. "Don't let your emotions about Jennifer cause you to do something dumb. I warn you, if I'm formally charged I won't hesitate to sue you and the city and the universe for false arrest."

Oxman turned back, his hand on the doorknob, and stared at Denton. He kept his anger in check by turning it into something cold and hard. "I noticed some bruises on Bonnie's arms. They looked like handprints. You might be surprised by who files charges against you."

"Let me suggest you leave Bonnie out of this. She's happy here with me, or she'd leave. She knows where the door is and how to use the knob."

"She probably isn't thinking straight," Oxman said.

"Yeah, and neither are you, Sergeant."

Oxman stepped into the hall and slammed the door behind him.

As he tromped toward the elevator, he tried to analyze his anger, to calm himself. What had really enraged him, he realized, was that Denton was right: He wasn't thinking straight. And he knew why.

Something had gained a grip on him and wouldn't let go.

A blossoming, genuine hatred for Zachary Denton.

Myra Deeber—10:30 A.M.

Myra got out of bed late, read *People* for a while over her coffee, then leisurely took a long, warm shower and got dressed. The seams of her pinstripe designer jeans were strained, and she had to lie on her back on the mattress and wriggle furiously to work the zipper. She decided to skip lunch.

A little before noon, she changed her mind. She'd been back from shopping for only fifteen minutes when she hurried to the kitchen of her cluttered apartment and opened the refrigerator door. Her workday began at four-thirty, and she ate late suppers in the restaurant's employees' lounge, where there was only the choice between the weekly special and standard stir-fried with rice. This would be her last chance of the day for a reasonably tasty meal of her own choosing.

She warmed a frozen cannelloni dinner in the microwave, along with half a loaf of garlic bread left over from yesterday. There was also some uneaten pecan pie, which she decided would be her dessert.

After the cannelloni and bread were heated, she put them on the kitchen's small, drop-leaf table, along with butter, parmesan cheese, and a generous slice of the pie. As an afterthought, she squirted some instant whipped cream onto the pie, swirling the gooey white mass into a heart shape. Then she poured herself a diet cola, unzipped her jeans, and sat down to eat.

As she forked food into her mouth, she kept an eye on the microwave's digital clock. It was almost time for the soaps to start. Myra would spend her afternoon immobile on the sofa in front of the TV, until it was time to leave for work.

Even unzipped, the jeans were constricting, so after lunch she struggled out of them and put on her loose-fitting terrycloth robe and her toeless slippers. It was difficult to get really involved in the soaps if your stomach was cramping and growling.

After adjusting the blinds so the living room was dim, she settled into the sofa and used the remote control to switch on the TV.

With mild dismay she found herself caught between worlds, in a hemorrhoid-medication commercial. Then a major-league shortstop was so pleased with his Toyota pickup that he jumped straight into the air. If there'd been a ball up there to catch, it would have been the play of the game.

Then "Ryan's Hope" began.

During the course of the afternoon, Myra would get up only three times. Once to use the bathroom, and twice to get soda and potato chips. It was a routine she'd followed for years. When she got to work later that day, the waitresses who hadn't been able to watch the soaps would come to her so they could be filled in on what had happened. To many of Myra's fellow employees, the characters on the soaps were as real as the supervisors who, in language sometimes hard to understand, ordered them to talk less and concentrate on their jobs. As real but less threatening.

It was between the trip to the bathroom and Myra's last snack time-out that something extraordinary happened.

She was watching "Shadowtown." Delia was in the cottage with Roger Maler. They were ensconced in the big soft feather bed and she was coaxingly and indirectly trying to get him to admit he was the father of Ivy Ingrams's baby. Delia had been to the foster home yesterday, trying to obtain demonstrable proof that the child's father was Roger, but the home's director wouldn't cooperate and was too old to be seduced. Delia was batting her eyes at Roger and talking about how terrible it must be for whoever had fathered Ivy's child to have Ivy's death on his conscience. How he was really innocent in Ivy's decision to try to abort their child but must long for someone in whom he could confide his agony.

Myra prayed Roger would be too smart to fall for the bitch's treachery; after all, he was doing everything that could be expected, even secretly helping the foster home to arrange for the best possible adoption.

Delia was twining the hair on Roger's bare chest when a figure appeared in the window beside the bed.

Neither Roger nor Delia realized the dark, caped form was outside the window, observing them from the shadows. The watching figure raised a clenched fist, as if in anger, then faded from the scene.

Myra was leaning forward on the sofa, her own pudgy fists clenched. There was no doubt about the dark figure's identity, shadowy and brief though his appearance had been.

The watcher in the window had been Edgar Grume.

What was this about? Myra wondered. She didn't see at all how the resurrection (if that was the proper term for a vampire) of Grume in the show could be explained logically, even in a soap opera. Everyone knew that Grume had been destroyed, transformed into dust and discarded. Everyone knew that—what was his name?—Allan Ames was dead. What was going on here? Had the scene been a mistake?

There was something eerie about it, the way Grume hadn't appeared to be a planned part of the episode at all, the way Delia and Roger had ignored his presence, though it was obvious Delia would have seen him when she moved to kiss Roger.

Myra ran the scene again in her mind and shivered. It was so real, yet unreal!

Then a startling thought struck her. Had she only *imagined* seeing Grume on her TV screen? Had she finally become too engrossed in the world of the soaps, in the strange and deadly games being played in "Shadowtown"?

No, she refused to believe that.

Another explanation, then. It was almost easier, and definitely more comfortable, to believe the appearance of Edgar Grume was a genuine phenomenon, that other viewers had seen his image in the cottage window. That he—Allan Ames, or Edgar Grume—had somehow actually returned. If not to life, then to a reasonable facsimile on "Shadowtown."

Myra glanced over at *People*, and at her stack of *National Enquirers*. Far stranger things had happened. They were documented.

The notion that Grume had returned to "Shadowtown" gripped her. She had to know what was going on. Had to find out if other viewers had seen Grume. What might soap-opera fans be saying about Grume's weird insertion into the show? What might the producers of "Shadowtown" be saying? Was this simply a publicity stunt, written into the episode? Or was it something far more difficult to explain, far more unsettling, and deliciously thrilling?

She punched the mute button on the remote control and scooted to the other side of the sofa, where she could reach the phone. In her haste, she knocked over a bowl of potato chips and some of them dropped between the cushions, but she ignored them. After leafing through the directory with trembling fingers, she dialed the number of Shadowtown Productions.

She dialed it again and again.

Again and again, she got a busy signal.

Smiley Manders—1:15 P.M.

Manders sat glumly behind his desk, staring blankly at the report of last night's activities at and around Lana Spence's apartment. What the fuck was going on? The stack of morning newspapers on the floor near his chair asked essentially the same question. Only they weren't as interested in the answer as Manders was, because for the news media the story meant added circulation; for Manders it meant added headache.

Wiping a hand down his long face, Manders closed his eyes, opened them, and tried to see the world more optimistically. It didn't work. And where the hell were Ox and Tobin?

He was about to go out into the squad room and see about the delay, when there was a perfunctory knock on the door and the two detectives walked into the office. They looked tired, worried, and haggard. Manders was sure cops aged faster than the general population.

Tobin leaned a shoulder against the wall near the window, watching Manders. Oxman stood at ease squarely in front of the desk, his weight evenly distributed on both sturdy legs.

"You really chase a vampire down all those flights of stairs, Ox?" Manders asked.

"Turns out I only thought I was."

"Is the protection in place for Lana Spence?"

Oxman nodded. "I checked it on the way over here. That's why I was late. She lives in an apartment that's easy enough to isolate, and we can escort her back and forth to the studio without too much trouble. Protection's tight, and right now Lana Spence is afraid and careful. But she's gonna get restless and do something unpredictable sooner or later. That's the kind of woman she is."

148

"E.L. knows her inside and out," Tobin said wryly. Manders saw Oxman shoot his partner a cautioning glance. If looks could kill, Tobin would be at least critically injured.

"Is it still strictly police work with Miss Spence?" Manders asked Oxman.

"Just that, sir. Artie's seen too many soap operas."

Manders was satisfied. Oxman seldom called him "sir" unless signaling that business was business. "Why do you think she called you to come see her?" Manders asked.

"To thank me for what we'd done for her. Lassiter was found dead and everybody thought we had this mess cleared up."

"Just to thank you?"

"That's what she told me."

Manders leafed through the report on his desk. He scanned the notes on Oxman's conversation with Zachary Denton. "What about this Denton?"

"I don't trust the bastard," Oxman said.

Manders picked up an uncharacteristic invective in Oxman's voice. He wondered about it, but he set his curiosity aside for the moment. "You think he was the one who pulled the knife on Lana Spence?"

"I'm not sure." The admission seemed to hurt Oxman.

"He was in the vicinity."

"But that was an hour after the vampire showed up on Lana Spence's doorstep," Tobin said. "And he had a reason for being there. Or so he says. My feeling is, if it was Denton he would've been long gone from the neighborhood by the time Ox thought he spotted him on the street."

"What do you think, Ox?"

"I think he could have laid low after running from the apartment building, ditched his vampire costume, and I saw him when he was on his way home."

"Too much time had passed," Tobin reiterated.

"Maybe," Oxman said. He seemed unwilling to give up on Denton.

"Another Edgar Grume costume's missing at Shadowtown," Tobin said.

"No surprise," Oxman said.

"There might be no connection between last night's incident and what happened before," Manders said. "I mean, maybe Lassiter *was* the one threatening Lana Spence, and we have now some different kook who likes to dress up and play Dracula."

"You believe that?" Oxman asked, reading him.

"No. It was the same guy. But we need to make a link to be sure of the connection between this and the previous acts. Like with cigarettes and lung cancer. Because there's an off chance we might be wrong."

"We oughta dig deeper than before," Tobin suggested.

Manders's droopy face creased in a smile. "Exactly. I want you and Ox to explore Lana Spence's past thoroughly."

"Meaning the men in her life," Oxman said.

"Of course. All except Calvin Oaks. Missouri authorities say the Keepers of the Covenant swear Oaks hasn't left the sanctuary in months."

"Keepers of what?" Tobin asked.

"Covenant. That's the religious cult Oaks joined after Lana Spence was finished with him."

"What kind of covenant?" Oxman asked.

Manders leaned back and pursed his lips. That was a question he hadn't considered. Maybe the group of zealots Oaks belonged to had for some reason worked vampirism into their ceremonial stew. Weirder things had occurred. Twisted religion could twist the people involved in it. In fact, that was the basic idea. "I'll have Missouri send me some information on the Keepers," he said.

"Plenty of Lana's former lovers should still be around New York," Oxman said. "All the ones who didn't get into movies or West Coast television."

"Find them," Manders said. "Hold them up to the light."

Tobin grinned. "Vampires can't stand light."

Manders ignored him. "The pressure's on us to get this one off the books," he said to both detectives. He didn't tell them about the phone call from Killbrellan, his contact in the commissioner's office. Killbrellan had told him in a veiled way that if this Lana Spence case wasn't resolved soon, Manders would find himself driving a desk in Traffic. One with a steering wheel and engine.

After Oxman and Tobin left, Manders tried not to think about how his career had become linked with the McGreery–Lana Spence case. He'd thought they'd gotten lucky when Lassiter's body was found. That should have been the last of the threatening notes, and of the real-life drama of "Shadowtown." The case would have faded in the news, and within a month or so it would have been mentioned only in show-business magazines and supermarket tabloids.

Manders lit a cigarette, inhaled deeply, then leaned back and stared at the exhaled smoke wending its way to the ceiling. He'd thought Fate was through fucking with him and making life difficult, but it seemed Fate had ideas of its own. Fate kept piling it on, seeing if Manders would break. Fate was one cruel cookie. Manders wondered if Fate was a he or a she. Probably a she, he decided. One that looked very much like Lana Spence.

At least for now, the telephone was quiet and Fate had ceased sticking pins in Manders.

A few hours later there was a knock on the door and Sergeant Felstein stepped in. His hair was mussed and he looked overwrought. He had a yellow pencil with a broken point propped behind his left ear. "I could use some help answering the phones, sir."

Manders put down his cigarette in the ashtray. "Help? Phones? Why?"

"Calls keep coming in," Felstein said. "Seems a lot of people saw a vampire on 'Shadowtown,' and they want to ask us about it."

"What do you mean, a lot of people? What kind of people would get excited over a television vampire."

"This vampire was supposed to be dead, sir, even dead as vampires go, only he turned up on the show and nobody seems to have an explanation for it, not even the show's producers. He appeared outside a window in one of the scenes, and he wasn't supposed to be there. He wasn't supposed to be anywhere in the show. Nobody can explain it. The people phoning in are mostly Lana Spence's fans, wanting to know what we're doing to protect her."

"And you're telling them? . . ."

"That **we**'re doing everything we can. Anything else you want me to say?"

Manders felt his stomach turning sour, and his piles itched. He wondered if tension had anything to do with piles.

He said, "Tell them she's wearing a garlic necklace, and all our men are carrying sharpened stakes in holsters."

"You gotta catch a vampire in his coffin to use a sharpened stake," Felstein said, "but the garlic might work."

Manders said, "Get the fuck out."

Sy Youngerman—1:30 P.M.

"Manny Brokton is scum," Youngerman said to Harry Overbeck.

Overbeck was pacing Youngerman's office at Shadowtown Productions, occasionally slamming fist to palm, as he was in the habit of doing when excited. "He's still our best bet to cast someone quickly, Sy. And don't forget we need some leverage, in case Lana gets a wild hair up her ass to leave the show. Then if we threaten to fire whoever Brokton comes up with this time, he might agree to talk sense into Lana and make her stay."

Youngerman studied his rumpled partner and wondered if Harry had been on something today. "When's Lana ever listened to sense? When's she ever listened to any voice except the tiny, tiny one in her skull?"

"Okay," Overbeck said, finally standing still. He'd actually created a scuffed path on the thick carpet. "You got a point there. But we need to take advantage of all this Edgar Grume publicity, and what better way to do it than to cast another vampire in the show?"

"I'd like to know how the old one got on yesterday's tape," Youngerman said.

"Me, too. But that's beside the point. The thing is, Sy, we've got to act fast. Everybody in every beauty shop and bar is talking about yesterday's show, but they won't be for long. You know the duration of the public's attention span—about as long as a gnat's pecker."

Youngerman looked down at his desk, at the idea Overbeck had put in writing. It was the product of a lot of hard work; Overbeck must believe firmly in what he was suggesting, that a character be added to

"Shadowtown," a mysterious male heartthrob known during the day only as Graveman, who becomes a vampire roaming "Shadowtown" at night. Adding such a character was a sound commerical impulse, Youngerman had to admit. And the show's writers liked the idea a lot. Or so Overbeck said.

"We catch the crest of this wave of public interest," said Overbeck, who to Youngerman's knowledge had never surfed, "and the show's ratings will climb back where they were, Sy. That's what we all want. Even Manny Brokton oughta want that, with his ten percent of Lana."

True, Youngerman thought. He drummed his fingertips and considered Overbeck's arguments. Some of them were compelling in a dollars-and-cents way. And what better way to compel?

"So I'll call him," he finally said, convinced. "We'll see who he's got available. You got anybody in mind?"

"Yeah, Sy. A young actor name of Brad Gaines. He's got the dark, brooding looks the part calls for."

"Can he act?"

"Not like Olivier. But he can think on his feet, ad lib with the best. He was an improv comic early in his career."

Youngerman liked the sound of that. A certain kind of balance and dexterity was necessary in a show that was ground out as fast as "Shadowtown."

"Believe me, Gaines is a can't-miss, Sy."

Youngerman's memory stirred. "Brad Gaines . . . He the guy played the cowboy in the 'Going West' mini-series on ABC last year?"

"The same. And he was on one of the new Hitchcock spots. Played a young gambler dying of cancer. Moody stuff. I looked over a tape of the show and he was great."

"I'll ask Brokton about him," Youngerman said. "See if he's committed to anything."

"If we pay enough," Overbeck said, "Manny Brokton will break a contract and uncommit Gaines. That's one of the advantages of dealing with scum."

"I'll feel out Brokton, see what Gaines has to have to play the part. Maybe we can tie his contract in with the show's ratings." Youngerman swiveled back and forth for a few seconds in his padded swivel chair. Scum. That was Manny Brokton, all right. "Harry, who do you think tampered with the tape and made Grume appear in that scene?"

Overbeck began pacing again, slower this time, his hands at his sides and his head bowed in thought. "I don't have a hint of an idea," he said at last. "In this business, who knows who might have the expertise to doctor the tape? And damn near everybody had the opportunity, if they wanted to take the trouble and accept the risk."

That's what was unsettling, Youngerman thought. Damn near everybody. Like at his party. He couldn't be sure himself who might have come and gone during the evening of Vince McGreery's death. And the same person might have gained access to the tape of yesterday's show.

Overbeck looked directly at him in a way Youngerman had never seen. "Maybe nobody tampered with the tapes, Sy."

Youngerman set aside the uneasy feeling that had crept into his mind. "Nonsense, Harry. You think a vampire's image just appeared like a force of nature?"

Overbeck ran a hand over his bristling brown hair. "Hell, I don't know, Sy. There are forces of nature we might not have fully explored. I'm no scientist."

Youngerman was astounded. "You saying you believe in vampires?"

Overbeck shrugged. "I'm not sure what I'm saying—what I believe or don't believe anymore."

"I mean, if you believe we've got a real vampire on the set, he might work cheaper than the one Manny Brokton comes up with."

Overbeck grinned. "Point taken, Sy. Guess my imagination runs riot now and then."

"Not much wonder," Youngerman said, "considering all that's happened around here lately."

But as Overbeck left his office, Youngerman did wonder. He'd never thought of Overbeck as the superstitious type. It was Harry's business judgment, his instinct, that had helped to make "Shadowtown" a leading soap, and everyone connected with the show knew it—including Youngerman.

It worried Youngerman that Overbeck's judgment might be impaired. Vampires, yet. Hoo, boy! But everyone connected with "Shadowtown" seemed to have been affected by what had gone on the past week, so why should Overbeck be any different? People believed in Allah and reincarnation and faith healing and faith killing and rabbits' feet and astrology. Maybe it was vampires' turn. For all things a season.

Youngerman told his secretary to get Manny Brokton on the phone.

It was time to order another vampire, even though one had been more than enough.

E. L. Oxman—3:30 P.M.

Oxman checked with Actor's Equity, then with various old show-business types who hung around the Carnegie Deli, and finally found out where Marv Egan lived.

He knocked on Egan's door, wondering what Egan looked like; he'd never heard of him as an actor, knew only that ten years ago he'd been Lana Spence's leading man in an independently produced film. And that their on-screen affair had generated some steam off-screen. The old-timers at the Carnegie Deli were eager to talk about Lana Spence, a burgeoning legend despite still being young enough to maintain her sex-symbol image.

"Minute," a deep voice grumbled on the other side of the door. But it was at least two minutes before the door finally swung open.

Egan looked too old to have played opposite Lana, even ten years ago. Oxman was reminded of the ravaged features of Burt Lassiter. But then he hadn't seen Lassiter alive. Egan's face was puffy and deeply lined. It was browned in a way that would have suggested he frequented an artificial-tanning spa, if it weren't for his impoverished circumstances. He was an average-height man, and his head was set forward on his shoulders in a manner that hinted at aggressiveness, even though he was smiling with perfect white teeth Oxman suspected were false. He was still lean-waisted, but with a definite stomach paunch bulging over his tight, faded Levi's. The Levi's and his red plaid shirt made him look more like the super of the decrepit building than an aging actor.

Oxman identified himself and said he wanted to ask some questions about Lana Spence.

"Ah, the bitch!" Egan said, grinning wider and stepping back so Oxman could enter. Maybe they *were* his own teeth. And maybe his full head of straight dark hair wasn't dyed.

Oxman stepped into the apartment and the stench hit him. It smelled as if someone ill lived there, a mixture of mentholated oil and stale perspiration often encountered in sick wards.

Egan must have noticed his reaction. "Got a damned cold," he said. "Trying to get well."

But judging by the sloppy appearance of the apartment—the sofa with its sagging cushions, a chair lying on the floor, yellowed drapes, grease-spattered wall in the kitchenette—Oxman thought Egan probably lived like this all the time. Maybe the menthol was used to cover up some other scent he didn't want anyone to notice.

"Wanna sit down?" he asked Oxman.

"I'll stand, thanks," Oxman said, eyeing the shaky-looking furniture. A large, dark roach zigzagged among some long-ago smashed fellow creatures on the wall and disappeared behind the sofa.

"I been following Lana's recent adventures," Egan said, tucking his thumbs in his Levi's pockets and standing hipshot. It was a young man's pose, cocky and poised, probably from one of his old play or movie roles. It didn't look right on him. "Seems she's mixed up in the occult."

"Only seems that way," Oxman said.

"Oh?"

"Unless you believe in the occult. Do you, Mr. Egan?"

"You mean like that story about the guy who was nailed to a cross and died and then came back to life?"

"You going to be difficult, Mr. Egan?"

"Me?" Egan grinned again. He was likable when he grinned. "No trouble from me, Officer. Tell you whatever you want to know."

"I want to know about Lana Spence."

"White-hot bitch. Was and still is, according to what I been reading in the papers, seeing on the news."

"Do you ever watch her on 'Shadowtown'?"

"Hell, no." He motioned toward the apartment's tiny black-and-white portable TV with its kinked rabbit-ear antenna. "I don't watch anything on that little idiot box. Helped to put me out of work."

"There's plenty of work for actors on television," Oxman said.

"No, Sergeant. Not for actors. Most of the people they call stars nowadays would be selling insurance if show business still called for acting skills. More work for stunt men now than for actors. Gotta be able to handle a helicopter or somersault onto a mattress. Study gymnastics instead of method and motivation."

"Lana Spence," Oxman reminded him, thinking about Lana somersaulting onto a mattress.

"We were a thing together for a while, about twelve years ago. When we co-starred in *Vixen's Revenge*. I played Roy the hunt master. No need to tell you who Lana played."

"She's had her share of men," Oxman said, trying to goad Egan.

"Ha! You don't know it all. Uses men and tosses them away like Kleenex, our Lana."

"Would you describe her as a nymphomaniac?"

"Naw. A real nympho doesn't actually enjoy sex, just has to do it again and again. Believe me, Lana enjoyed sex, enjoyed draining the life from her men. Goddamned black-widow woman."

"I've heard her called that before," Oxman said.

"I'll bet you have. She try to get you in the sack?"

"No." Oxman wondered if he was speaking the truth.

Egan was flashing his white grin in his lined, browned face, some of his old dash peeking through time. A swashbuckler but with years on him.

"When did you last see Lana?" Oxman asked, uncomfortable in front of that knowing grin.

"Oh, ten years. No, come to think of it, I ran into her . . . must have been four or five years ago. She was in Rumpelmayer's, eating a chocolate sundae. I kidded her, told her she was going to ruin her figure. She didn't laugh. I think she would've made a scene if I hadn't backed off and gotten out of there. Sometimes she's sensitive about her looks."

"Who do you think might send her threatening notes or try to kill her?" Oxman asked.

"Almost anybody who's ever met her."

"That seems a bit of an exaggeration."

Egan sighed and wiped the thick sleeve of his plaid shirt across his forehead. It was a warm afternoon for him to be wearing a shirt like that. "I guess she's genuinely liked by some people. Some men, even. At least the man who's balling her at the moment. I get a little carried away sometimes, Sergeant."

"Still hate her?"

Egan seemed to think about that. "No," he said after a while. "Or maybe yes, but not in the way you mean. She's something that happened to me, that's all. Circumstance. Like if I was caught up in a tornado. Lana was my bad luck, but I guess I don't hate her. No, not anymore."

"Did you know Burt Lassiter?"

"Never met him. I know he was an actor for quite a few years around New York. On and off Broadway. Saw him a few times at auditions, maybe at a cocktail party, but nobody ever introduced us. I heard he was another one of Lana's victims."

"He was. A lot of years ago, though."

"Yeah," Egan said wistfully.

"How long's it been since you've acted?" Oxman asked.

"Too long. I manage to collect unemployment, welfare, do a few odd jobs. The public forgets."

Oxman doubted that the public had ever really known Egan well enough to remember him. But then Oxman wasn't one to stay abreast with the lives of the stars, especially those of lesser magnitude. Egan had an actor's ego; that was for sure.

"How's she look?" Egan asked suddenly.

Oxman was surprised. "Lana Spence? Haven't you seen her on television or magazine covers?"

"I mean in person," Egan said. "Cameras lie. Oh, how they lie!"

"Still beautiful."

Egan nodded somewhat sadly, resignedly. Zinged again by life. It hadn't been a surprise.

Oxman felt sorry for Egan. The man, or what was left of him, was another of the human husks Lana Spence seemed to have left in her wake. Egan had described her accurately, Oxman thought. An erotic tornado, touching down and twisting out a path of psychic destruction, creating casualties before moving on.

The phone jangled. The abrupt noise caused Egan to start, as if he were unused to receiving calls. He picked up the receiver hesitantly, listened, then held it out for Oxman. "For you, Sergeant."

Oxman wasn't as surprised as Egan was by the call. He'd left Egan's number in case Tobin wanted to talk to him.

"E.L.," Tobin said, when Oxman had the ancient black receiver pressed to his ear, "we got more problems. Lana Spence received another threatening note, this time in the mail. The printing, paper and envelope are like the others. So's the kind of sick handiwork the writer promises to use on her."

"What about the postmark?"

"New York."

"How was the envelope addressed?"

"Same kind of generic printing as in the note, Ox. Nothing for a handwriting analyst to grab on to except to say for sure that this note and the others were written by the same person."

"Then we haven't moved closer to McGreery's killer and Lana Spence's antagonist at all," Oxman said. "We're at square one again."

"We spend more time there than the little green house spends on Boardwalk," Tobin said.

Oxman didn't bother replying to that.

Egan was staring at him, obviously wondering about the other end of the conversation. Let him wonder.

Oxman hung up, thanked Marv Egan for his cooperation, and was glad to get out of the crummy apartment. The place smelled like victim.

Brad Gaines—4:30 P.M.

"Consider yourself out of the contract, kid," Manny Brokton had told Brad Gaines, after Gaines told Manny he couldn't accept the "Shadowtown" vampire role because of the warrior movie he was to begin shooting in Australia next month. It was to be his second *Road King the Destroyer* movie. In this one his role had considerably more depth, but still he had second billing to a customized truck.

Gaines had been almost afraid to hope. The "Shadowtown" part could be a doorway to the kind of fame he'd worked toward for years. Not that the soaps provided much artistic satisfaction, but the people who worked in them were pros, and a couple of years on a top soap could make an actor rich, and able to choose his roles.

"Out of the contract how?" Gaines had asked, thinking of the heat and dust in Australia's outback country.

Brokton had leaned his pudgy five-foot frame back in his desk chair and grinned. He looked just like an evil Buddha when he did that, Gaines always thought. "No agent worth his percentage writes a contract without a kick-out clause, kid. That's so in case an opportunity like this one comes along, a client can grab it."

"Legally?" Gaines had asked.

"Legally enough," Brokton assured him. "This kind of thing's done all the time, and it never draws litigation." He seemed to put court action in the same category as flies: Something only moderately rotten might not attract lawyers. He dropped forward in his chair and was on his feet, though he was so short it was hardly noticeable that he was standing now rather than sitting behind the desk. "Go on over and talk

161

to Harry Overbeck. Make sure you feel comfortable with the role, then Overbeck and I will talk money. Plenty of money.''

Gaines had thanked Manny Brokton and left the agent's Broadway office. And now here he was listening to Harry Overbeck, one of the "Shadowtown" producers, explain the role of Graveman on the show.

The soap's director, bald Shane Moreland, whom Gaines had worked with a few years ago on a TV special about herpes, was also in the office, along with two of the show's writers. The writers were big guys with dark beards gone a little gray. They didn't say much, only listened, trying to draw a bead on exactly what the boss had in mind. Like most TV writers, they had about them the air of people who knew they were replaceable.

Overbeck had laid it out coherently. Graveman would appear in the next episode of "Shadowtown" as a handsome hitchhiker the mayor's wife picked up outside of town. The viewer would be led to believe the mysterious stranger had traveled on through town. But Graveman would appear in the last scene, in the mayor's wife's bedroom, and it would be revealed that he was a vampire.

From then on he'd be woven into the fabric of the show on a regular basis, as had been the Allan Ames character, Edgar Grume. Graveman would soon occupy the dark, soft place in female viewers' hearts that Grume had left vacant after Ames's death.

It didn't sound to Gaines as if this could be done plausibly, but judging by the expressions on the writers' faces, they were confident. Writers were like that. And this was the soaps. Plausibility was hardly a serious consideration; it was necessary only to play within the ground rules laid down early for the viewers. Soap fans weren't expecting Shakespeare—at least not in any form they'd recognize.

"So how's it feel to you?" Overbeck asked Gaines. "I mean, does it click?" It was one-pro-to-another time. Producers liked to think they had creative input.

Gaines put on his sincere expression and said what was expected. "I don't see how it can miss.''

"Not with the publicity we've been getting lately," Overbeck said. He ran his hand over his short brownish hair, a rumpled little guy whose enthusiasm was actually infectious.

"But is there room on the show for two vampires?" Shane Moreland asked. Maybe he was immune to infection.

Overbeck glared at him.

"Only kidding," Shane said. He looked at Gaines. "I guess you heard about somebody tampering with the tape so a vampire appeared in the background in one of our episodes."

"Difficult not to hear about it," Gaines said. "Nobody's talking or writing about much else."

"Will has got a script for you to look over," Shane told him, motioning with his gleaming pate toward one of the silent writers.

"That might seem a little premature," Overbeck said, "but I talked to Manny Brokton on the phone, and we won't have any trouble coming to terms. And we want to rush your inclusion in the show. I'm cabbing over to Manny's office now to finalize details, then we'll get together with you and you can sign a contract. It's one you'll be happy to sign."

"I'm sure," Gaines said. He accepted a bound script from Will the writer.

"Until then," Overbeck said, "a handshake deal." He smiled and held out his right hand toward Gaines.

Gaines said, "Deal," and shook. Overbeck had surprisingly long fingers and a powerful grip for a man his size.

Without either of them having spoken, the two writers left, and Lana Spence walked into the office.

Gaines had worked with a few top names in the business, but still he felt a twinge of awe when he realized he was in her presence. She was obviously between costume changes, wearing a bright-red silk robe with a flowered sash yanked tight around her lean waist. Her body moved smoothly beneath the reflecting material, playing over the imagination.

"Welcome to the show," she said to Gaines, and came to him and kissed him on the lips. She gave off a faint scent of lilac as she moved.

Startled, Gaines found he couldn't reply. His throat was dry, and he didn't want his voice to croak.

"I've seen what the writers have in mind," Lana said to the room in general, "and I'm looking forward to some glorious, bloodsucking love scenes with Mr. Gaines."

Mister, no less. "It's Brad," Gaines said. "Please."

She laughed and ran her hands along her hourglass figure. Casually, as if unconsciously checking to make sure there were no rough edges. There weren't. "Brad it is."

Gaines saw Shane and Overbeck exchange glances; Shane might have smiled.

What the hell? Gaines had heard about Lana Spence and her hot and cold affairs. But he was no cherry; he knew the deal. The publicity of an affair with Lana Spence, especially now, wouldn't hurt his chances of landing larger roles after his stint on "Shadowtown." In exchange for that career boost he'd become another notch on Lana's well-whittled bedpost. That struck Gaines as a fair deal at this point in his life. Actually more than fair; Lana Spence was a few years past prime, but still a dish to be ravished.

A youngish-looking guy knocked on the door, poked his head into the office apologetically, and said, "Sorry, Lana, but we need you now."

"On my way, Matt."

The silk gown swished in unsettling rhythm as she walked to the door; was she wearing anything beneath it?

"See you on the set," she said to Gaines, as she made a graceful exit. Her buttocks tightened and loosened against the smooth material.

"And off the set," Shane Moreland said, not bothering this time to conceal his smile.

Gaines, still hearing the rustle of silk on flesh, smiled back.

Art Tobin—4:00 P.M.

Lance Jardeen reminded Tobin of Burt Lassiter. Maybe most of Lana Spence's men ran to type.

Then Tobin realized it was similarity of the men's surroundings rather than physical resemblance that struck a chord. Like Lassiter, Jardeen lived in a tiny suite in a run-down residential hotel. Like Lassiter, Jardeen's possessions suggested he had little income. And there was a wasted quality about both men, evident even beyond Lassiter's appearance in death.

Unlike Lassiter, Jardeen was short. He had a pugnacious jaw and brilliant blue eyes. His nose was small and perfect, and Tobin suspected he'd had plastic surgery to shape it. Jardeen had wide shoulders and a dynamic way of moving, but it seemed somehow that the energy was being manufactured for Tobin's benefit, and as soon as Jardeen was alone again he'd collapse on the sofa and sleep for a couple of hours. To Tobin, Jardeen would never have been cast as a vampire—not tall enough. Yet through costume, lifts in the shoes, and carefully selected backdrop, magic could be worked to add six inches to a person's height. Or the impression of an additional six inches.

"Seven years ago," Tobin said, "you were Lana Spence's lover."

"A rather personal statement," Jardeen observed. "Do you know this for a fact, or are you fishing?" He seemed untouched by this intimate probing of his privacy, yet he was obviously wary of Tobin. As if there were moves in a game being made here.

"Fact," Tobin said. The room they were in was on the first floor; noise from outside was deafening. Tobin knew traffic could be heavy in this neighborhood, even late at night. He wondered how Jardeen managed to sleep.

"You've done your homework," Jardeen said.

"We call it legwork. Just like they call it on television. This is called an inquiry. You're supposed to answer questions."

"About the 'Shadowtown' case? And the vampire business at Lana's apartment?"

"That is not answering questions, Mr. Jardeen; that is asking them."

Jardeen smiled. His teeth were straight but yellowed. "Yes, Lana and I were lovers a long time ago. It lasted about six months—not a bad run for Lana."

"Were you ever in a movie or play together?"

"You mean other than our relationship?"

"What's that supposed to mean?"

"That's what our affair was to Lana, really, a very private play. A benefit. For her."

"I mean movie or play." Tobin was getting tired of this sparkling repartee.

"No. It appeared that we were going to be. At that time I was doing *Camelot* in a Chicago theater. I was lined up for a part on Broadway, a major role, but it never materialized. I found out later that Lana had a role in the play and preferred another co-star."

"This was *after* you broke off your relationship, I assume," Tobin said.

"Before," Jardeen said. "I thought you'd done your legwork; you should know how Lana operates."

"How's she operate?"

"She uses men. Really uses them. She's quite an expert at it. Her role on 'Shadowtown' is close to her genuine self."

"You watch her on 'Shadowtown'?"

"Not regularly."

Tobin listened to the roar of traffic as several large vehicles passed close together. They sounded like lions close by on the other side of the wall. "Where were you about ten o'clock last night, Mr. Jardeen?"

"Right here. Alone." He smiled and shrugged. "I can't prove it. But you can't seriously believe I was playing vampire at Lana's place, can you? I haven't seen her since we . . . parted."

"Was it an amicable parting?"

Jardeen raised his chin slightly, as if aware of a camera dollying in for a profile shot. "It was pretty bitter, actually. I confronted Lana with proof she'd torpedoed the Broadway role that would have been mine. She didn't try to deny it. In fact, she was amused. I got angry, then she finally did too. I left her fuming at a restaurant table, with the check. She could afford it; she was leaving the next day for New York and Broadway."

"To act in the play you were supposed to be in." Tobin shook his head; he found that he sympathized with Jardeen. Show business was tough, in or out of bed. "How'd she get her part in the play?"

Jardeen's yellow, bitter smile returned. "I used my influence in her behalf with the director. Then she used her influence with the producer. Not in my behalf."

Tobin looked out through a dirty window at a stone wall that had been stained by rusty water. Then he let his gaze play over the pathetic room. Some life, some graveyard for an actor's dreams. "We'd appreciate it if you hung around town for a while, Mr. Jardeen."

"No problem. I seldom go anywhere these days. I haven't been offered a decent acting job since Lana let it be known—"

"Let what be known?" Tobin asked.

"She spread the word that I had a serious drug problem, and that it had affected my short-term memory."

"Meaning you couldn't memorize lines?"

"Meaning a lot of things." Jardeen's squarish, tortured face seemed to age a decade in the harsh light. "Meaning mainly that I'd make other cast members look bad. That's how acting works; it's an organic process involving everyone on stage or in front of the camera."

"Did you?"

"Did I what?" Jardeen asked, frowning.

"Have that kind of drug problem?"

He laughed, too loudly. "In those days, no. That came later, and it was hell. I finally kicked it at a clinic in New Jersey. I've been clean since. I have to stay that way if I want to live. Before then, when I was acting in Chicago, I used recreational drugs lightly, but that's all."

"And you blame Lana Spence for your drug problem?"

Jardeen began absently running his fingertips over his chest in a circle, digging, as if scratching a persistent itch. "I blame only myself." He didn't sound very convincing.

"You have any idea who might have written death threats to Miss Spence?"

"I might have written some. But I didn't." The words seemed to boil up in Jardeen, erupt from his constricted throat, hissing with emotion. "The bitch deserves to die." He suddenly realized he was scratching himself and dropped his right hand.

"You're not alone in that opinion," Tobin said. "She seems to have a destructive effect on her lovers."

"That kind of impulse is in some women, but it rules Lana Spence. She stunts the self-respect of her victims, destroys the ego, then sows the ground with salt."

"Has she destroyed your ego, Mr. Jardeen?"

"Possibly. I've managed to con myself into thinking otherwise, but the truth is she marked me as a loser and it's a prophesy that's been fulfilled. By myself as well as through others."

Tobin looked into the brilliant blue eyes and saw the defeat Jardeen had described. Despite their brightness they had the unresponsiveness of a corpse's eyes. "What remains in your life, Mr. Jardeen?"

"Hate."

"For Lana Spence?"

"For myself. I simply don't have anything else."

Including an alibi, Tobin thought.

The door opened suddenly and a blond man in a tan safari jacket stepped in. He was smiling, but when he saw Tobin his moon-shaped face registered surprise, and, for an instant, terror. He knew immediately Tobin was a cop, and he knew Tobin realized that. They'd both had enough experience with their opposite numbers to recognize the moment.

"Phil, I'm busy," Jardeen said. Almost panicky.

"Sure." Phil was smiling. He toyed with one of the jacket's zippers. Tobin had never seen a jacket with so many pockets. They all had zippered flaps. Phil backed out of the room. "I'll drop by later, Lance."

"You sure?" The panic again, closer to the surface.

"Hey, of course."

Phil grinned, nodded to Tobin, and hastily closed the door behind him. It created a faint draft across Tobin's ankles.

"A neighbor," Jardeen said. "A pest, to tell you the truth. Always bursting in without knocking."

"Where's he live?"

Jardeen was in control again. Acting. "Gee, I'm not positive. On this block, I think."

Tobin knew better. "He looks familiar."

"Everybody says that about Phil. He's a type. A big Mickey Rooney."

Tobin wasn't sure if that accounted for the familiarity, or if he'd seen Phil before. The guy did, now that Jardeen had mentioned it, look like Mickey Rooney. "We might ask you to come to the station house and give a statement," he said.

That didn't seem to frighten Jardeen. "Okay. Glad to help. Though I don't know much." He managed a smile that was almost debonair. "I'm afraid it'll be a short statement."

"But maybe a sweet one," Tobin said. He apologized for taking up Jardeen's time and then left.

He waited outside, concealed by some rusting outdoor modern sculpture half a block away, until he saw Phil reenter the building. Phil was walking jauntily and had his hands stuffed into two of his tan jacket's many pockets. He even swaggered a lot like Mickey Rooney did in some of his movies; a short-man swagger, though Phil was average height.

When Phil emerged less than half an hour later, he hailed a cab and climbed in.

Tobin got to his car and followed him to an old apartment building in a seedy neighborhood near Tompkins Square.

The iron railing on the front steps was twisted as if a vehicle had come up on the sidewalk and bent it. Graffiti was spray-painted all over the walk in front of the place, and several of the building's windows had cardboard taped over holes in the glass. An old lady wearing a man's threadbare coat and oversized galoshes slumped next to the door, by a couple of brown shopping bags that probably contained everything she owned.

Tobin recognized the address at once.

This was where Marv Egan lived.

E. L. Oxman—4:45 P.M.

Oxman thought it would be a good idea to talk to Manny Brokton. He might well have represented some of her former lovers in their show-business careers. He might, in fact, know some secrets about Lana. Everyone seemed to know secrets about Lana, and she seemed to know them about others. If they were male, anyway.

Brokton's office was on Broadway near Fifty-fourth, on the twentieth floor of an office building whose lobby contained a variety of small shops. It was also the kind of lobby that provided a walkway to the next block, and there was a steady stream of people taking that shortcut, some of them slowing occasionally to gaze into shop windows. There was a lot of marble in the lobby, and the mingled sounds of footfalls and conversation had hard edges.

When an elevator arrived at lobby level, Oxman was surprised to see Harry Overbeck step out. Overbeck looked as rumpled as ever, wearing wrinkled slacks and a baggy gray sweater. He plopped one of those shapeless, crushable hats over his brush-cut hair as he dodged a woman lugging half-a-dozen large shopping bags.

Instead of entering the elevator, Oxman decided to find out what Overbeck was doing here. He walked over and watched Overbeck's fleshy, florid face register surprise, then a kind of polite pleasure.

"I've just been to see Manny Brokton," Overbeck said.

Oxman gently gripped his elbow and steered him toward a secluded area of the lobby where they wouldn't be overheard. "What about?"

Overbeck didn't hesitate. "Business. We're doing some casting for the show."

"I thought the show was cast."

"We're adding a character. Casting's an ongoing process with episodic television. Especially the soaps."

Oxman supposed that was true; he didn't watch enough television to know for sure. "Boob tube," was the term that came to mind when he thought about television. Not fair, maybe, but he was a practical man in a practical world and that was how he felt. "Do you know if Brokton represented any of the men in Lana's past?" he asked.

Overbeck smiled and shook his head. "Plenty of them, I'd imagine. He's been an agent for a long time, and actors tend to jump from agency to agency, especially early in their careers."

"Who are some of the people Brokton's represented?"

"Well, he was Allan Ames's agent. And he represents Jean Richards, who plays the mayor's wife on 'Shadowtown.'"

"How did Brokton and Lana get together?"

"Ha! How could they *not* get together? They were made for each other, in a business sense."

"Which means?"

"Am I speaking off the record?"

"Sure. If you want to be."

"They're both selfish and unscrupulous."

"Then how come you deal with Brokton?"

"Like Lana, he's damned effective at what he does. And if you want a particular actor, you have to deal with his or her agent. The thing about Brokton—"

Overbeck's face suddenly went pale and his jaw fell slack. He was staring beyond Oxman's right shoulder in a way that gave Oxman the creeps.

Oxman turned and saw the crowd of people standing near the elevators all looking in the same direction, toward the Broadway exit.

"What's the matter?" Oxman asked.

Overbeck actually rubbed his eyes. "I thought I saw somebody in a black cape just run from an elevator and out through the lobby." He gave a nervous giggle. "Hell, maybe I'm imagining things. Or maybe it was some kind of promotional stunt."

Oxman knew Overbeck hadn't been alone in what he'd seen— whatever it had been. He ran to the lobby exit, out onto the sidewalk, and realized he'd never catch up with anyone on the crowded midtown streets. And in New York, people didn't pay a great deal of attention to a man wearing a black cape. They encountered weirder sights every day.

Running back into the lobby, Oxman saw that the elevators had taken away most of the people who'd been waiting. A few remained. He approached a dumpy, middle-aged woman wearing a business suit that looked too small for her and flashed his shield. "Did you see someone run by here wearing a dark cape?" He felt foolish asking the question; it was like a line from a late-night horror movie. Or as if he'd somehow gotten caught up in a daytime soap.

"Sure," the woman said, as if she saw such apparitions regularly. "I figured he was in costume for an advertising stunt or something. Whazza matter, he steal the cape?"

A teenage Latin boy carrying a large, brown vinyl portfolio said, "I seen him too. He was in a hurry."

"Either of you see his face?"

Both nodded. "Yeah," the youth with the portfolio said, "but I never paid much attention to it. I remember he had gray or white hair. That's what caught my eye."

"It was white," the woman said. "I think."

"His face was kinda like white, too," the boy said. "Eerie-lookin', ya know?"

"It was, now you mention it," the woman agreed. "Real pale."

"Could either of you identify him if you saw him again?"

"Not me," the youth said.

"I'm sure I wouldn't be able to, either," the woman told Oxman. "You know how it is when someone brushes past you in a rush."

Oxman knew. Eyewitnesses were unreliable even in favorable circumstances.

"I need your names," he said.

"How come, man?" the youth asked, suddenly very alert.

"It involves a murder case."

The woman reached into her purse and handed Oxman a white business card with her name, Molly Sanderson, and a Soho address. The Latin youth scribbled his name and address on the back of another card supplied by the woman.

An elevator arrived and they looked at Oxman questioningly. "Go ahead," he told them. "And thanks for your help."

"I think we oughta get on the elevator, too," Overbeck said beside

Oxman. "I'd like to check on this with Brokton, see if the guy in the cape was one of his clients."

"Exactly what I had in mind," Oxman said. He moved into the elevator, which had become crowded. Overbeck squeezed in on the other side and contorted an arm to jab the button for the twentieth floor. Oxman noticed that the Latin youth was going to the fifteenth floor, the Sanderson woman to the thirty-second.

On the twentieth floor, Overbeck led the way down a carpeted hall to Brokton's office and opened the door.

A receptionist looked up from whatever she was reading on her desk and smiled. "Back again, Mr. Overbeck?"

The answer to that one seemed obvious to Oxman. He showed the woman his badge. "Someone leave here about five minutes ago?"

"He means besides me, Louella," Overbeck said, unnecessarily.

Louella, a pleasant-featured woman in her sixties, began to suspect something might be wrong. She puckered her lips and frowned like a concerned grandmother. "Nobody's come or gone since you have, Mr. Overbeck."

"Is Brokton in his office?" Oxman asked.

"Well, yes, he is. He left me orders not to let anyone in for the next half hour."

"I'm sorry," Oxman said, "but you'll have to make an exception. Mr. Brokton will understand after I explain."

"It's police business, Louella," Overbeck said gently, as if to reassure her she wouldn't incur Brokton's anger.

Louella nodded silently and punched an intercom button. She waited but got no reply.

"I know he's in there," she said. "He was a little while ago."

"I just left him," Overbeck added. These two liked to state the obvious.

"There another exit?" Oxman asked.

"Yes," Louella said. "It opens to a hall that leads the other way around the building to the elevators."

Oxman moved quickly to the light-oak door to the main office. "Hey, wait!" he heard Louella say breathlessly. He sensed Overbeck close behind him. He rattled the doorknob.

Locked.

"He never locks that door," Louella said. She was confused now, a little frightened.

"Something might be wrong," Overbeck told her, as if she weren't on to that notion already.

Oxman kicked the door open. It banged hard against the wall but didn't spring back.

"Oh, shit!" Overbeck said. "My God, my God, my God! . . ."

Louella drew in a breath that sounded like a file rasping on steel. But she didn't scream. Oxman moved into the office and stepped over a brass lamp that was lying on the floor.

Manny Brokton was seated behind his wide desk, bent over, with the right side of his face scrunched down on his green desk pad. He was a small man, and, except for his horrified expression, he resembled a tiny, pale schoolchild at nap time.

Blood was still worming sluggishly out of two ugly puncture wounds on the left side of his neck. There was so much of it on the desk and floor, Oxman knew he was dead.

Scene 5

Jennifer Crane—8:30 A.M.

The day outside the window was warm and bright, beckoning to Jennifer to forget work for the morning and leave the apartment. The Stick-and-Forget dentifrice artwork she was laboring over could wait. The deadline was a week away, and she was tired of painting false teeth biting into previously inedible food such as corn-on-the-cob and apples. She'd brushed her own teeth a lot since accepting this commission.

Ox was out on the job, engrossed again in the "Shadowtown" case. In dangerously close proximity to Lana Spence, and in the same orbit again as Zach Denton. Which meant that, by association, Jennifer was again in Zach's orbit.

And that, she realized, was what made her itch to leave the apartment. It wasn't going to be as easy to ignore Zach's existence here in New York as she'd thought. Not now, when every time she glimpsed a newspaper or turned on TV she was reminded of him. "Shadowtown" was everywhere. Especially now, after that theatrical agent's odd murder.

Damn Zach! He'd set himself up as a kind of authoritarian god, and it had worked! And was still working. Whatever he did or was suspected of doing, she was ready to find extenuating circumstances where none existed. Ready to forgive him, not because he deserved forgiveness but because he defied understanding. It was difficult to condemn someone you loved or had loved and whose violent side you didn't understand. Disorientation was anathema to hate. People like Zach knew that and took advantage of it.

But she *had* condemned Zach until she'd made the mistake of going to see him. Then had come the dislodging and whirling of selective pieces of the past, and the rebirth of compulsion.

Jennifer needed to explore those feelings further. The dark attraction was exerting increasing magnetism. It was a force she couldn't ignore, so she had no choice but to fight it. And right now, she wasn't confident of victory.

What would Ox think about her going again to talk with Zach? He hadn't really understood her reasons for the first visit, so she'd be wise to keep this visit a secret from him.

It made her feel guilty, dirty, sneaking behind Ox's back. He didn't deserve that kind of treatment.

But these emotions were associated with Zach Denton. Along with deeper, pleasurable emotions. And so, in an odd way, they were acceptable to her and didn't detract from her feeling that what she was doing was, in the long run, not only right but inevitable.

Life with Zach hadn't been one-hundred-percent miserable. In fact, the periods of agony were relatively brief.

Jennifer had thought she'd reasoned all of this out years ago, but apparently she hadn't. Or was it that reason didn't apply? It was impossible to awaken the pain without also awakening the pleasure, the curious but undeniable bonding. Punishment and twisted ecstasy. This was the sort of thing one read about, but that was only supposed to happen to other women, women who were masochistic fools and eager victims.

It was confusing. Love and hate and a rabbit hole to unreality, waiting for her.

The telephone rang. Again and again and again. She didn't answer it. Her mind's focus was fixed and not easily diverted.

She put away her air brush, slipped into slacks and a new purple blouse that set off her dark hair and her eyes, and looked over her reflection in the mirror. Didn't she look nice, the woman in the looking glass?

She left the apartment.

On her way to see Zach.

E. L. Oxman—10:00 A.M.

Oxman lounged in a high-backed wooden chair in a corner of Manders's office. The door was open about a foot, and the bustle and buzzing voices of the precinct house wafted in like toneless background music. Someone laughed, someone cursed, someone coughed as if he were in the last stages of consumption. Footfalls clattered past the open door; the walker was whistling a country-western hit about a girl who'd gone wrong and been sent to prison and married the warden.

Manders was standing at the grimy window with his hands stuffed into his back pockets, staring out at nothing; he was developing quite a large bald spot on the crown of his head, Oxman noticed. Half-dollar size. He wondered if Manders's middle-age hair loss was actually more severe than his own. He sure hoped so.

Tobin was perched on the only clear corner of Manders's desk. He'd just finished telling Manders about following Phil from Jardeen's place to the building where Marv Egan lived. Oxman had just finished telling Manders about the Manny Brokton murder. Manders had had about enough and probably wished he were someplace where there were no dead bodies or telephones or newspapers within miles. Everybody was on his ass again.

"Any thoughts on Brokton?" Manders asked, still staring out the window. Oxman felt like telling him there wasn't much chance of anything useful turning up out there.

"I don't think a vampire killed him," Oxman said.

Manders turned and glared at him.

"We gotta be crazy not to think there's some connection between

179

Brokton getting zapped and what's happened at Shadowtown Productions," Tobin said.

Manders snorted. "On that we agree. On that the press agrees. As does the chief and the mayor and every sonavabitch that can make my life miserable." He ran his tobacco-stained hand down his long, lined face. "Christ, I gotta take it easy." He tapped his chest.

"Heartburn?" Tobin asked.

"I hope," Manders said. "Someday, if we don't get to the bottom of this vampire bullshit, it's gonna be a fuckin' heart attack and a fatal one."

Oxman wished the lieutenant would ease up. They weren't getting anywhere this way, and Manders might be right about that heart attack. "We've got enough witnesses who saw a guy dressed like a vampire running from the building," he said.

Manders fixed a houndish, bloodshot eye on him. "Which means?"

"I think the guy wanted to be seen."

"Or didn't mind one way or the other," Tobin said. "Vampires don't give a fuck if they're seen or not. They're dead. What do they care?"

Oxman flashed his partner a warning glance. Manders was in no mood for jokes—if Tobin was joking. Oxman was beginning to wonder about Tobin.

"Vampires don't go dashing around in the daytime, either," Manders said. "You don't have to do a lot of research to know that."

"Whoever killed Brokton did it so he wouldn't tell us something pertinent," Oxman said. "The killer made a point of being seen so the murder would add to the 'Shadowtown' hubbub and get play in the press. He wanted to make sure Brokton's murder was linked to the show, on and off the TV screen."

"Hubbub," Tobin said. "That's a neat word, E.L. Haven't heard it in years, even from you."

Manders wet his flaccid lips with his tongue and paced a few steps toward the window, then back. He put on his somber smile. "Okay, that all figures neatly. Now tell me why the killer thought that way, Ox." Liquid brown eyes fixed on Oxman. "Why?"

Oxman shrugged. He had some ideas but he didn't know exactly the answer to Manders's "why," and he didn't want to speculate and get moving in the wrong direction.

"Ratings," Tobin suggested. "The murders and the vampire

publicity make for lots of media coverage and improved ratings for 'Shadowtown.'"

Manders shook his head. "People don't kill to improve a TV show's ratings, Art."

"They kill for money," Tobin said. "Every day. And in television, ratings translate into money."

Here was something hard to argue against. "Whad'ya think, Ox?" Manders asked. The whistler walked past the office again, blowing an old Hank Williams tune now. "Your Cheatin' Heart."

"It's possible," Oxman said. "It's more likely Brokton knew something about what's going on at 'Shadowtown' and was killed to shut him up. He was a greedy little bastard, from what we know of him, and if he had useful information he'd divulge it to anyone for a high enough price. Or to us if we threatened him enough. He was dangerous to whoever didn't want him to talk, so they killed him."

"Maybe he was even more dangerous than his greed and lack of moral fiber made him," Tobin suggested. "Maybe he knew something damaging and didn't realize its importance, might have dropped it in conversation anytime. Let a cat out of a bag. Cat that'd eat a lotta mice. So the mice killed him."

"Or mouse, singular," Manders said.

Could be, Oxman thought. He looked at Tobin and nodded. Tobin was plenty sharp, all right, when he took time out from playing the bitter black.

"I got men working the building where Brokton bought it," Manders said. "Questioning all the other tenants, as well as the eyeball witnesses to our daylight vampire fleeing from the scene."

"How come he didn't dissolve," Tobin asked, "exposed to the light like that?"

"I don't know," Manders said. "I never read the vampire rule book."

"Same vampire we been chasing," Tobin said. "It's gotta be. I mean, white hair and all."

"You live a couple of centuries," Manders said, "your hair might go white, too."

Oxman smiled. Manders glared. Oxman stopped smiling. On the outside.

"So we come to this guy Phil," Manders said, shifting gears with all the smoothness of a '50 Studebaker. "What do you figure he was doing going between Jardeen and Egan?"

"I think we should ask Jardeen and Egan," Tobin said.

Oxman knew where that would lead. Rather, where it wouldn't. "They'd either dummy up or lie," he said. "We oughta pick up on Phil again, find out who he is. Make the connection ourselves so we know it's right. Vice or Narcotics got any men working that neighborhood?"

"Are you kidding?" Manders said. "There's enough drugs and ass peddled in that area to keep emergency rooms and AIDS centers working round the clock."

"So have some undercovers ask around," Oxman suggested. "Let's see if we can find out about this Phil. Meantime, Art or I will do a loose stakeout on Jardeen's and Egan's apartments and see if Phil shows up again."

"Remember he only entered Egan's building," Manders said. "That doesn't mean he went there to see Egan."

"Hell of a coincidence if he didn't," Tobin said, getting up off the desk and stretching. Oxman actually heard his spine crackle, like knuckles being popped in quick succession. The sound made Oxman's back ache.

"Coincidence won't get you a conviction in court," Manders said. "Make the link and make it good. Hear, you two?"

"Hear," Oxman said. He stood up and stretched his own limbs, glad his spine didn't sound off like Tobin's. Or maybe that was healthy, to loosen the vertebrae that way. No, couldn't be.

He and Tobin left Manders's office and walked outside to the lot where their gray department car was parked between similar cars. It was sunny today, but a cool breeze sprang up and deposited something gritty in Oxman's right eye. He rubbed with his knuckle, only aggravating the eye.

"What you figure now?" Tobin said.

"You watch Jardeen's place," Oxman told him, "and I'll go talk to Zach Denton about Brokton's murder."

Tobin looked concerned. "Oughta be the other way around, E.L."

"Won't be, though," Oxman said.

Tobin grinned and shrugged. "Okay. But stay away from gut thinking, you know what I mean?"

"You mean keep my emotions out of any dealings I might have with

Denton." Oxman rubbed again at the eye, which still stung and had teared up and was watering profusely.

"That right, man. You street smart." Tobin was grinning wider, parodying the stereotype black punks he hated.

"It's good advice," Oxman said. "I'll take it."

"More advice, man: Throw a little cold water in that eye before you rub it blind." Tobin lifted a hand absently in a wave. "I'll take the department car, you take yours," he said, and walked away before Oxman had a chance to argue.

Uppity black dude.

Art Tobin—10:45 A.M.

Tobin was pleased. There was a coffee shop right across the street from the Waywind, the fleabag residential hotel where Lance Jardeen lived his miserable life. Tobin waited around until a booth by the window was cleared by a slat-hipped waitress who looked like a wasted junkie. He slid into the booth and smiled when he saw the unobstructed view he had of the hotel entrance.

There were littered steps leading up to two revolving glass doors beneath a broken neon WAYWIND sign, a regular door off to the left. Even from where he sat, Tobin could see that too much salt had been spread over the steps during recent winters, and the concrete was chipped and marred as if someone had gone at it with a ball peen hammer. He stared at the broken neon in the sunlight and tried to imagine what it might say lighted at night, which letters wouldn't glow. Or maybe the whole damned sign was shot. Neon was like that: pop! and some kind of gas escaped and that was it. Poisonous gas, Tobin thought.

"Ready?" the boy-hipped waitress asked, looming over Tobin. She had stringy brown hair and blue eyes with that nobody-home look that confirmed his first impression of her as being drug-ridden. Not so unusual in this neighborhood. His own eyes automatically checked her arms for needle tracks. Long sleeves. Ha! But she'd caught his glance and a change had come over her. She was concentrating harder now behind a studiously blank look that didn't fool Tobin at all. He'd seen so many junkies retreat behind that look that shouted "Hey, I'm doing my own innocent number, unaware of any wrongdoing anywhere in the universe; ask me about a needle and I'll think you got a button missing." Bull*shit!*

"Ready to order?" the waitress repeated, a little impatient now.

Ready to bust your flat ass, Tobin thought. But he said, "Make it a BLT and a Coke."

"Only got Pepsi, we don't carry Coke."

"Of course," Tobin said.

She smiled faintly at him, even knowing he was a cop; a measure of spirit left. He watched her walk away to place his order with the kitchen. Walked like a country girl from fucking Iowa or someplace, skipping imaginary furrows. Someone beyond the serving counter said something to her in Spanish. She turned away as if she hadn't heard. Tobin wished he spoke Spanish. You needed every edge you could get in this cesspool of a city.

The BLT arrived and he settled down to wait.

Stakeouts were no fun for Tobin. They required patience and often resulted in a waste of time. He thought, guy like that Phil, he oughta have a beeper planted in him surgically so he could be located at all times. Tobin had read in some law-enforcement magazine or other—or had it been a speech by some Supreme Court justice?—that implanting little electronic homing devices in known criminals was a practical concept and medically feasible, and possibly an idea whose time had come. It would sure make Tobin's work easier.

He pushed the sandwich away; the bacon was mostly warmed-up strips of animal fat, and who knew what animal? Then he lifted the large waxed cup of Pepsi so the straw was between his lips, and leisurely worked on the soda, hoping the carbonation wouldn't give him heartburn like Smiley Manders had bitched about a little while ago. Tobin got enough of Manders's complaining sometimes; damned guy oughta eat something other than pizzas and corned-beef sandwiches if he didn't want stomach trouble.

Tobin put Manders out of his mind and sat sipping Pepsi and gazing out the window at people and traffic passing on the street. New York was a funny place. You'd see a bum go past in handout rags, then somebody wearing ten thousand dollars' worth of jewelry along with new, cashmere clothes with some pansy designer's label sewn in to make the price exorbitant. People eating out of trash cans outside expensive restaurants because they were starving, while inside the waiters treated customers rudely to make them think dining there was worth the price and a privilege because the sauces were prepared a certain way. Maybe it was a microcosm of what the world was coming to in the next ten, fifteen years. It wouldn't surprise Tobin.

There was a blast of voices that quickly died, and he turned away from the window and saw that a TV mounted behind the counter was tuned to a soap opera. A rerun of "Shadowtown."

Delia Lane was propped up in a hospital bed. Town cocksman Arthur Sales—Roger Maler—was sitting in a chair next to the bed, talking to her sincerely. Tobin couldn't hear what they were saying and was glad. A doctor who looked about old enough to be playing quarterback on a high-school football team bustled in wearing a green scrub gown and a stethoscope. You just knew that beneath the scrub gown there was a stylishly cut suit and a tie, like the kid's graduation getup, only more hip. The doctor and Roger exchanged a few solemn words, then Roger left, looking pissed and worried. The young doctor leaned over and kissed Delia on her forehead and nibbled on an exposed ear. Some bedside manner. The scene faded to a commercial for false fingernails. Tobin loved the reality of these shows.

Then he looked around at the customers engrossed in the world on the TV screen and realized that in this neighborhood, maybe in any neighborhood, reality was often no less improbable than "Shadowtown."

"Wanna refill on that soda?" the waitress asked beside him, her head turned so she could catch "Shadowtown" when it came back on. She wanted to get her work out of the way during the nail commercial. The blonde on the TV screen took a swipe at the camera as if she were a cat, held up her long false nails, and said, "Now you can fight and scraaatch!"

"Sure," Tobin said, sliding his empty cup over for her to take away.

Seeing "Shadowtown" reminded him of Oxman going to see Zachary Denton. That was a dumb-ass idea, but he knew there was no way to talk E.L. out of it. E.L. had no business questioning a suspect who'd been married to Jennifer and had knocked her around. Old Elliot Leroy was weak in the knees over that woman, had damn near ended his career a while back by crossing over to Jersey and chasing down a psychopath who'd threatened her. That was how they'd met, through a series of murders the nut had done over on West Ninety-eighth, including some of Jennifer's neighbors. Tobin liked Jennifer and saw why Oxman did, too, but old Elliot Leroy had better keep his professional objectivity or he'd wind up stepping into deep shit for sure.

The waitress brought Tobin another Pepsi, along with a revised check. He nodded to her, sipped, then put the waxed cup down in surprise.

It never happened like this. It was too soon. And way too easy.

But there was Phil, still looking like Mickey Rooney, still wearing his jacket with all the pockets. He stood out on the steps of the Waywind, fired up a cigarette with a lighter, and glanced up and down the street. Not as if he was looking for anything in particular, just looking.

Tobin got out a five-dollar bill to leave on the table just as soon as Phil started walking, and he'd start following. He thanked whatever cop gods there were for bringing Phil to him so early so he wouldn't have to develop calluses on his ass from sitting in this wooden booth. His heart was pumping away hard enough for him to be aware of it; this next part was going to be fun.

Phil went over and opened the regular, nonrevolving door of the Waywind, but he didn't go all the way inside. He bent low and forward, as if straining, then dragged out a coiled hose. He coupled the hose to a spigot inside a metal panel alongside the entrance, then turned it on, adjusted the nozzle, and began squirting the sidewalk in front of the hotel. He paused while a couple of pedestrians walked past, then rinsed behind them as if they might have left dirty footprints.

Tobin's expectations fell and he took back his thanks to the god of cops. Phil was apparently some kind of maintenance man at the hotel; that was how he knew Jardeen. Simple as that.

Still, he'd left Jardeen and gone to Egan's place yesterday, hadn't he? Well, Egan's building. That had to mean something.

But Tobin knew it didn't have to mean a thing. Maybe Phil knew somebody else in the building. Maybe he got together every once in a while with the super over there to play checkers or gin rummy. Maybe this, maybe that.

In a disgruntled mood, knowing he had endless time ahead of him in the hard booth, sipping Pepsi and dealing with the hophead waitress,

Tobin settled back and folded his hands on the table. He watched Phil hose the dirt and cigarette butts off the sidewalk and into the gutter.

But a part of him was glad he'd made connections with Phil so soon. He hadn't been a cop for five hundred years for nothing; he felt in his blue-dyed bones that watching Phil would eventually bring results.

Zachary Denton—10:00 A.M.

Zach was surprised when the receptionist phoned back and told him Jennifer was here to see him. He hadn't expected to see her again, after the seeming finality of their last meeting. Unpredictable bitch in a lot of ways, he thought, and too predictable in others. But then, maybe that wasn't so true anymore. It had been years since he'd lived with her and known her in a day-to-day relationship.

He sat at a desk in the office where he kept his art supplies, drafting board, set photos, and samples. Samples were important to Zach, especially fabric samples. A lot of set designers didn't pay much attention to texture on television, thought it was flattened and lost between camera and screen, so why bother? Zach knew better; he often used rough textures that looked too bulky in reality, but transferred to the TV screen smoothly yet still with enough surface quality to give "Shadowtown" sets a kind of depth lacking on the sets of other soaps. That was a large part of the show's success, Zach knew, though most viewers, and certainly Youngerman and Overbeck, were too stupid to realize it. But it made no difference to Zach what anybody thought, as long as the show continued to thrive in the ratings and the money kept pumping in. And nobody could argue with the success of "Shadowtown." Not lately, they couldn't, what with the vampire commotion translated into dollars. Youngerman and Overbeck had a lot to be grateful for, if only they knew who to thank.

His thoughts were interrupted when the door opened and Jennifer peeked in tentatively.

"Wasn't sure I had the right office," she said. She stepped in and glanced around while he looked at her. She was wearing well-tailored slacks that showed off her ass nicely, and a purple blouse that made her hair and eyes seem darker. Sexy, all right. Nobody had ever accused Zach of poor taste in women. Not when it came to their looks, anyway.

"It's just an office where I can do impromptu workups when the situation demands," Zach said, standing up and smiling at her. "What brings you here, Jennifer? Wait, that sounds like I'm not pleased to see you, and actually I am pleased." He aimed at her what he knew was his warmest smile. "In fact, I'm very glad you came."

She shuffled her feet uneasily. He had the feeling she was experiencing strong emotions she hadn't felt in a long time. He could sense the power of this little get-together shifting to him, like in the old days. Still, he wasn't sure what she wanted.

She said, "I came here because . . . Well, I just don't think we should leave things the way they are, Zach. We were married once, even if it went sour. I guess we owe each other more than bad feelings. More than each of us trying to pretend the other doesn't exist."

He shrugged, putting his lanky arms and shoulders into it. "Sure, what'll it cost us to forgive and forget?" Shot the smile again. "Or, for that matter, forgive and remember?"

She tried a return smile, almost made it. "We owe each other more than trying to live without thinking about our time together. There shouldn't be doors in our minds we shy away from opening."

"That'd be unhealthy, all right."

"I don't want to live that way."

"Yeah, well, me either." Where the hell was this conversation going? Sounded like dialogue from yesterday's show.

"We oughta know a little bit about each other's lives," she said.

"Granted. What can it hurt, huh?"

Jennifer drew a deep breath and did manage to smile. She struck a pose as if she were poised and comfortable rather than painfully ill at ease. "So how's life with you?" she asked.

"It's good. I like my work. And everything's going well, except for all the bullshit about murder and the show. But, you know, even that's improving the ratings."

"Yeah, I suppose it is."

"An ill wind and all that, huh?" Zach said.

"What do you think about the murders? I mean, the latest one?"

"That Brokton creep? Listen, between you, me and the bedpost, he deserved it. Now, the old watchman McGreery was another matter. I mean, nice enough old guy with a wife, finally reached the point where he could take life easy, and zap, some punk dressed like Dracula kills him for kicks. That's not how life's supposed to treat people.''

"I thought you weren't sure about how the man running away was dressed.''

"All in black, in what looked like a cloak, as I told your friend Oxman. So much stuff in the papers and on the tube about vampires and the show, I guess maybe I remember it that way now more than I would have. If that makes any more sense than this whole rotten mess.''

"I know what you mean.'' She played with the pearl necklace dangling between her breasts. He remembered those breasts, firm and surprisingly large for her frame. "Zach, is there anybody in your life?''

Aha! "Yeah, sure. But not like you were, Jen.''

She tried to hide her pleasure at his remark but couldn't. The game was on, all right.

He moved out from behind the desk to stand near her. Watched her grow uncomfortable in his nearness. What was she thinking? He was beginning to get a vague idea. Maybe Oxman wasn't treating her right, not rough enough. Women got used to a certain way when they were young and couldn't shake it; didn't Oxman know that? "How are you and the cop getting along?''

"Okay—good.''

"That's fine. I wanna see you happy.''

"And I want that for you, Zach. I suppose I want that for both of us, and for it to end there, without us having to think about one another.''

As if he thought about her every day. "I know what you mean, Jen. I feel the same way. But the truth is, sometimes somebody gets under your skin and stays there and there's not much can be done about it.'' He rested a hand on her shoulder. "Except maybe act on it, huh?'' He gave an exploratory squeeze and she winced and backed away. But not far away. She wasn't sure. He wondered about her sex life with Oxman. Did he roughhouse her at all, tie her up or anything? She'd liked that kind of sex for a while, pretending she was just going along with Zach. Then he got too rough with her and she turned bitchy. Got fucking pregnant and caused him to lose his temper. Women were all alike, really. Eventually messed up everything. He smiled at her, contrasting gentleness with the tough act. She was confused; he could see that. Fine with him.

"Listen, Zach—"

But he reached for her again, pulled her to him and pressed her to his body hard. Jesus, she felt so familiar, so warm and soft! She was getting him going, all right. He felt his erection grow and press into her stomach, and she felt it, too.

Her eyes widened, full of innocence. It was going to be the surprised act. Well, *he* wasn't surprised.

She tried to pull away from him, but he had her arms pinned. "Dammit, Zach, you've got the wrong idea!"

He laughed and tried to insert his tongue in her ear. "Do I, Jen? Or do you just think I do?"

"Zach, please! Don't do this!"

"Do you like to beg, Jen?"

She worked an arm free and tried to hit him. He grabbed her wrist. Her free hand darted up and slapped his face. Not hard, but hard enough to cause him to release her. She backpedaled away from him like a lightweight boxer. Zach raised his fingertips toward the sting in his cheek. His eyes were watering. He was beginning to get mad. What was this cunt doing, waltzing in here putting on the moves— definitely putting on the moves—and then turning him away? She had to know what was going on—nobody could be that fucking dumb! Without thinking about it, he took a step toward her. She got pale with fright and seemed rooted to the spot, couldn't do anything but wait for him in her fear. He liked that; he could feel his erection start to return.

"I know you must prefer it the old way sometimes," he said, moving in on her.

"Oh, goddammit, Zach!" He could see the resignation, the denied desire, in her eyes, which she couldn't avert from his own.

"Tell me that's what you want. Go ahead, tell me!"

"No! That isn't why I came here, Zach!"

"Sure it isn't."

There were two loud knocks, then the door opened.

Zach froze and swallowed. He wasn't concerned about an erection now.

Oxman stood in the doorway. He'd looked surprised for only an instant, then he recovered and his cop's mask was back on tight. He might have been staring at something inanimate all of a sudden. His flat eyes went from Jennifer to Zach, taking it all in. Everything. The bastard missed nothing! Zach felt a little spiral of fear, along with his anger at having his scene with Jennifer ended when it was going so well. She'd been backing herself into a corner, probably on purpose.

Well, she'd come around again. She'd been well on her way to where he wanted to take her. She'd want to go the whole distance. He remembered now; she was like that. So many of them were that way.

"Interrupting?" Oxman asked.

"No," Jennifer said, recovering neatly herself. "I just dropped by to iron out some personal matters with Zach. We've finished talking."

Zach was aware of Oxman staring at his right cheek, where Jennifer had slapped him. The stinging sensation was gone but the flesh would still be reddened, Zach knew. He'd had experience in such things. The cop was boiling inside behind those calm eyes; Zach was sure of it. He was also sure Oxman knew nothing—at least, he didn't know enough.

"I've got a few things to say to Denton myself," Oxman said.

Zach didn't like the way he said it. Fucking cop was putting on the Clint Eastwood act. That could be bad, but so what? All cops had limits and stayed inside them. *Had* to stay.

"Always glad to try and help the law with whatever it can't handle alone," Zach said, knowing he was making things worse but not caring, letting his anger at being interrupted with Jennifer carry him past his fear.

Zach made up his mind not to take any shit off this hard-on Dirty Harry today. None at all. A sacred vow. A guy could take so much and then no more.

That was how Zach felt, and that was it.

No matter what.

Tobin had drunk his fill of Pepsi. He worked on his third cup of nasty coffee and kept an eye on the Waywind Hotel entrance. Several people who looked about as down-and-almost-out as Lance Jardeen came and went through the revolving doors. It wasn't the sort of hotel a jewel thief was likely to choose as hunting grounds. The guests and tenants were strictly cubic-zirconia types, if they had any jewelry left unpawned.

Tobin added more cream to the coffee to cut some of its bitterness. His legs were getting stiff and his ass felt as if it had grown into the hard wooden-booth bench. If he stood up suddenly, the whole damn bench would come with him. He'd have to drag part of the booth around for life.

My mind's slipping, he thought. Too much sitting here. Too much "Shadowtown." He thought about "Shadowtown" and some of the other soaps he'd watched the past few years. Real worlds—or virtually real—to millions of faithful viewers. Now and then a real-life personality would guest on a soap, playing him or herself. Tobin remembered seeing Gerald Ford on one of the daytime dramas. What the hell? Ford was real, so why not the rest of the package? Then there was the guy who did cold-tablet commercials on TV, claiming not to be a doctor but to be someone who played a doctor in one of the soaps. People believed the man, bought the pills. Must, or the advertisers wouldn't keep trotting him out in front of the camera. Real? What was real? Why not "Shadowtown"? Why not vampires? Ox wouldn't believe anything he couldn't see and touch or figure with mathematical certitude. You couldn't kill a guy like Ox with voodoo, but voodoo killed nonetheless.

Tobin stopped his rumination and did a double-take worthy of a daytime soap actor. He stared out the restaurant window.

Phil had pushed out through the revolving doors and was standing on the Waywind's steps. He'd changed to tight-fitting faded jeans and white jogging shoes, but he still wore the many-pocketed jacket. In his right hand was a partly rolled-up brown paper bag; looked like an ordinary lunch bag.

Now what? Off to a second job? Maybe Phil was a school crossing guard.

As Tobin watched, Phil carefully rolled the bag even tighter, then slipped it into a side pocket of the jacket and worked a zipper. Then he swaggered down off the steps and began walking along the sidewalk.

Tobin stood up and dropped a five and some one-dollar bills on the table to pay for everything he'd drunk and the stale doughnut he'd forced down. He nodded good-bye to the slat-hipped waitress, who nodded back blank-faced and slack-jawed, as if she were bidding him a nonchalant farewell on her deathbed. He wondered how much he'd tipped her.

Another soap was coming on the TV behind the counter as Tobin left the restaurant and fell in behind Phil on the sidewalk, matching the speed of the bobbing blond head half a block ahead of him.

I'm following goddamn Mickey Rooney, Tobin thought. That's exactly what he felt like he was doing. What he looked like he was doing, if anybody on the street noticed what was going on. Not that Phil looked quite enough like Rooney for someone to stop him and ask for an autograph. But in the flesh and to his fans, did *Rooney* look that much like Rooney? How many people would have thought he looked older, younger, taller, shorter? Tobin thought again of "Shadowtown." What the fuck was real? Delia Lane in a hospital bed? Or Tobin tailing an oversized Andy Hardy down a crowded Manhattan street? A lot of people were confused about reality, and Tobin couldn't blame them. Today he felt he was joining their numbers.

Phil was some walker. After about five blocks, Tobin's heart was hammering and he was short of breath. He stayed with Phil, though, out of sight. This was his reality and he knew his stuff. He was sure Phil had no idea he was there.

The blond head kept bobbing along, swerving to avoid oncoming flows of pedestrians, crossing streets against the lights, keeping up a steady, rapid pace.

Phil walked down Broadway through the Village and turned right on Houston. Cut back to Bleecker and then wound around some side streets. Not as if he seriously thought someone was tailing him, but as if taking routine precautions in case some Village junkie or mugger might latch on and follow him.

A huge man wearing a black-leather jacket on whose back was lettered "Losers of a Dying World" did seem to take an interest in Phil, walked behind him for about a block, then peeled off to enter a used clothing shop. Get a new jacket, Tobin thought. Jesus, get a shampoo, take a bath. Cheer up. People paid a lot of rent to live in the Village. Tobin wondered why.

Phil finally stopped in front of an old brick building that housed a cheap used-book shop and, above that, what looked like run-down apartments. He glanced around, absently touched his fingertips to the pocket containing the rolled-up paper sack, and entered the book shop. Young asshole wasn't even breathing hard. Tobin resented that.

He waited a few minutes, then moved closer to the shop. Through the dirty window he could see most of the narrow aisles of books. Phil wasn't browsing, as far as Tobin could tell. The shop was very small, and seemed empty except for a thin young man with a mustache, leaning behind the counter and leafing through a magazine.

Back door? Evasive maneuver by Phil? That'd be just like the Mickey Rooney jerkoff.

Tobin considered sprinting around the block to look for Phil, but he realized that would probably prove futile. Besides, he wasn't convinced Phil had left the shop.

A couple of guys in baggy pants and distressed-leather bomber jackets entered the place. They had white scarves wrapped around their necks. Looked as if they were going on a World War II mission over Germany, drop some bombs on the Huns.

Tobin waited. Ten minutes. The two young bombardiers hadn't emerged from the shop. He moved in even closer and peered through the window again, couldn't see them. The place ate customers.

When three more people entered, one of them an elderly woman, Tobin counted to ten, then went into the shop behind them. These were conservative-looking types, probably tourists.

The man behind the counter glanced at Tobin and Tobin smiled and nodded a polite hello. He began browsing while the three customers who'd entered before him quizzed the clerk about the latest Ludlum thriller. The woman couldn't bring the title to mind. "I know it has three words in it," she told the clerk.

Tobin gazed disinterestedly at the rows of books. The place had a section on natural foods, there were shelves of hetero- and homosexual-oriented sex manuals, some used novels, diet books, home craft instruction books. Hey, there was a Ludlum, all right! Three words. Tobin thought about pointing it out to the elderly woman questioning the clerk, but he decided against it. Instead he roamed toward the back of the narrow shop, seeing no sign of Phil or of the two guys dressed for war in the air.

He did see a door. Possibly a way out the back of the shop.

The clerk was still busy with the tourists and the elusive Ludlum. Tobin rotated the knob on the door, pushed, and found the door unlocked.

It didn't lead outside, but to a narrow stairwell that ran to a landing, then right-angled to climb to the upper floors. Unintelligible graffiti marked the walls, and the stale smell of urine was almost overpowering.

Tobin didn't hesitate. He stepped into the stairwell and quietly closed the door behind him, hoping that if the clerk noticed him missing, he'd decide Tobin had left the shop during the mild confusion about Ludlum.

As silently as possible, Tobin crept up the stairs. The damned things creaked, so he stayed near the wall to keep give in the boards to a minimum. Light was provided by a filthy broken window on the landing, but the stairwell was still dim. Swirling dust rioted quietly in slanted sunbeams that found their way in but somehow provided little illumination a foot beyond them.

On the second floor Tobin paused and looked down a hall lined with doors, most of which were closed. The floor was dusty and littered, and showed no signs of recent passage by anyone. He moved to the nearest open door and peered inside.

The door led to a two-room apartment that was uninhabitable. Debris was piled in a corner, wallpaper hung in damp shreds, lathe showed where plaster had crumbled and fallen to form yellowed patterns on the floor. There were rat tracks in the dust.

The next opened door revealed two rooms similarly ruined.

Apparently the building was due for rehab and had stood vacant except for the downstairs book shop for a long time. The place was going to be gentrified, and would soon rent for monthly fees that would keep the city's undesirables out on the street and waiting for the occupants to emerge and become fair game.

There was a scuffing noise above Tobin's head. Then what might have been the sound of a man's voice. An icy finger probed Tobin's spine. He remembered the "Shadowtown" vampire. "Myth," he whispered softly, wanting to hear his own voice in the dim emptiness. "Myth and publicity and an overactive news media." *And murder. Don't forget murder.*

He went back into the hall, calculated where the apartment the noise had come from would be on the third floor, then walked stealthily toward the stairs.

The third floor was a duplication of the second. Tobin worked more cautiously here, though. He crept from door to door, pressing his ear to faded paint and dried-out wood. A voice inside him told him he was in danger, urged him to cut and run. Tobin had heard the voice before; he refused to listen.

Halfway down the hall, he heard a voice other than the one in his mind. It said, "The shit oughtn't to be that expensive, you know."

He crossed the hall to be closer to the source of the voice, and leaned against a closed door. There were faint sounds of motion inside, but no more voices.

What the hell? Tobin thought, and actually stooped down and peeked through the keyhole. He felt like a character on "Shadowtown" himself now. He couldn't remember ever peeking through a keyhole before in his long career on the department.

The view was limited. Keyhole-shaped. Tobin smiled. This reminded him of those countless camera shots through keyholes seen in movies and TV detective shows. A nice effect on film, but not very revealing in real life.

Or was it?

He moved to the side to take in a section of the other half of the room, and saw a pair of bare feet. A man was lying on the floor. Another was slouched in an old armchair. A third sat beneath the window with his head thrown back. He was staring fixedly at something on the ceiling. Tobin thought he recognized the void in his eyes.

"Oughtn't to be that expensive," a man's voice said again. "Gettin' to be a fuck deal. But who you gonna complain to?"

"Squeezing the supply," another voice said.

"No bargain, my friend."

"Ain't any of my business."

"Your business shit!"

Tobin focused his gaze on the end of a table, barely within his vision. There was a candle on it, not burning. And a spoon. A flexible thin rubber hose. A couple of bottles. Paraphernalia for free-basing. This was a shooting gallery, a safe place where hard-core addicts went to shoot up and not worry about interference from police or friends or family. A kind of Moose Lodge for the bad guys.

One of the men who'd been talking walked into Tobin's vision. He was Marv Egan. Tobin figured the other talker was Phil.

And there was the link between Egan and Jardeen. Phil was a narcotics courier, and Egan and Jardeen were addicts. That might explain the momentary interest in Phil by the black-jacketed big guy. Probably Phil was known to carry drugs, and would have been a vulnerable mark without the protection he no doubt enjoyed from higher-ups in the operation's chain.

A creaking noise made Tobin's heart jump. Somebody was trudging up the stairs.

Tobin straightened up halfway and ducked into the vacant room across the hall. It smelled like shit, literally, and came furnished with crumpled newspapers and empty cans and bottles. There was a yellowed poster of Farah Fawcett Majors on one wall with obscenities scrawled on it, some of them violent. Went with the show-biz territory, Tobin thought. Didn't Lana Spence know that?

He eased the door shut and listened as someone walked along the hall and entered the shooting gallery to join that lively and inspired group. The people over there were past the lofty and beneficial stages of their habits. They were into the hell of desperate need and dependence. Now they could only delude themselves that they were riding the beast that owned them, instead of it being the other way around.

Tobin nudged a dusty wine bottle out of his way with his toe, then crossed the room to the window. No need to open it; there was no glass in the frame.

He wedged his thick body through the window and out onto the metal fire escape.

He drew a deep breath, then plunged down the steel stairs, causing a clamor and then a loud squeal when he rode the metal drop-ladder to the alley.

A voice shouted, "Whoozat out there? Hey!"

Hit the pavement running! Tobin told himself.

And he did. His right knee bumped an empty metal trash can, sending it toppling and rolling, its lid spinning like a thrown hubcap. It didn't slow him down at all.

He was back out on the street and jogging away from the place within seconds. The trash-can lid was still warbling and clanging behind him as it settled onto the pavement. His tie flopped against his chest and his holstered gun jounced beneath his arm.

It didn't bother him that he'd made noise, as long as he got away unseen. This was a neighborhood full of bums and burglars who prowled the buildings. He didn't want anybody thinking cop.

He was sure he hadn't been seen.

Jennifer Crane—1:00 P.M.

Jennifer shivered. Oxman had been so calm, but at the same time so fierce. She'd never seen him quite like that. His hate for Zach had blazed through those quiet eyes, like something burning deep within murky water. She could see that even Zach had been a little frightened, after his initial show of bravado.

Zach had made the mistake of advancing on Oxman after Ox had interrupted them at the "Shadowtown" studios, scowling at him with intended menace. It had been foolish of him, after his mocking tone when he'd agreed to cooperate with the police.

Ox hadn't felt menaced. Not at all. It was almost as if he were glad Zach was moving in on him and might try to get physical. In an apparently friendly fashion he'd rested his hand on Zach's bony shoulder and continued asking his questions. All so routine. Then Jennifer had noticed the grimace of quiet pain on Zach's face, seen that he was twisting, trying to pull his lean body away from Ox without loss of dignity or admission of agony. The tips of Ox's fingers were white where they were digging into Zach's shoulder.

Jennifer didn't even know what Ox was asking Zach. It simply didn't register. Something about a man named Egan, she thought. And some other men whose names she didn't recognize. It was about the vampire murders—what else? And Lana Spence's name was mentioned.

Then Oxman had released Zach, and even thanked him for cooperating. Detective Oxman, the professional. Still in the routine; the protective routine that shielded from emotion. In this case, dangerous emotion. Dangerous to Ox and to Zach. Zach seemed to know it.

"Want a ride home?" Oxman had asked Jennifer in his strangely level voice.

She'd shaken her head no. She was frightened of him just then, afraid of what they might say to each other if they left together. There was something poised in delicate balance and they both realized it.

"I've got some shopping to do," she'd said, and watched him nod and walk from the room without a glance at Zach. There was nothing in Ox's face to suggest what she knew he must be feeling.

"Smart-ass bastard," Zach said to the closed door, when Ox was gone.

"He was polite," Jennifer said.

"Yeah, he was that." Zach grinned and rubbed his shoulder where Ox had applied pressure. "The law likes to shove people around, polite or not."

"I'll be leaving," Jennifer said. She stepped toward the door.

"Jen?"

She stopped and turned, making sure she could get to the doorknob before Zach could reach her. "We've been through it all, Zach."

"Yeah? I thought we were starting to reach an understanding before Dick Tracy came in."

"No, we weren't. Let's you and I let it rest."

"For how long?" He moved closer. Or did he merely lean his long body in her direction?

"Forever."

He turned his best smile on her, the one that prompted memories good and bad. He edged nearer. "You don't really feel that way, Jen. I know what it is you like."

"You don't know, Zach. Never did." She shrugged. "Sorry."

"Hey, you and I understand each other, Jen."

"I understand us, Zach; you don't." She looked into his eyes and realized she was smiling sadly. "Good-bye, Zach."

But when she moved to leave he was suddenly next to her; he'd measured distance, caught her a few feet from the door.

And he had her by the shoulders and was shaking her; she was aware of her hair flying, whipping and webbing across her face and eyes. She tried to speak but her teeth knocked together. She knew how ridiculous she'd sound if she *did* manage to say something, so she clenched her jaws. "Goddamn cop!" Zach was saying, playing out on her his frustration with Oxman. Jennifer knew how that worked. She was afraid she'd lose consciousness. She opened her mouth to scream and only bit her tongue.

"Goddamn cop and cop's whore!" Zach hissed. She felt spittle fly into her face.

And suddenly he released her.

She stood dizzily, leaning with her shoulder and hip against the closed door.

"You're a devious bitch and always were," Zach was saying. His voice sounded muffled, as if he were speaking through a thick blanket. But he was calmer now. "Always were . . ."

The room leveled out and the dizziness passed. She felt nauseated; she knew her mouth had the slackness of someone about to vomit.

Zach smiled down at her. He raised a finger and flipped her lower lip so it made a tiny slurping sound. "Or maybe you like rough stuff the way you used to, huh?"

"Damn you," she said slowly and with soft deliberation. "I hate you, you bastard." She swallowed something thick and bitter. "I mean I fucking *hate* you!"

He slapped her, sending a shock of pain through her jaw and jolting her head around. But that seemed to clear her mind.

"I'm leaving, Zach. And I'll scream like you never heard if you try to stop me."

He wasn't smiling. *"Stop you?* Who's trying to stop you? Go! Get out! Go to your crummy cop you're shacked up with! He use his handcuffs on you, Jen? I bet you like that, don't you?"

She opened the door, then stopped and turned back to face him. "How do you know we live together?" she said.

He wiped his arm across his forehead, and his expression changed; the long face took on a blank look of feigned nonchalance. He obviously didn't like her knowing he'd been interested enough to check on her.

"I been told," he said. "I don't remember by who. Go to your cop. Marry him, why don't you? Mr. and Mrs. Mediocre. That's where you belong."

Jennifer went out and slammed the door behind her. Slammed it on her past.

Zach was right about one thing. She belonged with E.L. Oxman. They belonged together.

She knew that now with certainty.

Sy Youngerman—2:40 P.M.

Youngerman was going to enjoy doing it to her, but he knew he'd better pretend otherwise—and pretend well. She could cause a lot of trouble, and probably would anyway, no matter how he broached this subject. It was in her genes, apparently. Maybe it was what made her such a success, gave her the kind of drive and ruthlessness usually associated with top-level corporate executives instead of actresses. Or with successful serial killers.

Youngerman had his dark hair fluffed and combed straight back in its fifty-dollar salon style, was wearing his white sweater and dark slacks. He looked almost collegiate, if about ten years too old for the Ivy. He planned his appearance this way; he didn't want to come across as the heartless show-biz mogul cutting the throat of a friend. Hell, Lana Spence had never been a friend.

He leaned back in his desk chair in his Shadowtown Productions office, carefully held a neutral expression, and said, "It's been decided you're not going to recover from your car accident, Lana."

She cocked her head at him, dark hair cascading over a lean shoulder, as if she hadn't heard correctly. He was going to like doing this even more than he'd thought. He remembered the almost daily turmoil she'd caused on the set, the clash and crush of male egos. The subtle, exquisite cruelty.

He made what he'd told her more easily understood. "We're going to kill off the Delia Lane character, Lana. We've been thinking about going with an occult angle anyway. Now . . . Anyway, Lois Smith will be the show's new vixen—a female vampire."

She was an actress, all right. Her features set in an almost casual expression, as if he'd told her rain might spoil her picnic. But a twitching beneath her right eye gave hint of the rage she must be feeling as the significance of his words penetrated and gained full impact.

Lana edged forward in her chair, as if she might spring up and over the desk at him. Like in the old "Wonder Woman" series. Youngerman had a moment of uneasiness. Might she actually get physical? Violent?

"You can't do that," she said with exaggerated calm. "Haven't you read my contract?"

Youngerman nodded. "Even the fine print, Lana. Especially the fine print. The lawyers have been consulted. We can and will do it. We have no choice, if we want the show's ratings to climb. All the numbers, the reaction tests we've been doing—"

"Reaction tests?" she interrupted. "You mean to tell me a roomful of yokels off the street with sensors attached to their fingertips are going to knock me out of this role?"

"Those sensors measure metabolic rate, Lana. They're scientifically reliable. And the test subjects aren't yokels, they're a carefully chosen cross-section of the television mass audience. Average people. Good Americans."

"And I suppose their average metabolism sank when I came on the screen."

"No, no, not at all. But it rose whenever anything relating to the occult was shown. Especially in regard to a female vampire. Women like the idea of a lady bloodsucker, and most of our viewers are women. Jesus, maybe it's some kind of subconscious sicko sex thing, but it exists and it creates a wider audience for the show, so we gotta go with it. Lana, you know how this business is."

She got up, couldn't stay seated any longer. Without thinking what she was doing she began to pace like a tigress, faster and faster, in front of Youngerman's desk. She'd lost roles before, like every other actress; what was the big deal?

But he knew what the big deal was—this was by far her most successful role, the biggest fame- and money-maker of her career. Its end might signify the beginning of her inevitable decline. And that's why he was getting his kicks doing this to her, because she deserved it.

So many ruined men in her past, so many stories about her, most of which were true. One lousy stunt after another, one victim after another for her to step on during her climb to star status. Not too many people would feel sorry for Lana when they read in the trade papers that her "Shadowtown" role was being terminated. That she was another victim of the show-business long knives.

He said, "It's not just the metabolic responses, Lana, telephone surveys correspond. Everything has to end, unfortunately. Even a character as brilliantly played as you portrayed Delia Lane has to run its course. You know the game, Lana. It's time for something new. The caravan moves on, kid."

" 'Kid,' is it? It was 'Lana' or 'Miss Spence' yesterday."

"Sorry, Lana. I didn't mean to be flip. But yesterday's dropped into the past. The show, and you, have got to look ahead."

"What's Overbeck think of this idea?"

"He and I agree on it. But it isn't anybody's 'idea,' Lana. It's what the facts dictate. The murders, all this vampire publicity, it means we'd be stupid not to give the show an occult slant—and we have to move right away."

Her pacing had slowed but she was shaking her head. "I can't believe this, Sy. The way my goddamn life's been going lately. First someone wants to kill me, and now you want to kill *me!*"

"Not you, Lana—Delia Lane." The look in her eyes struck Youngerman as kind of creepy. How closely did she identify with Delia? After all, Delia and Lana were quite similar in a lot of ways. So similar it was sometimes uncanny. And certain actresses, with certain roles, sometimes had difficulty stepping out of character when they walked offstage.

"Manny won't—" She stopped herself, suddenly remembering.

He reminded her anyway that her sleazy protector was no longer around to wheedle and threaten and find contract loopholes. "Manny Brokton's dead, Lana." He sighed and stared at his hands folded on the desk. "That's a shame, like a lot of things that've happened lately. A deep-shit, black-hole shame. But that's the way it is. The way it has to be."

She sat back down, calmer, staring icily at him. "Few things in this world *have* to be one way or the other."

"You're wrong about that, Lana. I'm afraid it's something every beautiful woman has to learn."

"And how do you intend to work this out?"

"The writers have already figured how to write Delia out of the show, in a matter of days."

"Jean Richards isn't going to bite me in the neck, is she? I won't have the Lois Smith character kill Delia."

"No, not that. Lois's bite would make Delia a vampire, according to the writers," Youngerman said. He waited, watching, secretly delighting in the light of desperate hope that flared in her eyes.

"Well, why *not*? Why not have two female vampires on the show? If your response tests and ratings numbers indicate a positive upward trend for the occult and for female vampires, why not hit the audience with both barrels? Give them even more of what all the murder publicity has made them want?"

He pretended to think it over for a moment, then firmly shook his head. "No, Lana, you know that'd only dilute the impact of both characters. Besides, we've already got Graveman, the Brad Gaines character. Three vampires would be too much; two women would destroy the balance. We need one—and only one—strong female occult figure, and Lois Smith is it. You'll suffer a relapse of your auto-accident injuries. Complications will develop and you'll die in the doctor's arms. It'll be a great scene, one the audience will remember for years. Bigger than the wedding on 'Hope's Other Life.'"

Lana's mouth twitched bitterly. "Yeah, where's Hope now?"

Youngerman shrugged. "Hope's Other Life" had been cancelled six months after the ballyhooed TV wedding of its main character, and the actress who'd played Hope was doing peanut-butter commercials. "So the viewers wouldn't accept Hope as a married woman," he said. "Viewers are fickle."

"Not so fickle they'll accept Delia Lane's death," she said haughtily.

"So fickle they won't accept her alive the way they used to, Lana. This is nobody's fault. It's simply time for you to move onward and upward, accept some of those major film roles Manny told us keep coming your way." He stood up behind his desk, signaling her the conversation was over. An executive decision had been reached, and that was that. Business. "I'm sorry, Lana."

She didn't move. "You don't fool me, Sy."

He felt a tickle of alarm at the back of his mind. "About what?"

She laughed at him then, as if he were something less than human, born of woman solely for her amusement. He couldn't be sure if she meant it, or if it was an act to cover her anger and sense of loss. His own anger rose hot and bitter in his throat, but he swallowed and held his calm attitude.

"I didn't want this to get nasty," he told her.

"Oh yes you did, Sy. Only you wanted to control the nastiness."

She walked to the door. Her slender body was as tense as he'd ever seen it. Fluidity of movement had deserted her. She'd been struck in the heart for sure. He smiled faintly, briefly, at her rigid back.

The smile disappeared when she turned to face him, preparing to leave. No doubt she'd thought of an appropriate exit line.

He was disappointed by her lack of imagination when she said, "I won't take this lying down, Sy."

"That's a cliché we'd write out of the show's dialogue, Lana. The way we're going to write you out."

"This isn't script dialogue, Sy, this is real life. My statement stands." She went out and slammed the door hard enough to make him wince.

That was better, Youngerman thought, that "statement stands" line. It had a newspapery, *Front Page* ring to it.

He picked up the phone, punched a Lucite button, and said, "Have Zach Denton come in here."

Then he sat back and crossed his arms. He'd enjoyed his conversation with Lana so much he actually felt guilty about it.

And at the same time, he was somewhat uneasy.

What was this business doing to him?

As soon as he entered the Twenty-fourth Precinct station, Oxman saw Tobin sitting at his desk reading a morning tabloid and smiling. When Oxman got closer, Tobin looked up and grinned wider.

"How about this, Ox?" he said. He cocked his head to the side and read from the paper: " 'New TV vampires draw blood in ratings wars. Real vampire still seeks jugular juice.' "

"Imaginative," Oxman said.

He'd talked to Tobin earlier by phone and wanted more information on this Phil character. A known drug courier, Tobin had said. Evans of Narcotics knew right where to find Phil. So where was Evans? Where was Phil? *Who* was Phil? And did he fit into this the way Oxman and Tobin figured? "If you can tear yourself away from the so-called news," Oxman said, "give me the info on our friend Phil."

Tobin folded the paper in half and tossed it onto the desk. A black-and-white still photo from an old Bela Lugosi movie showed at the fold. Lugosi was leering into the camera, his mouth distorted by dark stains. Oxman didn't want to read the caption. He recalled that Lugosi had been buried in his full vampire costume; that seemed important to Oxman but he couldn't figure out why.

Tobin leaned far back in his swivel chair; he did that habitually. Oxman often felt like extending a foot and nudging him onto the floor, just to erase the smug expression he sometimes wore. Tobin was wearing that expression now. He knew he'd done a solid piece of police work with Phil.

"Phil Malloy's his full name," Tobin said. "Narcotics knew all about him. Small-time courier, delivers drugs for an operation that works out of New Jersey. The DEA's watching them now and plans to move when they get a little more evidence. Anyway, Phil runs drugs for the suppliers of both Marv Egan and Lance Jardeen.''

"A link," Oxman said. "Along with Lana Spence."

"On the other hand," Tobin said, "it's not all that unlikely that these two guys would know one another and make connections with the same drug supplier. You know show-folks and drugs. And a couple of used-up actors like Jardeen and Egan might hang out in the same places and tell each other how the world and their agents fucked over them."

"Not unlikely they would," Oxman agreed, thinking that was something he should have thought of long before now. Maybe Phil Malloy could bring them up to date. "Where's Malloy now?"

"Upstairs in an interrogation room, getting uneasy while he's waiting for us. Evans picked him up on a possession charge forty-five minutes ago."

"The Jersey outfit will send a lawyer, won't they?"

"Yeah, he's on his way. Fella name of Singer."

"Izzy Singer?"

"Yeah. Know him?"

"Vaguely." About six months ago, while waiting in court for a homicide case to reach the docket so he could testify, Oxman had seen Singer represent a defendant in a drug case. Singer had worked the judge beautifully, and the defendant got probation even though it was his second sale-of-a-controlled-substance offense and he had an assault record. That had left a sour taste in Oxman's mouth. Maybe the fix had been in. And Izzy Singer had been such an unctuous, obviously insincere yet somehow effective performer in the courtroom that Oxman remembered him vividly and with loathing. Good cops put criminals into courtrooms; good lawyers like Singer arranged for them to walk out. Hell of a system.

"What'd Phil have on him?" Oxman asked.

"Couple of pellets of crack. No big deal. Unless you got two previous felony convictions behind you, like Phil does."

"Gives us something to bargain with," Oxman said. "What's Evans say?"

"Narcotics would rather have Phil on the street right now, actually. They like to see who he talks to and why, and they think he can be turned into an informant. They say bargain away. Some future date, it'll make their arm-twisting all the more persuasive."

"I suppose he's not talking until Singer gets here."

"Yeah, that's his position," Tobin said. "Guy's been around the block and knows the moves. On the other hand, he's jumpy."

Oxman unbuttoned his sport coat and adjusted his shoulder holster. "So let's go talk with him, Arty. Maybe he'll change his mind and volunteer some information."

"You intimidating bastard," Tobin said with a grin, and followed Oxman to the steps.

Phil Malloy was seated at a walnut table in a small, green-walled room on the second floor. The table was nicked and scarred and had one leg slightly shorter than the others; it wobbled if you put your elbows on it and leaned. The room had a fluorescent ceiling fixture boxed in with wire, and had no furniture other than the table and four wooden chairs. It had one window, with rusty grillwork over the glass. There was a large, square mirror on one wall that looked as if it might be two-way. But Oxman knew it was just an ordinary mirror. There was the unmistakable scent of perspiration and fear in the room, along with tobacco smoke. Phil should shower more often, Oxman thought, being careful not to show his revulsion as he picked up the pungent smell of rancid sweat and unwashed flesh.

The window was lowered about two inches on top, and smoke up near the ceiling was oozing through to outside, as if Phil's spirit were escaping even if his odorous bodily husk remained slumped despondently at the table. He'd been puffing Winstons; a near-empty pack and a matchbook lay on the table before him, next to an old metal beanbag ashtray full of ashes and butts. Today wasn't going well for Phil. It would get worse. He looked as if he knew that it would and was wondering how much worse.

Oxman thought immediately, The guy looks like Mickey Rooney, only bigger.

Phil stiffened in his chair and his blue eyes rolled from Tobin to Oxman. "Singer here?" he asked. He started to light a cigarette, changed his mind and shook the match out and dropped it in the ashtray.

"He's on his way," Oxman said, watching Phil. He was wearing a jacket with about two thousand pockets. Oxman wondered if every zippered compartment had been searched.

Phil didn't like being watched. He squirmed uneasily. "I told the other guy, Evans, I didn't wanna talk till Singer got here. He said that was okay with him."

"It's okay with us, too," Tobin said.

Phil wriggled some more. He was a man who couldn't stand silence. He'd be easy.

"You gotta go take a piss, Phil?" Tobin asked.

"No."

"Okay." Tobin gazed down sleepily at him. "You let us know if you do."

Phil unconsciously picked viciously at a wart on the back of his left hand. He suddenly hurt himself and stopped. He slid the right hand out of sight beneath the table. "I mean, I had this small amount of junk a friend asked me to hold for him. Hell, it ain't such a big deal."

Oxman watched Tobin shrug. "Could be big enough to mean a lotta years, Phil."

"Well, Evans didn't seem to think so."

"He's Narcotics," Oxman said. "Maybe he knows."

Phil looked surprised and worked his lips. A lock of blond hair flopped down onto his forehead. "You guys ain't narcs?"

"We're Homicide," Oxman said.

"Huh?" Phil got pale and brushed the hair back. It flopped onto his forehead again, exactly the way it had been.

"Don't you remember me?" Tobin said. "I saw you in Lance Jardeen's room the other day at the Waywind Hotel."

Phil peered up at Tobin, and his moon face was transformed by sudden recognition. "Yeah, yeah. Now I remember. Jardeen said later you was there about a—"

"Murder," Oxman finished for him. "A series of murders, actually, Phil."

But Phil had swiveled his body in his chair and was staring out the window. "You don't mind," he said, "I'll wait for Mr. Singer."

Oxman looked at Tobin, who shook his head.

"We don't mind, Phil," Oxman said.

That was the thing to say, because the door opened and Izzy Singer stepped into the room.

He was only about five-feet-four, and reached that with his built-up shoes. His pinstripe blue suit must have cost a thousand dollars and had probably paid for itself many times over in court. A gold watch peeked out from beneath white French cuffs fastened with gold cuff links. There was a huge gold nuggetlike ring on his left hand, a smaller gold pinky ring on his right. He had a handsome if somewhat pinched face, dark eyes, thinning black hair that was combed severely sideways in a careful but futile attempt to disguise a bald spot, and a smile that sort of crept onto his features like something that might suck eggs. It was a smile that seemed to conceal rather than express amusement. He looked exactly like what he was, a high-priced criminal lawyer who could connive and arrange the best possible deals for his clients. Phil couldn't have afforded him on his own; Singer was on a retainer in New Jersey.

"Trying to trick my client into giving up his rights?" he asked, using the weasel smile even though he was serious about his question.

"Sure," Oxman told him. "We can't shut him up. Something about shooting the president."

Singer left the oily grin on, introduced himself formally, and officially told them he was representing Phil Malloy. Then he sat down next to Phil. Tobin sat down across the table from Phil. Oxman remained standing.

"They say they're from Homicide," Phil said.

Singer looked alarmed, but only for an instant. "I thought this was a possession charge," he said.

"It is," Oxman said.

"So. You think my client knows something about a murder," Singer said. "You want him to tell you what that something is, in exchange for dropping the possession charge." Quick little bastard. He didn't have time to fence with them, he was letting them know. Get to the point; busy, important attorney they were dealing with here, representing bigger fish than Phil Malloy.

"Dropping the charge?" Oxman said, pretending to be thoughtful. "Well, I don't know about that . . ."

"Don't be a hard-on, Sergeant."

"It's not up to me to make any deals," Oxman said.

"I suspect that at this point it is. I think the matter's been cleared. I think that's why Mr. Malloy was arrested in the first place."

"That wouldn't change anything," Tobin said.

Singer nodded. Light glanced off the bald spot beneath strands of greasy black hair. "No, it wouldn't," he said. "May I talk to my client alone?"

"Sure," Oxman said.

He and Tobin left the room.

They waited about ten minutes, then returned and took up exactly the same positions. Singer and Phil appeared not to have moved at all. Everyone was being very careful now.

"Mr. Malloy says he knows nothing about a murder," Singer said.

Oxman put out a palm and propped himself against the wall. "It's the people he deals with who might know about murder," he said.

Singer's dark eyes shifted between the two detectives. His mind must be going like a rat in a cage, Oxman thought. Phil rested his arm on the table and leaned forward. The table wobbled and he withdrew the arm and sat back.

"This has nothing to do with drugs," Oxman said, and watched Singer relax. His real clients in New Jersey weren't the supposed killers. The establishment wasn't being threatened.

Singer said, "If Mr. Malloy cooperates, will the possession charge be dropped?"

"If he cooperates fully," Oxman said.

Singer looked at Phil, who looked back eagerly but with doubt on his rounded features.

"Lance Jardeen," Tobin said. "Tell us what you know about him."

Singer nodded, giving the okay.

Phil shrugged. "He's an old guy I sometimes run errands for, is all. Lives in the Waywind, where I work in maintenance."

"No bullshit, now," Oxman cautioned.

"I really do work at the Waywind."

"Your boy's gonna log some jug time," Tobin said, "if he don't loosen up."

"You deliver drugs to Jardeen," Oxman said. "That's what we want confirmed."

"I want our deal in writing," Singer said.

Tobin let out a long breath. "Fuckin' writing, no less."

Singer smiled. "That's how it is, business being business." He reached into his thin black attaché case. "I've got a form."

"Jesus," Tobin said, "he really does."

Singer made a few initialed changes on an agreement of immunity-in-exchange-for-information, then handed copies to Oxman and Tobin.

Oxman read his copy, wadded it tightly into a ball, and tossed it onto the table. "You're going to have to take our word that nothing said here gets outside this room. We're working a murder case; we don't give a damn about this piss-ant junkie delivery boy."

Phil looked injured. Singer's expression didn't change. He considered, tapping his gold pinky ring lightly on the table.

"The choice is that or Narcotics puts Phil away until the twenty-first century," Oxman said.

Singer said, "You're a hard man, Sergeant."

"Honest one, too."

"And your friend?"

"I vouch for him."

"Means nothing."

"Of course not. But you've got no alternative but to buy what I say."

Singer looked at Phil. "I think you better tell them what they want to know," he said.

"You believe these guys?" Phil asked.

"Yes. And I know the room's not wired for sound or tape." Again the creepy smile. "I've checked these things out, Mr. Malloy. And as the sergeant promised, it's talk and walk. I believe him. And we can deny the conversation if he breaks his word."

"Yeah," Phil said, "okay," liking the idea of walking out of the station that day.

"Lance Jardeen," Oxman repeated.

"He pays me and I deliver drugs to him," Phil said.

"And Marv Egan?"

Phil glanced at Singer, who nodded.

"Same deal with Egan," Phil said.

Tobin said, "Tell us what you know about them."

Phil thought for a moment. "Just a couple of burned-out old guys. Actors. But they ain't acted in years."

"Where'd you meet them?" Oxman asked.

"A shooting gallery. That's where people go to shoot up on drugs."

"We know. In the Village?"

Phil looked worried.

"Don't answer," Oxman said.

"I seen 'em now and then at The Last Reel," Phil said.

"What's that?"

"Place down around Eighth and Broadway, where a lotta washed-up show-business types hang out. I mean really washed up. They get a buzz on, mostly on cheap liquor, and bitch about things in general."

"Who else do you deliver to, who hangs out at The Lost Reel?" Oxman asked.

"*Last* Reel," Phil corrected. He couldn't keep his eyes off Singer now. He was nervous.

"Who else?" Oxman repeated.

"Nobody. Not anymore."

"Why not anymore?"

"Well, the guy was killed, I read in the papers. Friend of Jardeen's and Egan's. I seen 'em drinking together lotsa times."

Oxman looked over at Tobin, who was studying the burnt matches and butts in the beanbag ashtray.

"Lassiter," Phil said. "Another old actor. Burt Lassiter, I think his name was. Is it his murder you guys are trying to solve?"

"Among others," Oxman said. Singer was observing him with exaggerated casualness. "Did you hear about his death from Egan? Jardeen?" Oxman asked.

"Naw, it was in all the papers. You know, the way he was the 'Shadowtown' vampire. But I guess that turned out not to be so, huh?"

"Seems that way," Tobin said.

"You mean Jardeen or Egan didn't even mention Lassiter's death?" Oxman asked.

"Nope. And I didn't bring it up. Shit, I only saw those guys a few times a week." He glared at Tobin. "And one of 'em, *you* had to be there."

"The breaks," Tobin said, pulling his gaze away from the ashtray and smiling at Phil.

"What did the three old actors talk about when they were together?" Oxman asked.

Phil put on an earnest expression. "Now, that I don't know. I mean, I wasn't one of their buddies, you see. Ours was a strictly business kinda relationship. You gotta be show-biz if you wanna get treated human by those people at The Last Reel. Tell you true, I don't even understand what they're telling each other half the time. Show-business words and sayings. And show business is all them has-beens at The Reel ever talk about, like they was still getting movie parts instead of scrounging for a living."

Oxman stared up at the ceiling for a few minutes. Then he lowered his eyes again to look at Phil. "That's it," he said.

"That's it?" Phil said unbelievingly.

"Uh-hm. You can go. Thanks, Mr. Malloy."

"Come on," Singer said, and stood up.

Phil grinned, just like Mickey Rooney after Andy Hardy and the gang had raised enough money with their play to save the starving widow.

He stood and said, "Thank *you*, Sergeant Oxman."

"Let's go," Singer insisted. "The sergeant might be fickle." He shepherded Phil out the door ahead of him. Didn't say good-bye.

"What do you think, Ox?" Tobin asked, when they were alone.

"I think tomorrow's Saturday," Oxman said.

"Huh?"

"Never mind." Oxman extended his arms and stretched the kinks out of his back. Shadowtown Productions would be closed down for the weekend tomorrow, he knew. It provided a perfect opportunity to snoop around the place without interruption and see what evidence against Zach Denton was available. But it would be better not to mention to Tobin what he had in mind. Tobin would cluck at him like a moralistic old maid and suggest Oxman was going out of his way to nail Zach Denton.

Oxman wasn't sure; Tobin might be right.

Phil Malloy—10:15 P.M.

Fuckin' cops! Phil was still shaking, even after downing half a bottle of Laurel Springs bourbon in his room at the Waywind. They'd sure as hell messed up his evening. Murder, was it? He looked at the bottle on the table by the bed; that was the only thing he'd ever killed—a bottle.

That and a toke or two of Mexican brown. He could use a hit now, that was for sure. Instead all he had on hand, all he could afford, was booze. Well, a man had to make do with—

The door opened.

Phil sat straight up on the sagging mattress, where he'd been reclining and half-watching something on television; it had a lot of sexy-looking women in it, so he'd left the set tuned to that channel and put down the remote control and picked up the bottle.

But he wasn't looking at the women on TV now; he was staring at a tall guy dressed in a dark overcoat. He had a long blue muffler wrapped loosely around the lower half of his face, like he didn't want to be recognized. Or on the way in he hadn't unwound it all the way. Not that it mattered; his face was in shadow anyway, what with the only illumination in the room coming from the flickering TV screen.

"Who the fuck are you?" Phil asked, trying to bluff away his fear. It had all happened so suddenly, the way the guy burst into the room, it didn't seem quite real. It might have been something happening on TV to somebody else.

"I came to see you about that talk you had with the police," the man said softly, from behind the blue muffler.

Phil thought back through his alcoholic haze; he'd locked the door he was sure of it.

"How'd you get in?" he asked.

"I got a knack with locks," the man said, and crossed over to stand near the bed.

Phil didn't like the guy looming over him like that, so he climbed up out of bed and stood facing him. The intruder was an easy six inches taller than Phil's five-foot-ten.

"So whaddya want?" Phil asked.

"To talk," the man said, "like the cops."

"So sure, I'll talk," Phil said, relaxing a little. He was getting some idea where this guy was from.

"You'll listen," the man told him, still in that soft voice. He had on black gloves, Phil noticed.

"This is my place," Phil said, determined not to take any more shit than he had to. He'd had a rough night already and wasn't in the mood for any more shoving around, with him the shovee. He'd done what Singer said, nothing more. He had nothing to hide or be ashamed of, did he?

"Yeah, your tough luck," the man said, unperturbed. "Thing is, Phil, it's no good you chatting to the law. It's no good them being onto you. Once they stick to a fella they keep on sticking, like Velcro. They won't shake, not the cops."

"You're from Jersey," Phil said.

"Half the people in Manhattan are from Jersey," the man said. "This is an island, Phil. A small island where once somebody like you comes to the attention of the law they try to bend him. They *do* bend him."

"I won't bend." So that was it! Phil tried to laugh and almost choked. Nerves! He didn't really want to laugh anyway at a time like this. He *sure* as hell didn't! He said, "I don't cooperate with cops. Don't matter how small Manhattan is."

"It matters."

"I got friends, though. They know the ins and outs and can keep the cops off me. Like the song says, 'No man is an island.' Jack Jones, I think, sang it. Or maybe The Commodores."

"Sounds like Barry Manilow shit to me," the man said. "This is an island, full of millions of people who're islands themselves, just like you. Only now there's a bridge to you, Phil."

Phil wanted to bolt for the door, but his legs were trembling, threatening to buckle. The effects of the bourbon were fading fast.

"You think I don't know why you're here? Listen, we can talk this out!"

"Sorry, Phil, the world don't work that way."

"It can! There's as many worlds as there are people. All them islands you mentioned. You'd be surprised what can be worked out!"

The tall man's eyes darted to the TV and then back to Phil. "You watch that crap?" he asked, as if amazed. Guy was a snob.

"Yeah, sometimes."

"Then you deserve what you're getting," the man said. There was a metallic click and his gloved hand darted forward so fast Phil thought it might have been an illusion. Like a magic trick.

Suddenly there was a numbness all over Phil's body, except for something very cold low and deep in his chest. There shouldn't be any coldness way in there, his dazed mind realized. "Wha—what is this?" he asked indignantly. Not understanding. Not wanting to understand. What was going on here couldn't be real. Impossible!

"This is death," the man said, and Phil saw him lean forward and twist his right arm and hand that seemed attached to Phil's chest.

Nothing happened at first. Then the room got dim, then black along the edges of Phil's vision. The black area closed in, gradually at first, then very fast. Faster.

The pain! . . .

Scene 6

Art Tobin—1:45 P.M.

Tobin liked the way things had been breaking lately. He could sense that the case was drawing to some kind of close, in the way an old war-horse senses when it's headed toward the barn. Nothing factual, but a tightening of the psyche, a familiarity with the landscape. As if the subconscious mind were operating on a sublimely logical level impossible to the conscious; fitting facts together, shuffling through mental file cards and selecting and rearranging until finally a pattern appeared.

He had a feeling that, if he could delve into his subconscious, he'd get some inkling of the meaning of the murders and the vampire scare, and the "Shadowtown" mania that had swept the country and boosted TV ratings—and network advertising revenue.

Elliot Leroy didn't understand the importance of those ratings, and the immense sums of money that pivoted on a tiny percentage of audience share. Ox wasn't a show-biz kind of guy. Maybe that was why Lana Spence was hot for him. Or pretending she was. Ox was something different for Lana the black widow; a diversion. Poor Ox.

Bullshit! Tobin smiled. Lots of men would gladly trade places with Ox in Lana Spence's affections, whether she was sincere or acting. What the hell, the lady was a star.

As Tobin left his car and walked toward Marv Egan's crummy apartment building, he concentrated again on the specifics of the case rather than on Lana Spence. Couldn't blame a vampire for nibbling on that neck, though, he thought, before he cleared the vision from his mind. Tobin the black vampire, having a hell of a good time. White meat and red blood, all the same to Count Tobin.

223

The background investigation of Lana and Burt Lassiter had led to a link—other than Lana—between Lassiter, Egan, and Jardeen. They were all down-and-out semijunkies who frequented the same haunts and even shared the same supplier. Tobin was sure that if he questioned Egan and Jardeen again, carefully, he'd learn something pertinent. He could let them know that drug charges might be brought against Phil Malloy, and good old Phil might talk and the drug investigation might spill over to them. Better to nip that in the bud, Tobin would assure them, and keep the police department's attention focused on the "Shadowtown" case.

He stood in the vestibule that smelled like aged paint and boiled cabbage and pushed the button beneath Egan's brass mailbox.

There was no answer on the intercom. No sound from up above.

Tobin stepped back and shook his head. The damned bell and intercom had worked the last time he was here. But that was last time. Maybe vandals had gotten to it. Or maybe Egan wasn't home. That was the most likely explanation, though Tobin didn't want to believe it. He knew he'd have to take the stairs and check, and he didn't want to do that. He'd rather simply leave the building and drive over to try to catch Jardeen at home and question him first. But he wouldn't; he'd climb the stairs and knock on Egan's door. Every year, it was harder to be a cop.

"You policeman?" a voice with an Oriental accent asked from the lower landing.

Tobin moved away from the bank of mailboxes and buttons and looked up. A frail Chinaman in his sixties, with hooded eyes and a thatch of white hair over his forehead, was peering down at him. He had a scraggly little beard that looked like a handful of bean sprouts he'd pasted on the point of his chin.

"I'm police," Tobin said. "How'd you know?"

The Chinaman smiled. Silly question. Tobin smiled back.

"I'm Sam Lee," the slender little man said. "The building super. I saw you talking with Mr. Egan other day. Ah, I knew you were police."

"And you're nosy," Tobin said. "You want to know what's going on."

"Yes and no."

"Don't be inscrutable," Tobin said. "Out with whatever you have to say."

"Mr. Egan's gone."

"I figured that. I've been ringing his doorbell and not getting an answer. But thanks for telling me he's not home, saving me some steps."

"I don't mean not home," Lee persisted, with a concerned expression that remotely alarmed Tobin. "I mean gone. Mr. Egan's gone."

"Gone how?"

"Don't know."

"Gone where?"

"Don't know."

Damn! Tobin thought. What *did* this guy know?

"He wanted me to put a new washer in his sink faucet. I was supposed to do that this morning. I knocked on door, no one answered, so I let myself in with the pass key. Mr. Egan never minded that, honest."

"I believe you," Tobin said. "Go on."

Lee nodded, bobbing his head and smiling, as if he'd seen too many Charlie Chan movies. "I go into the apartment, see no one home. Food still on the table, half eaten, cold. No one home, though. And Mr. Egan hasn't come home."

Tobin scratched his head. "Why's that so alarming? Maybe he went out for a walk."

"No. Not without his shoes."

"Huh?"

"Mr. Egan isn't a rich man. Only pair of shoes he has is still on the floor by the bed."

"Could be he bought another pair you don't know about."

"No," Lee said. "Not likely. Mr. Egan has other things to spend his money on."

That's for sure, Tobin thought. Like cocaine or heroin or bargain booze.

"You going to check?" Lee asked.

"Let's take a look," Tobin said, and started up the stairs.

Marv Egan's tiny apartment smelled almost as bad as the vestibule. But at least there was no graffiti here. Only faded paint and peeling wallpaper.

Tobin saw what Lee meant. The brown dress shoes by the bed were old but had recently been resoled and heeled. And Egan wasn't the sort to have that done and then rush out on impulse and buy new Nikes for jogging.

"You ever seen him in any other pair of shoes?" Tobin asked.

Lee, standing a few feet inside the door, shook his head no. "Mr. Egan always dress the same. Small wardrobe."

An understatement, Tobin thought, glancing in at the tattered garments visible beyond the closet door that was hanging open. Egan probably hadn't been to Saks Fifth Avenue in weeks.

A soft dripping sound caught Tobin's attention and he stepped to the side and peered into the kitchen. Water was oozing relentlessly from the faucet and striking more water.

Tobin walked into the kitchen. The dripping faucet was a lot louder in there; he could see why Egan had wanted it repaired. There was a half glass of orange juice, an entire egg fried sunny-side up, and a whole piece of toast and full cup of coffee on the table. The meal had been there awhile. Roaches were over everything, scurrying madly as if they'd never had it so good and couldn't believe their luck. Bug heaven.

Tobin touched the back of his knuckle to the toast and egg, dipped his forefinger into the coffee. Everything was at room temperature and might have been there for a long, long time. The margarine had soaked completely into the cold toast. The yellow in the egg was unbroken; it looked like a fake egg of the sort sold in magic shops for sight gags. A roach crossed the egg white and skirted the yellow, as if obeying traffic rules on its way to the other side of the chipped plate. Tobin looked away.

"Mr. Egan ever leave suddenly before?" he asked.

"Never," Lee said. "And he told me for sure he'd be home while I fixed faucet. We were supposed to meet."

Tobin delicately peeled a loose shred of flesh from his lower lip. "You two good friends?"

"Pretty much, yes. We talk all the time, play backgammon every now and then. Mr. Egan taught me; he's good at backgammon. I'm worried about him, the way it looks like he just got up and walked out. I haven't seen him all day, and he's never gone for more than a few hours at a time."

Somebody walked across the floor of the apartment overhead. Out in the hall, an infant began to scream. A woman cursed in Spanish at the child. Doors slammed, and the building got quiet again. "Well, maybe there's nothing to worry about," Tobin said. He glanced at his watch. "It's just two o'clock, and he's only been gone since breakfast."

"No, no," Lee said. "Mr. Egan never eats breakfast. This his supper. He always eats an egg for his supper. He says it's the easiest way to keep his strength up, but I know it's all he can afford. Egg cheaper than meat. And the bed, he hasn't slept in it. He left last night and never returned."

Tobin stared at Lee. "Why didn't you tell me that in the beginning?"

Lee shrugged and said nothing, being inscrutable again.

Tobin curled his upper lip and walked around the apartment. Egan had gone suddenly and unexpectedly, all right, and hadn't left a note. That was for sure. But there might have been a logical and innocent reason. Maybe he'd been about to sit down to supper when the phone rang and he was told a relative was sick and in the hospital. Maybe he'd won the state lottery and was out considering Rolls Royces. Maybe.

Tobin pulled open a few drawers. Egan didn't own much. He probably really was too poor for a second pair of shoes, even without the drugs and liquor that drained his meager finances.

In one of the kitchen drawers under the sink, Tobin found where Egan kept his paperwork. A few receipts for groceries, an unpaid electric bill, threats of legal action from a department store unless Egan settled his account, some old letters.

Tobin read a couple of the letters. They were all from a theatrical agent named Ruthley and were dated in the early seventies. Business letters. None of what was written interested Tobin.

He tossed the letters back into the drawer and began looking through some yellowed old business cards. The usual thing: a card from a liquor store over on West Forty-seventh, one from an insurance agent in Jersey, another from a writer named Collins who'd scribbled that he was interested in doing Egan's show-business biography as soon as he was finished with a biography of one of the Three Stooges. Tobin smiled at that one; he liked the Stooges. And a biography didn't have to be dull just because it was about someone relatively obscure. Egan might make it as a subject. After all, he'd put in sack time with Lana Spence. Some world it was. Not quite real at times.

Tobin was about to turn away when he noticed that the liquor-store card had something scrawled in pencil on the back. The writing was faint and barely legible. It was a phone number, nothing more.

But it was a number Tobin had seen before. Phone numbers were something he seldom completely forgot.

He stood staring at the card, flicking its edge on the sink counter, listening to the little snapping sound it made.

Then he remembered.

It was Harry Overbeck's home number.

Tobin stopped playing with the card on the chipped porcelain and stood watching the water drip into the puddle in the bottom of the sink, creating ripples. Overbeck and Egan, Egan and Jardeen, Jardeen and Lassiter. Moe, Larry and Curly. And Lana Spence.

"Christ!" he said softly. He stuffed the card in his pocket and hurried from the apartment, almost knocking over Sam Lee.

"About Mr. Egan—" Lee called behind him.

"I'll take care of it," Tobin said. "I'll take care of it."

He broke out onto the street at a fast walk and crossed in the middle of the block to get to his car. He hoped the tie-in between Overbeck and Egan meant what he thought it might. The way to get a better reading on that was to talk to Overbeck.

This was Saturday. Shadowtown Productions would be shut down, but maybe he could catch Overbeck at home. Tobin didn't want to phone first to make sure; he wanted Overbeck surprised to see him.

He ignored a horn blast by a furious cab driver who'd almost run over him, then he slid behind the steering wheel of the department car and started the engine. The cabbie had pulled to the curb and cranked down the taxi's window and was swearing at him, but Tobin was barely aware of it.

He didn't use the cherry light or siren, but he drove fast toward Overbeck's Central Park South apartment.

Arthur Sales—1:15 P.M.

Sales strode down the block and entered the Clover Lounge. Except for a young couple in a back booth, there were no other customers. Sales mounted a stool near the front of the bar, away from the early-boozing lovers, and tapped a quarter on the side of a pretzel bowl.

Irish Jamie swiveled his head around and smiled. "Hey, Mr. Sales!" He ambled behind the bar in Sales's direction. His dark hair was particularly stringy and greasy today, and he had a complexion that made the surface of the moon look smooth. Yet Sales envied him for his youth. "Early for you, ain't it, Mr. Sales? Come to think of it, I ain't ever seen you in here before on a Saturday. Special occasion?"

"Not hardly, Jamie." Sales and Wendy had arguments all too often these days for them to be called special occasions. Though this morning's had been especially cruel and mutually destructive. It would never be the same for Wendy and him, Sales had realized. She'd never be able to forgive him for his affair with Lana Spence. Lana had destroyed his marriage as surely as if she'd poured acid on it, and it had eaten away for months and then struck something vital.

"Mr. Sales?"

Sales snapped out of his bitter remembrance of the morning.

"Here you go, Mr. Sales." Jamie set the usual Scotch-on-the-rocks in front of Sales, centering it on its coaster. "You okay?"

"Couldn't be better," Sales said, flashing Jamie his best actor smile. The dashing grin he'd used in a hundred leading roles. Jamie bought it and moved a few feet down the bar to assume an attitude that invited conversation but at the same time accepted silence.

Sales had been better. Much better. Wendy had accused him of drinking too much lately. She'd harped at him, as if he were disgustingly ill. As if he were some kind of mental case or genuine alcoholic.

Sales had snapped back at her. The argument had gotten nasty then, and they'd both known they were on the familiar track toward loathing and exhaustion. There was no stopping or turning around as they traded accusations, recriminations, insults, and ugly threats. The interaction of their lives had produced something grotesque and unquenchable. And impossible to kill.

Today's argument had been about Sales's drinking, so naturally he'd left the apartment and come straight here, to dimness and comparative anonymity and expensive Scotch.

"Jamie?" Sales said.

"Yes, sir?"

"You ever known me to drink way, way past my limits?"

Jamie wiped his hands on a red towel and stared innocently.

" 'Course not, Mr. Sales."

Good lad, Jamie. "Notice me looking kind of old lately?" Sales asked. *Notice me dying by inches?*

Jamie grinned. "You? Old? Come off it, Mr. Sales. Guys like you don't really get old till they hit eighty."

Sales glanced at his reflection in the back-bar mirror and found that his vision was partially blocked by the cash register. He caught only a glimpse of flawlessly groomed hair over an ear, the curve of his right cheek. Good bones in that cheek. He still had that; flesh eventually sagged, but good bones were forever. And ever and ever.

He knocked down the rest of his Scotch and ordered another. The lounge was soothingly dim, but the sun was bright outside. He didn't like the idea of going back out there. He decided he'd nurse his next drink along slowly and not leave for a while.

Maybe not for a long time.

He'd just sit here and soak up good Scotch.

The public wondered what soap-opera stars did with their real lives on weekends, Sales had read somewhere. Well, this is it, baby, he thought, propping his elbows on the bar.

This is it.

Lana Spence—1:00 P.M.

It had become a Saturday ritual. A few lines of coke, a warm bubble bath, that was what unwound Lana and built confidence when she really needed it. And God knew she needed it now, after yesterday's conversation with Sy Youngerman. After what she'd learned they were doing to her. She'd been awake most of the night and had slept only fitfully this morning, dozing from vision to vision. It was depressing. Dreams; she hated to dream. Write her out of the show, would they? Make that flat-chested, brush-headed Jean Richards the "Shadowtown" vixen, a sexy female vampire. How implausible! How unfair! But that one was no dream; it was real. The bastards!

But Lana knew they could do what they wanted with her part. With her. It was a crock of shit, but that was the way it was. How the business went. The creative people were at the mercy of the incompetents who ran the show. What a pity that was for the fans as well as for professionals like Lana. Maybe it wouldn't be that way for her if Manny Brokton were still alive.

Lana told herself to relax. It was an easy instruction to follow in the private, quiet bathroom.

She slipped deeper into her bubble bath and felt the warm water engulf her breasts. The suds touched the tip of her chin. She extended her tongue and tasted soap.

Right now "Shadowtown" seemed important, but it wasn't the sun her world revolved around. She had to admit there was even a certain modicum of sense in what Sy had said about emphasizing the occult aspects of the show. That's what the viewers wanted, after the vampire murders. The media, friend and enemy, having their effect, playing the occult and real-life murders for everything possible. And a hell of a lot was possible with a story like that.

For a moment the water seemed cool, and Lana shivered as she remembered the dark figure that had appeared outside her door and obviously intended to kill her. With effort, she rejected that image.

Then she felt safe again. Her police protection was down in the lobby. Hortensia, her part-time maid, was cleaning the apartment while Lana relaxed in the tiled sunken tub. If anyone tried to kill Lana they'd surely murder Hortensia first, and Hortensia would no doubt scream. Lana would be alerted. She couldn't help but smile, even in her sudden distress, when she realized exactly what that meant. She'd at least be able to climb out of the tub and die with her robe on rather than be turned into an obscene spectacle for the tabloids, photographed dead in her bubble bath. Soap star meets soapy end.

Morbid thoughts, she told herself. But who could blame her for thinking them, the way things had gone for her lately?

There was a knock on the door. "Miss Spence?"

Lana turned her face toward the voice in alarm, then felt her heartbeat slow. Only Hortensia.

"Miss Spence?"

"Come in, Hortensia."

The door eased open and the maid stepped in, not shyly. She'd been in the large bathroom before when Lana was bathing. To ask about having the next week off, as Lana recalled.

Lana noticed Hortensia staring at her. The maid had been with her almost a year now, and had been recommended by her previous employer, a female country-western singer who was a well-known dyke. Lana was sure something had gone on there.

Hortensia was a tiny, dark-eyed Puerto Rican woman in her thirties, with lean hips and perfect brown skin. Lana watched the maid lick her lips. Deep, Latin eyes and delicate features took on a fixated expression.

Lana had occasionally toyed with the idea of making it with another woman. Why not? Anything for escape.

Maybe someday, she thought, and raised her body slightly so her nipples became visible through the suds.

"Well, what is it, Hortensia?" Precisely the right tone of detachment and impatience in her voice. Her secretary voice from the light comedy with Gig Young too many years ago.

"Uh, Mr. Youngerman was on the phone."

"Was?"

"I told him you couldn't come to the phone right then and he said to just leave you a message." She was staring at Lana's exposed breasts as the bubbles settled.

"What was the message, Hortensia?"

"He said he'd be doing some work in his 'Shadowtown' office, and if you can, will you come to see him in an hour."

"Thank you," Lana said, and slid back down the gentle curve of the tub, deeper into the warm bubbles.

"Is that all?" Hortensia asked.

"Yes. Please close the door as you leave."

Alone again, Lana mulled over Youngerman's message. It could be that Sy and Harry had a change of heart. Or a change of mind about what would make them the most money. Anyway, if Youngerman wanted to see her, it might very well be to take back what was said about writing her out of the show. Maybe Manny *had* protected her with fine print in her contract. Fine print had been Manny Brokton's specialty. They should engrave his headstone that way, Lana thought, with letters chiseled so tiny and fine anyone would need a magnifying glass to read them.

Lana sat up straight and began climbing out of the tub. She slipped on the smooth tile and dropped back down onto her bare ass, causing quite a splash. Very undignified. Hell with it.

The door opened again; no knock this time. "You okay, Miss Spence?" Hortensia asked, sticking her head in and doing a good job of looking worried.

"Just fine," Lana said. She flashed her wicked Delia Lane grin. Hortensia could probably get off on Delia, all right. Delia had no scruples whatsoever.

"I'm fine," Lana reiterated.

Hortensia cleared her throat and backed out, closing the door behind her. After a while, the hollow drone of the vacuum cleaner found its way into the quiet bathroom.

Lana began another effort to lift herself out of the soothing water. Then she changed her mind. She smiled and settled back down. The water was so warm and comfortable, and she still had a bit of a buzz on.

Sometimes reality seemed to be falling away from her, she reflected.

Possibly she'd played Delia Lane too long. But that wasn't all there was to it. Getting older had something to do with it, Lana decided. Aging was particularly difficult for an actress like her—not that she wasn't still one of the industry's truly beautiful and desirable women. But she wasn't all that she'd been, of course. Maybe that was the thing about Oxman that attracted her; he was so solid, beyond being bothered by mortal agonies. Men like Oxman were like sturdy oak trees that matured and then seemed impervious to time. She tossed back her head and smiled. Was there something phallic in that sturdy oak-tree analogy? Probably, she admitted. She ran her hands over the swell of her firm breasts, shivering as her soapy palms massaged her erect nipples. She sank deeper into the warm water and thought about E. L. Oxman. Drugs, sex, and bubble baths. The great escapes.

"Sometimes I feel like I'm someone else," she said softly, startling herself with the sound of her own voice. *Who? Delia Lane?*

Lana closed her eyes, opened them, and stared at the gold-faced clock on the vanity. Time seemed so disjointed and unpredictable lately. That was why she'd been late so often on the set. But she had plenty of time to dress and get to Shadowtown Productions to meet Sy Youngerman.

She raised a languid hand and flicked a few glistening bubbles out of the tub. One of them rode the air, gleaming, and then popped.

Let Sy wait. He'd said an hour, so Lana decided to appear at the "Shadowtown" studios in an hour and a half. She'd show him she didn't really need the goddamn part. Didn't need Sy, or anyone else, for her career to keep on thriving. She was a star, and she still burned bright!

Well, maybe she'd make it an hour and fifteen minutes.

Overbeck looked more rumpled than usual today, Tobin thought, when the "Shadowtown" producer invited him into his high-rise Central Park South apartment. He had on a camel-colored sweater, beige corduroy slacks, and tan suede shoes. A vision in brown. Everything but the shoes were wrinkled, and a checked, twisted shirt collar protruded unevenly out of the wooly sweater and writhed around Overbeck's pudgy neck like an affectionate boa constrictor.

"I guess, to the police, Saturday's like any other workday," Overbeck said.

"Yeah, crime never takes a day off." Tobin moved inside and shut the door behind him. "Crime's like that. Inconsiderate."

Overbeck stepped down into his sunken living room and crossed the plush carpet to where the sliding glass door to his balcony was open about six inches. Tobin noticed a small telescope on the balcony's ledge and wondered if Overbeck spent much time out there, spying on his faraway neighbors across the green rectangle of Central Park. Was that, in fact, what Overbeck had been doing before Tobin arrived? There was a vaguely guilty expression on Overbeck's flushed features, as if he might have been watching something intensely personal through a distant window. Voyeurism was a pastime for a lot of New Yorkers.

"Great day out there," Tobin said, probing. "Nice and clear."

Overbeck smiled. "I wouldn't know; I was just about to step outside and check on the weather when the doorbell rang."

For the first time Tobin noticed a hardness, a sheen, to Overbeck's eyes. Did he spend his off days doing drugs? Did he know Phil the way

Egan, Jardeen, and Lassiter had? One thing he had in common with them: He seemed to hate Lana Spence.

"You didn't come here to talk about the weather, Detective Tobin," Overbeck said. There was a hint of trepidation in his voice. And Tobin couldn't remember anyone else outside the department ever referring to him as "Detective Tobin."

"Nope, I didn't," Tobin said. He stepped down into the living room and sauntered over to where Overbeck stood near the sliding door.

Overbeck seemed bothered by Tobin's nearness. He swallowed, then ran a hand over his brush-cut hair. "Why *are* you here?" he asked.

"Because I know," Tobin said, playing on Overbeck's nerves.

Overbeck feigned impatience, though actually he wasn't at all eager to hear what Tobin was about to say. "Know *what*?" he asked, pacing toward the balcony and then back. He did want to hear it, but then again he didn't. Agony.

"You on something, Mr. Overbeck?"

"On something? Wha—why, no! You mean drugs, don't you? Hell, no! I don't do drugs. You don't last long in my business if you're part of the drug scene."

Toby almost laughed at that one. He liked the way this conversation was going, all right. He decided not to tell Overbeck about his phone number turning up in Egan's apartment; he'd let Overbeck think he had something even more damning than that.

"Are you going to tell me what it is you know?" Overbeck asked. "Or are you going to search the apartment for controlled substances?"

Ah, Tobin thought, a show of bravado. He said, "I know about your connection."

"Connection?"

"With Egan, Jardeen, and Lassiter."

Wow! There went the bravado. Overbeck's face changed from ruddy to chalk-colored. He palmed his crewcut again, as if trying to make it stand a certain way and set his world right. "Burt Lassiter? The man who died?"

"The same," Tobin said. "And Marv Egan and Lance Jardeen. All former lovers of Lana Spence. As you are, Harry." Tobin liked the "Harry" touch; Harry and Detective Tobin.

"Is that your connection between us?" Overbeck asked. "Lana Spence?"

"I wouldn't be here if that was all there was to it," Tobin said. He noticed that a big console television was on in a corner, playing a tape of a "Shadowtown" episode. Lana Spence herself was rolling around on a mattress with a young man wearing only swimming trunks. They both looked as if they were having one fine time. The camera zoomed in on Lana's half-closed eyes and she rolled them back as if experiencing an orgasm. Just like real life, Tobin thought. Almost, anyway.

Overbeck stuffed his fists into the pockets of his baggy corduroys. "I don't exactly know what we're talking about here," he said, but not with much conviction.

Tobin took a chance and dived in. "You better figure it out, Mr. Overbeck; you're up for three counts of homicide."

The camera was pulling away from Lana and the young guy on the bed. Suddenly they were gone and replaced by a reed-thin woman munching a popular brand of diet cookies. She bit into one and rolled back her eyes the way Lana had.

Overbeck broke. By degrees. He seemed to shrink into his wrinkled clothes and age ten years right there in front of Tobin, a year every second. He stumbled to the low sofa and slumped down into a corner of the soft cushions. He was having a problem catching his breath. His lips were parted in shock.

Tobin waited until the rasping breathing leveled out. Then he said, "What's happened to Marv Egan? Where is he?"

Overbeck gazed up at him with zombie eyes. "Egan? What do you mean? Is he missing?"

"I didn't say that," Tobin told him. "I asked you where he is."

Overbeck bowed his head and buried his face in his hands. A vein in his forehead was pulsating with blue ferocity. "I don't know where Egan is, and that's the truth."

Tobin sat down beside him. What he didn't want was for Overbeck to ask if he was being formally charged. To clam up and wait for his lawyer before he talked. But Overbeck was obviously consumed by guilt and not thinking straight. Fine, Tobin thought. Smooths the way.

Very gently he asked, "What else is the truth, Harry?"

Overbeck pulled his hands away from his face, then flung himself even deeper into the cushions, so the back of his head was resting on the sofa and he was staring through watery eyes at the ceiling. As if there might be something playing on a screen up there.

Tobin was going to hear it now, at last; he could feel it. Overbeck was ripe to talk, had to give it release before it devoured him from the gut out. That was the way guilt worked. Tobin had seen it this way in hundreds of interrogations.

"You're right," Overbeck said. "The four of us did this together."

"You, Lassiter, Egan, and Jardeen," Tobin said, not asking a question, but as if he knew and was merely commenting.

"Yeah," Overbeck said in a weary voice. "Those three—washed-up old actors—were into drugs. They went to the same shooting gallery down in the Village to trip out. They used to talk about the good days, when they were working and prosperous. And they talked about Lana, about how they hated her. They concluded, maybe rightly so, that she was to blame for their ruined careers. After Allan Ames's death, they decided to use some of their acting skills to terrorize Lana with threatening notes and glimpses of Ames's vampire character Edgar Grume. It started as a practical joke.

"Then, when Egan was on the set to plant one of the letters, the watchman, Vince McGreery, caught him. And Egan panicked and killed poor Vince.

"After that, he and Lassiter and Jardeen blamed Lana not only for the loss of their careers and dignity; they blamed her for making them murderers."

"They told you this?" Tobin asked.

Overbeck nodded, still staring at the ceiling. "The night of McGreery's murder, I'd slipped away from Sy's party to get something from my office, and I saw Egan outside the studio. In the Edgar Grume costume. Lassiter was with him. They told me what had happened; they knew I hated Lana as they did. I thought about what they told me—thought about it too long. It would have looked funny if I'd gone to the police and changed my story about the night of the murder. Instead of turning them over to the law, I struck a deal. I wanted them to continue the Edgar Grume appearances, to generate publicity and boost 'Shadowtown' ratings, which had begun to slip." He rolled his head on the sofa back and gazed beseechingly at Tobin. "After all, Vince was already dead; what did it matter?"

Tobin shrugged as if he might agree; not breaking the momentum, keeping Overbeck talking. He knew confession was a catharsis and everything would come out of the festering conscience, if only he was patient and there were no interruptions.

"Then they tried to take advantage of me," Overbeck said.

"Lassiter came to me and demanded a role in 'Shadowtown' in exchange for his silence about the McGreery murder. He said nobody could prove he was at the studio when the murder occurred, and he'd tell the police Marv Egan had confided in him and confessed while drugged up. I went to Egan and told him Lassiter was breaking. Egan went to see Lassiter and they quarreled, and Egan killed him."

"To keep him from talking?"

"Of course," Overbeck said. "Lassiter was an aging egotist who'd gone completely around the bend. He would have confessed eventually just for the publicity."

Tobin thought about that. Lassiter had been an old actor with an actor's compulsions. "Probably," he agreed.

"So he had to die, don't you understand?"

"Yeah, I guess so," Tobin said.

"But somebody frightened Egan out of Lassiter's room before he could get the Edgar Grume costume from Lassiter's closet. And the police found it. It was like Egan and I were in on Lassiter's murder together. No turning back for me then, no way at all. So I decided to keep going and make the best of it. I doctored one of the 'Shadow-town' tapes to include a background glimpse of Egan in Edgar Grume makeup. That was a mistake."

"It sure boosted ratings," Tobin said.

"But it also really got Egan going. He began to live the role. He killed Manny Brokton, whom he'd always hated—along with half the people in show business—and punctured Brokton's neck with the bent tines of a fork. The idea was to build on the publicity and vampire myth and perpetuate the case's occult aspect that was confounding the police. And you *were* confounded. Admit it."

"Confounded," Tobin conceded.

Overbeck sat forward and began laughing in a way that scared Tobin. The producer's eyes were so animated they seemed about to leap from their sockets like separate, vibrant beings. Here was a glimpse of absolute madness. It was a madness that lay, deep down, in everyone, even Tobin, and he couldn't look directly at it.

Then the laughter burbled to silence and Overbeck was serious again. "Do you know what fools soap-opera fans are, Detective Tobin?"

"Tell me," Tobin said.

"To capitalize on all the vampire publicity, we're introducing a new character, Graveman, another vampire with sex appeal. They're going to watch the show in the millions and millions! Graveman is my idea, and it's going to work!'' Overbeck gave that laugh again, a sound like thin glass breaking. "Don't you get it?'' he almost shrieked. "Graveman! Shuffle the letters around and they spell Marv Egan.'' He laughed again, sending ice up Tobin's spine. "My idea! Mine! And nobody out there would catch on!'' He became solemn again, instantly. "Not just a joke though—not at all. It would keep Egan in line, keep him from getting extortion ideas like Lassiter. He could hardly say he hadn't been involved in the murders when all the time I had a character on the show named after him. Don't you see—that proved he was an accomplice and I anticipated trouble from him, that we were partners in murder and I feared him and needed some insurance against his greed and vampire evil. Against his insanity.''

Tobin stood up. He'd heard enough. And he was afraid Overbeck might lose control completely and make things difficult. "Well, I think we better go uptown, Harry.''

"Uptown? Oh! Sure. I see what you mean. To the police station. Usually the station's downtown on television. You know, the writers use that expression too much these days. On our show, too, though it isn't a police show. But you use a similar expression in real life, I see. There's not as much difference as some people think. The soaps are like parallel universes. You ever think of them that way?''

"No,'' Tobin said, waiting for Overbeck to stand. Was this going to be a problem? He didn't want a hassle, didn't want to have to wrestle Overbeck to the floor and use the cuffs.

The phone rang.

Overbeck stared at it as if he'd heard a sound from a thousand miles away. One that didn't quite make sense. He wasn't going to answer it.

Tobin walked over and lifted the receiver.

"Harry?''

The voice sounded familiar. With a dash of desperation in it. "No, this is Art Tobin.'' Tobin noticed the commercial was over and Lana was back on the bed with the guy in swimming trunks.

"Tobin . . . the detective. Good! Great! This is Sy Youngerman, Tobin. Listen, why I called, I phoned Lana Spence and her maid said Lana wasn't home, that she'd gotten a call from *me* asking if she'd meet me at the 'Shadowtown' studio. But I never made that call, Tobin. What I want to know is, did Harry?''

"When was she supposed to meet you?" Tobin asked.

"Now. She's there now. And it's Saturday; the place is closed down and empty today. Ask Harry and see if he called her, will you?"

"Sure," Tobin said. He put down the phone and turned.

Overbeck was gone.

"Damn!" Tobin said, cursing his carelessness. His glance flicked to the door to the hall, but he immediately realized he'd have glimpsed Overbeck in the corner of his vision if he'd sneaked out that way. Overbeck might have gone into the bedroom.

Tobin took a few steps in that direction. Then, with sudden cold paralysis, he made a more accurate guess. He stood motionless and listened to the ocean roar of blood in his ears.

Within a second he could move again, and he ran across the living room to the sliding glass door to the balcony. Even as he approached, he could see that the door was open wider than when he'd arrived.

Then he was outside, feeling the bite of cooler air and skidding across the balcony's concrete floor on leather soles. He hit the ledge with both hands, his momentum almost enough to tumble him over.

He swallowed, leaned dizzily out over the ledge, and looked down.

Twenty stories below, a crowd was gathering around a bundle of rumpled brown clothes. The scene reminded Tobin of ants closing in on a dead insect.

He rushed back into the apartment, depressed the phone's cradle button, phoned the Two-Four and asked for Oxman.

As he sat with the receiver getting slippery in his sweating hand, he realized it was probably Egan who'd phoned pretending to be Youngerman. Egan who'd set up the appointment with Lana Spence.

Oxman wasn't there, Murray Felstein said, and no one there knew where to reach him.

Tobin started to report Overbeck's leap to hard death, but he heard sirens reaching crescendo below, and more wailing in the distance. Somebody had notified the police already.

"A call just go out on a jumper?" Tobin asked, to make sure.

"Yeah. Central Park South. You near there?"

After telling Felstein what had happened, Tobin left the apartment, made his way through the swelling crowd on the sidewalk, and headed for his car to drive to Shadowtown Productions.

For some reason he remembered the television set still on in the apartment, Lana Spence—Delia Lane—in ecstasy while Overbeck lay dead on the pavement below. "Like parallel universes," Overbeck had said of soap operas. Said that in the madness of his guilt.

And the steamy love scene, and Delia Lane, were more real now than Harry Overbeck.

E. L. Oxman—3:00 P.M.

The entrance to Shadowtown Productions should have been locked. Oxman had felt certain that the security guard would have let him in, but if there'd been a problem he was going to call Youngerman or Overbeck and have them clear him to go in and search for evidence. Either way, he wanted to get inside and snoop around when the place was deserted, to find out what he could about Zach Denton. Wanted to see the bastard hanged by his balls, guilty or innocent.

But he wanted Denton to be guilty. *How he wanted it!*

Oxman opened the door a few inches and let it swish back to its heavy metal frame. The door should have been locked. Even if someone were working today in one of the offices, they surely would have locked the door behind them. Especially after what had been going on here.

He shoved the door open again and stepped over the threshold.

It was cooler inside. And dim. The few windows in the converted warehouse had been painted over so illumination was controllable on the sound stages. There was a faint yellow glow near the end of a long hall, like light filtered through thin, ancient parchment. Oxman wasn't sure if it was from a dim fixture or was light spilling out from a partly opened door.

He walked silently toward it.

He was halfway there when a noise off to his left made the back of his neck tingle. It might have been a woman's scream, stifled within an instant of its birth. A muffled, gagging sound that fell abruptly to dead silence.

Oxman drew his revolver from its holster and moved toward the sound. He was in another dark hall, one without a ceiling, leading toward the sound stages. He could sense airy spaciousness above him, and it made him feel exposed. Vulnerable.

Vampires flew, didn't they? Sometimes as bats, sometimes as wisps or ethereal webbing. And who could say what *wasn't* known about vampires?

Don't be a superstitious ass, he told himself. Don't remember those black-and-white, light-and-shadow, terrifying movies you saw as a child. And the dreams afterward. So real.

But he hunkered lower as he crept down the darkened hall. Something in him more ancient than his childhood was urging caution, arousing fear in the far corner of his mind where nightmares waited to happen.

There was only silence now, but somehow it seemed to echo. Seemed ominous. Oxman wished he knew where to switch on some lights. Or would it be better to take whoever was in here by surprise?

If the sound he'd heard was of human origin.

If it hadn't been his imagination.

If there really *was* someone other than Oxman in the studio.

But the door *had* been unlocked!

Better to leave the lights out, he decided, and maintain the element of surprise. *And perhaps not have to face what might be waiting*.

He reached a door, rotated the cool metal knob, and swung it open slowly, ducking low and holding the revolver extended before him with both hands, arms braced for the impact of the gun's kick. His mind and body were tight, tensed for anything.

In the muted light he saw that the room was empty except for a rack of costumes along one wall, and some metal folding chairs arranged around a table. And a mirror at the other end of the room, reflecting darkness.

The muscles in his back bunched up as he heard a faint sighing sound, like breathing.

Something was behind him! *Close!*

He swallowed, felt himself weaken and begin to tremble, and was about to whirl when something clutched his arm.

He heard his own sharp intake of breath, a muted shriek. *He was in one of those childhood horror movies!*

"E.L., what the fuck you doin' here?"

Tobin! For Christ's sake it was Tobin! Beautiful Tobin!

"You look scared," Tobin said, still in a whisper. "What's got you spooked, Ox?"

"The front entrance was unlocked. I heard what sounded like a woman start to scream, then it was cut off."

"Lana Spence, or whoever came here to meet her, left the door unlocked," Tobin said.

"Lana?" Oxman tried to connect the woman's stifled scream to Lana but couldn't. Or was it because he didn't want to think of her as the source of the brief, horrified cry?

He listened as Tobin quickly filled him in on Overbeck's confession and suicide. Overbeck! It all dovetailed. It made sense. And the phone call to Lana made a terrible kind of sense, too.

"Egan must have phoned her," Oxman said, when Tobin was finished.

"That's the way I figured it; that's why I'm here."

"You call for backup?"

"It's on the way," Tobin said.

"Meantime, let's figure out how to get some lights on. I was gonna try to surprise whoever was in here, but if Egan and Lana are here, we'd be better off with light."

"You mean because vampires can't stand light, E.L.?"

Oxman aimed a cold look at him.

"Nonbeliever honky," Tobin said. His voice had a slight quaver in it. "I'll go throw the main switch." He drifted off into darkness.

Oxman moved forward slowly. The dim interior of the vast warehouse was quiet. He imagined seeing himself from above, a tiny, ineffectual figure advancing through endless space, hobbled by a part of himself he didn't understand.

But not alone!

Suddenly he was on the floor, his shoulder aching where he'd been slammed down from behind.

A towering figure in a dark cloak flew over him, then fled down the hall and merged with the shadows. The cloak had cracked like a sail in a wind with the force of its passing.

"Egan!" Oxman screamed, struggling to his feet. "Halt, god-dammit!"

The figure became visible again for a fleeting instant as it crossed a dim patch of light.

Oxman sprinted after it, hoping he wouldn't trip over something in the dark. He couldn't seem to build speed; he was running in a nightmare, trapped in an unfamiliar landscape.

A woman's scream chilled him and made him skid to a stop in the hall. So high-pitched and echoing was the terrified shriek, there was no way to judge from which direction it had come.

His heart fluttering in his heaving chest, Oxman held the revolver steady and edged forward again, toward where he'd last caught sight of the fleeing dark figure. His shoulder was throbbing, making it difficult to keep the heavy gun above waist level.

There it was again! A hurtling black form with flowing white hair— here and then gone! Almost as if it were unreal, without substance.

"Oh, Jesus!" Oxman heard himself moan.

But he got off a round, feeling the gun buck in his hand. The crack of the shot reverberated through the vast studio and sang in the steel girders. He was sure he hadn't hit the thing. It had all happened too fast for accuracy.

He cursed himself, realizing he'd fired more from panic than judgment. He had to rein in his emotions, not act on dangerous impulse.

Running footsteps sounded behind him. He whirled.

Saw nothing.

Nothing!

And a terror he hadn't thought possible speared into him, doubled him over. He heard a low whimper and knew it was his own. His limbs were jointless and his bowels were water. He was helpless.

The lights flicked on.

The place was full of blue uniforms.

Hunched against the wall, Oxman felt naked in his primitive fear.

He straightened up immediately. Reality flooded in with illumination and human company.

"Search the goddamn premises!" he barked. "And be careful!"

The young cop nearest him stiffened, drew his Police Special from its black-leather holster, and jogged down one of the halls. Several uniforms behind him spread out in similar fashion. Everyone had on his cop face, cheeks rigid, expression blank, eyes disguising the fear scrambling behind them. Professionals in a job that sometimes scared holy shit out of them.

Tobin was beside Oxman.

"You okay, Ox?"

"Yeah, I guess." Oxman's legs felt weak and the acid taste of terror still lay thick on his tongue.

He made himself walk.

He and Tobin moved down the hall, then tried a couple of doors that led nowhere.

The third door opened onto one of the new occult sets. There was a brass and mahogany coffin resting on fake-marble twin pedestals. The furniture was dark and Victorian. Phony cobwebs were draped gracefully in wispy arcs in the corners. It all conveyed a sense of timeless authenticity and menace. Oxman knew Zach Denton must have designed the set. It was creepy enough, all right; give the bastard that.

"Let's go, Ox," Tobin said, and started back out the door.

Oxman was about to follow when he heard a steady *plup! plup! plup!* Water dripping on something soft.

He tapped Tobin's shoulder, then turned and looked around.

It took him several seconds to notice that the red carpet beneath the casket was soaked. An even darker red stain was rapidly spreading over it.

It wasn't water he'd heard dripping—it was blood!

He rushed to the coffin and set himself to heave the heavy lid open. The fetid stench of blood rocked his stomach.

Even the coffin wasn't real mahogany and brass, only make-believe, like everything else on the set.

Almost everything else.

The unexpectedly weightless lid flew open and banged against the far side of the coffin. Struck twice more, lightly.

Oxman stared inside and was electrified with horror. He began to gasp. Couldn't breathe! Couldn't move!

"Ox, what the fuck is it?"

He heard Tobin walk up behind him, shoes squishing on the soggy carpet. Heard Tobin's breath hissing.

"Aw, Christ, Ox!"

Oxman's gaze was glued to the two figures in the satin-lined coffin.

Marv Egan was sprawled to the side but still mostly on top of Lana Spence. The black cape he wore was wound tightly around both of them. Like a dark shroud. His visible eye was unblinking and glazed.

Oxman had hit Egan when he'd fired at him. There was a nasty exit wound above Egan's left shoulder blade.

It was hard to tell if that was where most of the blood was coming from, or if it was flowing from where Egan had his teeth sunk into the white column of ·Lana's neck.

Egan had played his final role to the hilt, gotten inside the part and believed. *Really believed!*

And had made Lana believe.

Lana's eyes were open wide. Her mouth was gaping.

Moving without sound.

No, she was trying to say something!

Oxman leaned close so his ear was near her lips. He could feel her breath brush the side of his face like powdery soft wings.

"Real," she was whispering over and over. *"Real! Real! Real! . . ."*